Carrion

Betsy Reavley

First published in 2014 by Bloodhound Books

www.bloodhoundbooks.com

No one ever told me that grief felt so like fear.'

C. S. Lewis

'People once believed that when someone dies, a crow carries their soul to the land of the dead. But sometimes, something so bad happens that a terrible sadness is carried with it and the soul can't rest. Then sometimes, just sometimes, the crow can bring that soul back...'

James O'Barr

For my husband.

Introduction

18 October 2012

When I looked into those eyes I knew nothing would be the same again. The blackness from within the stare was spellbinding. It was an echo of something long forgotten, something dangerous and pure. It spoke of horrors beyond my wildest nightmare and I doubted the fabric of my existence.

But I told myself I was being stupid. It was just a bird, a harmless bird. Then I came back. I looked past the shattered windscreen and the spatters of blood and brains that decorated the world. All I saw was the crow. He sat on the wire, watching. Perfectly still, like our car.

The smell of petrol mixed with burnt rubber mingled with the stench of fear and caught in my throat. I stopped looking at the bird and remembered where I was. I could feel shards of glass sticking into my face. The seatbelt was tight around my torso, making it hard to breathe. My neck ached. I looked down at my trembling hands and felt the warm blood drip off the end of my nose.

I looked to my right. It was like I wasn't there. This was not happening. I watched myself examine reality with a detached calm. I could not see the face. The body was hunched, lifeless, over the steering wheel. A mass of bloody hair covered a smashed skull. I could see the inside of the head. It was pink and messy, like a child's first attempt at decorating a cake. Until I could lift the head and see the face it would remain unreal.

My ears were ringing. Smoke poured from the collapsed bonnet. Above us stood the solid trunk of a tree. This was not where I was supposed to be. And then I felt a kick. I glanced down at my round belly and remembered the life growing inside me. A lump was pushing out of my pregnant bulge, a lump that had not been there when we left. The muscles were contracting around my belly. This is a mistake, I thought, staring around at the mess of crunched metal and glass and blood.

I willed myself to move but my legs were trapped, pinned down under the weight of the car bonnet, which had been crushed in on itself. I tried to wriggle free. I could not see my feet or ankles. I thought they were moving. I thought they were.

The car felt hot. The slimy fabric of the seatbelt cut into my neck. I needed to release it, and I fiddled with the button but it wouldn't come out. It was stuck.

I looked over to the driver's side again. The body hadn't moved. Wake up, I thought. Come on, wake up. It looked bad. There hadn't been any movement. I sat very still and watched for signs of life, the rise and fall of the chest. There was nothing. I felt frantic as I stared at the wrist, hoping to see a pulse. The flesh looked alive and warm but I could not bring myself to reach out and touch it.

My head was spinning. More smoke poured from the front of our silver car. Panic surged through my body with the speed of the crash. And then I remembered my mobile. I felt about for my bag. Where was it? Oh shit, it was trapped along with my legs. If I could have got my fingers through the contorted metal then maybe...

Then I felt those eyes on me again, piercing my soul with a deadly grimace. And I looked up to see it was closer. Standing only a few feet away. It sat on a branch of the tree we'd collided with. It was looking down at us. Emptiness surrounded everything. The world had decided to hide and all that was left was the blood, the crow and me.

CHAPTER 1

When I arrived at the hospital I thought I might be sick. I had known something was wrong. It was a feeling that I'd woken up with and had been unable to shake. Walking along the corridor towards the intensive care unit I focused on the echo of my footsteps. For a hospital it seemed very quiet. I passed a nurse in a blue uniform alongside a young man, her hand around his shoulder. He sobbed. I walked faster.

Pushing open the heavy swinging doors, I ignored the sign that told me to wash my hands. I didn't have time for that now. My daughter was in there along with my grandchild, and I needed to get to them.

An elderly Nigerian nurse with grey hair around her temples stood up from behind a desk at smiled at me. I gave my name, Ingrid, and my daughter's, Monica. The nurse stopped smiling. The matron nodded gravely and whisked me towards one of the closed doors. My stomach did a flip.

'You's can't go in dares. Wet for dem dactars. Day will tell you's what's is happenin'. Sit yourself dawn and I'lls get you a nice hat cap of some din to help steady dem nerves.'

I did as she was told and perched down on a plastic chair by the door. I didn't want tea. All I wanted was to be with my daughter. I fiddled with my keys, busying my hands. Glancing at a clock on the wall I saw that it was nearly five o'clock. Then I remembered I was meant to be at the hairdresser getting my roots done. I should not have been sitting outside a room waiting to hear the fate of my family.

The nurse turned and slid away to fetch me a drink as I sat in the eerie silence of the ward. All I could hear was the beeping from life support machines and it made me want to cry. I am meant to die first, I thought to myself. I hoped and pleaded I would never have to bury my child.

For the first time since I was a little girl, I prayed. As a young teenager I'd lost my faith, much to the disapproval of my pious parents. I closed my tired eyes and imagined my daughter recovering. Suddenly I felt old, as I looked down at my hands and noticed the ageing skin. They were not soft like Monica's hands. Monica had lovely soft white skin and long delicate fingers. I wished I could hold my daughter's hand in my own.

As I got up out of my seat deciding I would seek out a doctor and demand to be told what was happening, the doors into the ward swung open and I saw Mary and Richard approaching.

Richard was a short, portly man who was balding and always appeared to be frowning. He had deep lines around his eyes and on his forehead. From behind him appeared Mary, who looked ashen white. Her hazel eyes were sunk back into her skull and her dyed strawberry blonde hair looked dry and brittle. She was a bony woman with a large nose and plump mouth. I liked them both but we had nothing in common apart from the marriage of our children. We shared a friendly but formal relationship. I suspect I was too bohemian for them. Mary and Richard were nice enough, but square.

Suddenly I felt very guilty. I hadn't given much thought to the wellbeing of Tom. The couple approached me, and Mary and I hugged. Mary began to cry while Richard walked over to the door and tried to peer through the frosted glass to see inside. It was hopeless.

'Hello, Ingrid. What have they told you?' Richard was brisk and to the point. No time for niceties.

'Nothing as of yet. I'm waiting to see a doctor.'

I held tightly onto Mary's skeletal hand. Mary's eyes were pricked with tears and she couldn't bring herself to speak. Her husband looked around furiously as though he was hoping to find a more satisfactory answer.

'I'm sure they will all be all right. We would have heard if…' My words trailed off as the kindly nurse reappeared holding a steaming polystyrene cup. 'Richard Bowness, Tom's father,' he said, extending a hand formally as though it was a business meeting. The nurse, who wore a badge bearing the name Denise, handed the cup of beige liquid to me.

'You's need to come wit' me,' she addressed the couple, 'Dis way, please.'

Mary turned and I saw the horror that filled her eyes. I gestured encouragingly and sat back down as my in-laws were led away down the corridor. I was alone again and could not shake the feeling in the pit of my stomach that something was seriously wrong. All I wanted was to be close to my daughter. With sudden urgency, I stood up and pushed open the door into my daughter's room.

It was a small sterile space filled with machines and wires and tubes. The room smelt of disinfectant. I held my breath as I took a few tentative steps towards the large mechanical bed. The woman lying in front of me, purple and swollen, did not look like my daughter. Suddenly I felt giddy and reached out a hand to steady myself.

Monica was attached to various machines and had a large tube coming out of her mouth. Her face was covered in splintered cuts and there was a large gash over her left eyebrow that had been recently stitched. It looked sore and raw and I wanted to stroke it and sooth her pain away.

I inched closer and gently rested my hand on top of Monica's. It felt small and warm. There was no response from my daughter. I hung my head and let out a long sigh. At times like this I wished my husband were still alive.

Jim had died nearly three years earlier. When playing tennis at his club, he had suffered a fatal and unexpected heart attack. Both Monica and I had been devastated. He was a wonderful father and a doting husband. I had gone to Addenbrooke's hospital in Cambridge to identify his body. Now I was there in the Whittington Hospital in Archway, this time standing over the battered figure of my daughter. My stomach did a somersault.

I jumped as the door opened behind me. A

young male doctor with trendy glasses glanced down at the notes that hung on a board at the end of Monica's bed. A freckled nurse with a short boyish haircut and a number of stud earrings in her lobes stood inspecting the various monitors.

'I'm her mother,' I said, stepping out of the nurse's way while she read long reels of paper decorated with indecipherable charts.

'Ah, yes, Mrs?'

'Whitman,' I answered.

'Mrs Whitman, you'll be glad to hear the operation was a success.'

The doctor fiddled with a biro, repeatedly clicking the end.

'Operation? What operation?'

From where I stood by the machines I could feel the nurse glaring at the doctor, who moved uncomfortably on the spot.

'The hysterectomy.' The young doctor looked grave. I looked down at my daughter. None of it made sense.

'Hysterectomy? But she is pregnant...'

The words echoed around the room. The doctor looked down at his tan loafers and I noticed how tall he was. I could see that, although he was young, his mousy hair was thinning. He stopped playing with his pen and lifted his face to look at me.

'What do you mean?' I grew aware of the high pitch of my voice. 'The baby ... her baby ... what about the baby?' my words lost momentum.

'I am very sorry.' The words travelled through me like a bullet. Monica was only thirty-one years old. Her whole life should have been ahead of her.

The nurse in blue overalls approached and put her hand on my shoulder.

'Can I get you a cup of tea?'

I sank into a grey chair and put my head in my hands.

'No. No thank you. I don't want any more tea.'

The nurse addressed the doctor, 'Her stats look normal.' He gave a small nod of satisfaction as she excused herself and left the room. I remained slumped in the chair and could feel the doctor's eyes burning into the top of my head. Slowly he approached and pulled up an orange plastic chair close beside me.

'Mrs Whitman, I am Dr Frampton, your daughter's consultant.' He had a soothing voice.

'I suppose Tom gave you the go-ahead?' I sounded defeated.

'We had no choice. She lost the child in the crash. She was bleeding heavily. The operation saved her life. She should make a full recovery.' The doctor paused. I could see he was struggling with something else he wished to say.

'I'm afraid I have to inform you that your son-in-law passed away. His side of the car took the brunt of the impact. He was brought to us with severe head injuries. He suffered a fatal brain haemorrhage. There was nothing we could do. I am very sorry.'

I shook my head. This could not be happening. All the information that I needed to absorb swirled around my head. My daughter had lost everything: her husband, her child, her womb. As I looked over at the small skeletal figure that lay lifeless in the bed, my eyes filled with tears.

'Oh, dear God, my baby.' I squeezed my daughter's hand tightly.

'For the moment we are keeping her heavily sedated. As I say, she has lost a lot of blood and sustained some quite serious injuries. She has two cracked ribs, damage to her neck and has broken one of her legs. We have put pins in it and she will be able to walk without any problems but she'll need weeks of bed rest. For the moment we are going to keep her here in intensive care but she should be moved to one of the other wards in the next twenty-four hours. If you would like to stay, we have a relatives' room. Do you live nearby?'

'No. No, I've come from Cambridge.'

Dr Frampton looked at my face. He looked at me as though I reminded him of a favourite teacher who had taught him at school.

The young doctor stood up and edged towards the door. My gaze was fixed on my daughter's wounded face.

'I have other patients to see.' He was apologetic.

'Yes, of course. Thank you.'

'Denise, the ward matron, will be doing her rounds and can be found at the reception desk any time. I appreciate this must be a very difficult time for you but your daughter will be all right.'

He slipped away quietly, pulling the door closed behind him.

'My poor darling. My poor, poor darling.'

I tucked my daughter's white bedsheet up under her chin and felt a wave of exhaustion swell along with a gush of tears. The moment I received the news, I'd driven as fast as my ageing red Volvo would go. I had come home that afternoon to discover a number of messages from both Mary and the hospital on my answering machine. I cursed myself for not having a mobile. I'd been convinced that owning one was unnecessary and now I bitterly regretted it.

My fingers gently brushed the dark fringe off Monica's brow, as I used to when she was tucked up in bed before I told my little girl I loved her and kissed her goodnight. Her pale forehead felt clammy to the touch. She looked much the same now as she had done as a child. I remembered her as a ten-year-old, in bed with flu. I was glad to be able to touch my daughter and thought of Tom. Poor Richard and Mary. I felt torn. Part of me wanted to stay with my daughter but I knew I should go and be with the grieving parents. I crossed my arms on the bed and rested my forehead. The sheets felt cool and smelt clean. I wanted to go to sleep and for it all to be just a bad dream.

The noise from the various machines whirled around my head. I felt sick and watched as my hands began to shake. How was I going to tell Monica that she had lost her baby and her husband? My brow furrowed with pain as I looked at my child.

'Sleep now, my darling, sleep. I need to be with Richard and Mary. I will be back soon, I promise. I love you.'

I kissed my child's fingers and touched the top of her head as I got up out of my seat. Before leaving the room I took a last look at my delicate girl lying in the hospital bed. Then I closed my eyes and quietly said to myself, 'Dad is going to look after you, my angel. He will watch over you while I'm gone.' Although I have no faith in religion I believe strongly in the spirit world. I left the room and made my way back towards where I had met Tom's parents.

Returning to the waiting room, I looked around, not knowing where to go. A young Indian man was pushing a mop around the vinyl floor, listening to an MP3 player and bopping his head. I shifted in my boots and rubbed my heels together. What could I say when I saw them? What *should* I say? I remained there locked inside my own thoughts when I noticed that the hospital worker had stopped mopping and stood with his head cocked to one side, watching me.

'Is you all right?' the young man asked.

'No, not really.' I responded with more honesty than I intended. The tall slender man rubbed his forehead and looked at the floor.

'I need to find a couple who are here. I saw them earlier. They're not ill, they are relatives. Where might they be?'

'All depends where de patient is, like.' He rubbed the mop between the palms of his hands. I ruffled my blonde hair and tried to think.

'I need to find them now. They aren't here to see a patient. It's their son. He's dead. He died.'

My eyes began to fill with tears. It suddenly hit me that the death of my son-in-law would have a momentous effect on me too. I had only been thinking of Monica before and the emotional impact it would have on her. Now in the stark waiting room the sadness of it all hit me. Losing all control I crumpled to my knees, while the young man stood helplessly in front on me. I could feel his awkwardness but was unable to restrain myself. The floor felt hard and cold through my trousers. I realised it was still damp from mopping.

After a few moments the young man bent down.

'Can I do some fink for you?' He was kinder than his rough exterior appeared.

'I ... I ...' I blubbed. The man inched closer.

'I can take you's to the relatives' room if you like.'

My shoulders shook but no sound came out. I felt like a fool. How dare I react like this? I still had my child, unlike Monica. Unlike Richard and Mary. That thought snapped me out of the misery.

'Do you think that's where they'll be?' I wiped my eyes with the sleeves from my jumper, smudging mascara down my cheeks. A small drip of snot hung from the end of my nose and I gave a quick deliberate sniff.

'Well I can't be sure but it's worth a go.'

I nodded silently and got up off the floor and gestured with my hand for him to lead the way. He put his mop back in the bucket and pushed it against the cream-coloured wall. Then the man sunk his hands deep into his overall pockets and headed along a corridor I had not been down. He took long quick strides and I tottered along behind, struggling to keep up on my chunky high heels. The sound of us walking echoed around and bounced off walls that were decorated with various murals intended to inspire peace and tranquillity.

After working our way through a maze of corridors that all looked the same, we came upon a door marked 'Relatives' Room'. I felt lost, both physically and mentally. The cleaner who had been so kind took a step back and waited for me to enter. I stood still, holding my breath. I needed to be ready and wanted to be strong for them. A rush of cold ran over my body and I hugged myself.

'Good luck.' The young man with dark eyes stepped away and hurried off back in the direction from which we came. The solid door was all that stood between death and I. It was an unusual feeling. I pictured Mary inside and it pulled my heartstrings. I straightened myself and lifted my head up. Then, holding my breath, I slowly pushed open the laminate beech door. In doing so, I noticed my knuckles turn white.

CHAPTER 2

When I woke up, the first thing I noticed was how dry my throat felt. It took a few minutes before I realised I was in a hospital bed. Gradually my circumstances became clear. My leg was in plaster and my body in a brace. The needle from a drip was sticking into my right arm, secured by medical tape. A blue paper curtain was pulled around my bed. On a table next to me stood a get-well card, a potted azalea and a vase of yellow lilies. Mum had been here. I knew that much. Yellow lilies meant my mum had come.

I tried to swallow but found the pain too much. My throat felt like a cheese grater. The rest of my body felt numb. It was a strange sensation. I couldn't really move, although if I had been able, I am not sure where I would have gone. I looked down at my static frame and wondered whether I was paralysed. And then I began to think. How had I got here?

It took a moment for my memory to order the events and begin to process my reality. I was in hospital. I felt battered and bruised. I was scared. I was alone. Panic started to set in when I realised I couldn't remember how I had ended up there. And then the sudden memory flashed across me like a comet. Being in the car. The crash. And Tom.

I tried to move. I hadn't believed I was capable of it at first but the thought of Tom, the sense of him, made me try. I wriggled in my cast. My leg swung about as though it belonged to a puppet. Claustrophobia set in out of nowhere and I tried to scratch the drip out of my arm.

Someone must have heard me struggle because it was at that point that a fresh-faced nurse arrived and efficiently pulled the curtain back.

'Well, Hello!' She spoke as if we knew each other. 'We've been waiting for you to wake up, love.'

I hated that expression. How could she call me love? What did it even mean? All I wanted was answers. I didn't require her patronising kindness.

'Tom,' I croaked. 'Where is Tom?'

By now she had a hand on my shoulder and was forcefully guiding me back into a lying position. She had more strength than I expected. Her narrow face and dirty scraped back blonde hair gave the impression of someone weak and naïve. From a glance into her eyes I established I was wrong. She was a strong young woman in every sense. It had been a mistake to underestimate her.

'You need to lie back. I am going to get the doctor. You've been in an accident. The doctor will be along to explain. Just lie back please.' By then she had restrained me and I was helpless once again, a victim in a hospital bed.

Once she was satisfied that I was going to obey her, she stood back and straightened her uniform and then my bedsheets. Her glare held the authority of a true professional and I accepted I was powerless. I let my chin drop to my chest and gave a loud sigh of acceptance as she pulled back the curtain. It sounded like a zip being fastened and my eyes flashed open with surprise. Noises sounded strange, like they were one-dimensional. Perhaps it was the drugs they had me on.

As the short blonde nurse disappeared, I looked around the ward I was in. It was a large room with five other beds. Only three were occupied. The other patients were so different from one another. There was an old boy, who must have been in his eighties, who lay motionless staring into space on his bed. His body was skeletal and his skin was so thin and frail it was almost translucent.

On the bed opposite him was a young man with both arms in casts. He had a thick dark beard and long dark hair he wore in a ponytail. His face was round and chubby and his cheeks glowed pink. He was wearing an AC/DC T-shirt instead of hospital robes. As I glanced at him, he offered me a friendly smile. I didn't feel like smiling back.

On the other side of him was a bed surrounded by people. I could just make out a woman in her fifties lying there. She was ghostlike, her skin was so pale. Her lips looked blue and her hair was colourless. I was sure she was dying.

I was snatched away from absorbing my surrounding when Mum appeared in the ward and rushed towards me, arms outstretched.

'Oh, my darling girl!' she whimpered. I surprised myself by smiling.

'Mum.' The word sounded good to my ears.

'God damn bloody bad luck. I've been here for hours! I wanted to be here when you woke up but

I needed to pee, and oh, it's just typical.'

She parked her bony frame down on the bed and somehow managed to jolt it.

'Mum...' My voice was distant. She immediately reached for a jug of water and poured some into a small plastic tumbler.

'Here, shhhh,' she said, 'drink, sweetheart,' and held the cup to my lips.

Since my body was confined to the brace, it made drinking difficult. She did her best to help but most of the lukewarm water ended up dribbling down my chin. Still, it felt good.

'Mum, Tom...' I managed to say more clearly. 'Where...?' The words petered off. My mother couldn't look at me. She silently put the cup back down on the bedside table and looked down at her feet. It seemed like an eternity before she spoke.

'Monica, darling...' Her words trembled and it seemed that time stood still. 'The accident. Sweetheart, what do you remember?'

I clenched my fists and tried hard to get to grips with a memory that danced just beyond my reach.

'We were driving along ... the car.'

The pictures were jumbled up in my brain and the memory was a mess. Mum had hold of my hand. Her grip was firm. 'Tom was taking us ... we were going out...'

Mum's eyes were wide and searching my face. Surely she was the one with the answers.

'Yes, you were in the car...' She let the statement hang unfinished in the air. And then like a tidal wave it hit me.

'The crow! I remember. The blood ... Tom. Oh

fuck, Jesus, the crow!'

The vision came pouring back over me, like photographs from the past. I felt my body tense and my heart rate increase. I remembered those dark eyes staring into me, cold and unforgiving. My mother looked confused.

'No Monica, calm down. The accident, darling ... you were in an accident.' Her words were restrained and calming. She brushed my brow and I felt like a child again. I sank back into the bed. Everything was muddy. 'Shhh.'

Her mouth sung the sound and I noticed how busy her mouth was with teeth. 'Shhh now.' She repeated the words over and over until I had relaxed again. Her fingers brushed my hair again. I noticed that although she did have make-up on, her hair was unkempt. It was so unlike her.

'Monica,' she said gravely, looking me right in the eye, 'I have some terrible news. It is not going to be easy for you to hear but I'd rather you heard it from me. It's Tom.' By then my heart was in my throat. 'Darling, he's gone. I'm so sorry. He's gone.' It took a while for the words to compute. My face must have given away my lack of belief. 'Monica, sweetheart, I am so, so sorry.' I looked around the room again. I thought maybe I would find him there in one of the beds. 'You were in a car accident. We don't know exactly what happened but you crashed. The car hit a tree and Tom...' She didn't need to say anymore.

I think I stared blankly at my leg in its cast. That's all I can remember from that moment – the sight of my broken, bandaged leg. I didn't say anything. I couldn't.

'There's more,' my mother added, but I doubted there was anything else that could be worth mentioning.

'The baby…' Just those words were enough to snap me out of my daze. *The baby*. I tried to sit up, forgetting I was held down by the brace around my torso. My baby. I looked frantically at my stomach. I could find nothing.

'My poor girl.' She gripped my hand in between hers. 'The baby didn't make it.' By this point it all became too much for her. Her resolve crumbled and her mask fell away. She hung her head so that I couldn't see her face but I watched as her shoulders shook up and down.

I instantly felt sick. The hollow space, which had once been home to my unborn child, began to ache. I'd been thrown onto a violent rollercoaster that would not stop. I closed my eyes to try to escape the nausea but it was pointless. The entire bed began to shake with the tremor that travelled through my body. I don't know where it came from or why. Something alien had hold of me and I needed to expel it.

Mum jumped up off of the bed and brought her hands up to her mouth. I watched as her lips formed the words 'N-U-R-S-E!' but I heard nothing. A woman in uniform appeared and began pressing buttons on the machine next to me. I felt my eyes go back into my head and then there was darkness.

***

When I came too, the first thing I saw was my mother sitting at the end of my bed reading a book. Her trendy red glasses were perched on the end of her strong nose. She's in her mid-sixties and has steely eyes. Her hair is shoulder length now, peroxide blonde and wavy. It frames her narrow face. A charcoal-grey mohair jumper hung loosely from her slender frame and she was wearing tight black jeans. She is a slight woman who looks like she knows how to enjoy herself. She always wears chunky silver rings on her fingers and that day had deep brown painted nails

I didn't speak. I just watched her for a while. During that time I had forgotten what I had been told moments before. The only thing in the world I thought about was my mother. I watched her silently as she thumbed through each page she read. She had no idea I was awake; her book had total control of her concentration. I was glad she had some way of losing herself. Looking at my beaten-up body, I wished I did too. And then I remembered. I remembered what my mother had told me about Tom and the baby.

My skull began to ache. For a second I entertained the idea that perhaps it was just a sick joke or a nightmare. I closed my tired green eyes and let out a long breath. Just then I felt Mum's movement on the bed and my eyes sprung open. She smiled as she closed her book and removed her glasses. Lightly, she placed her hand on the sheet which covered my leg and gave a squeeze. She didn't speak. Clearly she didn't know what to say. But I wanted her to say something. I wanted her to tell me that everything would be fine and that nothing bad was going to happen, but the worst had already happened and there was nothing in the world either she or I could say to change it. We just looked at one another for what seemed like an eternity. For the first time, my mother looked old to me. It was as if the news of the accident and everything that came with it had aged her ten years.

My mind felt heavy with medication. All I wanted to do was sleep again. I felt like I'd done ten rounds with Mike Tyson. Suddenly the world felt like a very unfair place. I tried not to think about Tom. I couldn't deal with it. It was too raw. It made no sense. I hadn't had a chance to say goodbye. What had my last words been to him? What were we talking about before the crash?

And then I remembered the crow; its black eyes staring into me. In that moment I knew it was the crow that caused the accident. I couldn't explain how it did it but I knew it was responsible. And it had been deliberate. The crow had taken my life away from me but left my body behind.

My mother cleared her throat and asked if I was hungry. I shook my head. What was the point in eating? I wanted to die, to be with Tom and our child.

'Was it a boy or a girl?' I asked urgently.

'What are you talking about, darling?'

'My baby. Was it a boy or a girl? I want to know.'

'I…' The confusion swept across her face. 'I-I don't know darling, but I can find out for you.'

The words were helpless and hung in the air

along with the smell of the yellow lilies. It seemed morbidly appropriate that they were Mum's favourite flower.

'Yes, please.'

My mother patted my leg and got up off of the bed. Before leaving the room she turned,

'Would you like me to get you a magazine from the shop or something?'

'Quite frankly I don't give a fuck what William, Kate and George are doing in their happy bubble. Thanks anyway.'

'Sorry.' My mother blushed and looked embarrassed.

'No Mum, I'm sorry. I just don't fancy reading at the moment. I can't take in any more words. I have enough going round my head at the moment.'

'I know, darling, I know.' And she slipped out of the room.

I lay static, staring at the card my mother had brought. It featured a large bunch of watercolour flowers lying on a sun-drenched table. It was a warm scene but I felt cold. I only had a sheet over my body and outside the grey October wind clattered the world. I remembered it had been windy on the day of the accident. I wondered how long I had been in hospital. My head ached as I tried to search my memory for answers. Why had we crashed? I couldn't remember. It seemed so unkind of my brain to withhold this information. I had nothing left. My husband and my child had both been taken from me and I needed answers.

CHAPTER 3

Monica had been in hospital for a week now. As I walked towards the reception desk my legs felt wobbly beneath me. It hadn't occurred to me to wonder what sex my dead grandchild had been, and I didn't like the idea of knowing. As far as I was concerned it was easier not to know. Knowing whether the baby had been a boy or girl would somehow make it sadder, if that were possible.

When I reached the desk I was greeted by Denise's kindly face. The black woman was standing up and I noticed how small she was. She had seemed somehow bigger before. She waited patiently for me to speak.

'My daughter has a question.'

'And what might dat be?'

'She wants to know about her child. Was the baby a boy or a girl?'

I felt sick as I heard the words leave my mouth. Denise looked serious and said she didn't have that information but she would find out. I thanked her and headed down to the hospital forecourt.

For half an hour I sat nursing a cup of watery tea. I couldn't face being with my daughter. I felt useless and unable to deal with the magnitude of the situation. Worst of all I knew there was nothing I could say or do to fix things for her. It was impossibly hard seeing Monica lying in the hospital bed, fragile and broken.

Psychically she looked much the same – a small nose, those bright green eyes, pointy chin and ebony hair. As a child she had a fringe and wore it in a bob. Now she had long locks and was even more beautiful. I once told her I missed the fringe but she laughed at me and told me not to tell her how to wear her hair.

She'd always been a force to be reckoned with, even as a small child. Monica knew her own mind and could never be told anything. Her father and I used to chuckle at her dogged, independent personality, which sometimes meant she backed herself into a corner.

At school she was so sure she could climb the large tree in the playground she ended up stuck at the top and the fire brigade were called to rescue her. But she was not embarrassed by the event. I remember she rather enjoyed the extra attention and carried the story around with her as if it were a badge of honour. No other child had ever made it as high up that tree as she had and Monica was quick to remind everyone of that fact.

Jim built her a tree house at the end of our wild garden one summer, and she spent many hours there playing and flexing her vivid imagination. Monica once told me that she had decided to become an architect one afternoon as a child in the tree house. She admired the idea of being able to turn an empty space into a home. For as long as I can remember she wanted to build the perfect home. That extended to her work life as well as her own.

I thought about Monica and Tom's history

together. They had met at University College London where Monica took a degree in architecture and Tom studied design. Since it takes seven years to complete an architect's degree, Tom had gone on to get a job with a web design company while Monica finished university. They had shared the rent on a small lower-ground-floor flat in South Kensington for a number of years before they both started to make money and decided to buy a place of their own. Since both their families coincidentally lived in and around Cambridge, the young couple had chosen North London and Crouch End as a place to build their nest.

Tom was a man's man. He was a bit rough around the edges and when I'd first met him I didn't know what to make of him. He wasn't the sort of chap I would have ever imagined Monica with. She's a creative, sensitive, impulsive, outgoing, rather wild girl and Tom was the opposite. He liked things to be just so. He was confident, rational and calculated. He never reacted without thinking first. I hadn't believed their relationship would last but when they announced their engagement I was happy for her. If he was the man she wanted then I would back her all the way. At the time it seemed to be a case of opposites attracting, but I had always worried he wasn't exactly right for her. Still, it seemed their marriage had been working and the memory made me want to burst into tears.

People buzzed around me getting hot food from the canteen. The smell was as unappealing as the appearance of the meals on offer. I felt sick as it was and sitting there was making matters worse. I stood up and shook myself off in a bid to regain some composure, knowing I needed to return to Monica again. It took a huge effort to push away the hollow feeling left by the void of the grandchild I had never met.

Monica was my only child. Jim and I had planned to have two but my pregnancy with Monica was troublesome and the labour horrific. She was four weeks premature and in those days it was touch and go. We vowed for me never to get pregnant again and promised to instead spend all our time concentrating on the wonderful little life we'd already made.

When I returned to the ward, Richard was there, waiting to greet me. His face was ashen and he looked short and hunched over. The effect of his son's death was plastered across his grey face.

'Mary is at home.' He spoke with a rasping voice. 'She couldn't be here today. It was too much for her. Jenny is with her.'

He rubbed his hands together with nervous energy. There was a long silence while he ordered his words. I waited patiently.

'How is she?' He seemed unable to speak his daughter-in-law's name.

'Devastated, Richard. She hasn't cried. It is almost as if she doesn't believe it is real. I'm seriously concerned about her.'

'Yes, right, yes, poor girl.'

'You can go and see her if you'd like? It might help the both of you to...'

Richard nodded decisively and took steps

towards the door before he froze and began to shake. Immediately I put a hand on his shoulder and guided him to a seat nearby.

'I don't think I can go in there. It's ... it's too much.'

His hands quivered and little beads of sweat decorated his high brow.

'Richard' – I perched on the chair next to him – 'you should go home and be with Mary. I'm here for Monica. Go home to your wife and daughter. You can visit when things have sunk in a bit more, when you feel stronger.'

Large pools of tears gathered in his eyes.

'I can drive you home if you'd like.'

The man who was normally so matter-of-fact and together seemed like a pathetic orphan. He wiped his eyes with the sleeve of his Marks and Spencer's jumper and shook his head. Then he stood up and straightened himself.

'Please tell her we will come and visit her soon and our prayers are with her.' He paused. 'And Tom's funeral – we will wait until she is ready.'

'Thank you.' I rose out of my seat, noticing I was at least three inches taller than him.

Richard left and I watched the distance between our bodies grow with each step he took. I nearly jumped out of my skin when Denise tapped me on the shoulder.

'Gosh! I'm sorry. I was miles away.'

'I ave dat information you's was after.' Denise handed over a piece of printed A4 paper. 'It's all in dare. Tell er dat she can bury de child when she feels ready.' I nodded with solemn gratitude and made my way back to my daughter.

Monica lay staring up at the high ceiling. The glare in her green almond eyes contained more intensity than I was prepared for. The answers can't be gained from looking at that spot, I thought, lowering myself gently onto the bed.

'Where were you?' Monica sounded frantic.

I decided not to mention my conversation with Richard. Taking a deep breath I handed the death certificate over to my daughter.

'Here is what you asked for, sweetheart.'

The colour drained from Monica's petite damaged face. She was not prepared to see it in black and white yet. Her bottom lip quivered while her eyes scanned the words. Slowly and deliberately she lowered the paper and folded it in two. With painful difficulty she placed it on her bedside table and looked at me.

'It was a boy.' The words cut through the air. 'I had a son. Tom and I, we had a son.'

I swallowed hard and inched closer to my daughter, cupping her head in my hands as a river of tears snaked down her cheeks. Watching my daughter, my baby, in such pain was too much. We both cried. We clung to each other and tried to ride the wave of emotion that crashed into us.

Afterwards, we lay together on the bed embracing in silence. We had cried all the tears we could that day. Stroking my daughter's dark silky hair, I spoke to her softly.

'The nurse says you can have a funeral for your boy.' I felt Monica tense.

'Shhhh,' I whispered soothingly. 'You don't need to think about that now. When the time is right you can put him to rest. Just concentrate on getting better now, darling.'

I think she was too exhausted to argue. A numbing agony seemed to encase her. She held onto me the way she had done as a heartbroken teenager when her first boyfriend had broken up with her. I could sense she felt safe wrapped in my arms. It was all too much for her to cope with now. How could she start to think about burying someone she had never known? Internally, we both pondered the same question. As I read my daughter's thoughts, even if her doctor advised against it, I just knew she was determined to see the baby's body. I dreaded the visit we would have to make to the morgue.

Moments later, two male police officers walked in. They approached Monica's bed and stood silently while we composed ourselves. In an officious manner, the older of the two informed us he had come to ask Monica further questions regarding the crash.

'My daughter has already answered your questions. She has lost her husband and her child for goodness sake!'

Monica would normally have chastised me for interfering but this time she was grateful for my Rottweiler mode. I did not see what good going over it again would do. And besides, she still couldn't remember anything. A sensation of paranoid dread poisoned the air around her bed.

'I understand this must be a very difficult time for you but we do need to get a clear statement. We are just doing our job.' He spoke with inflated self-worth. I disliked the man.

'Now look here, officer...' I stood up, hands on hips and fixed him with a stare. 'I don't really give a damn about protocol at the moment. My daughter was not driving the car. She does not remember anything and the only thing you are achieving by being here is to cause her more anguish. Unless you leave here right now I will be making a formal complaint to your department. Have I made myself clear?'

The younger policeman had already taken steps back towards the exit. He knew better than to argue with a mother who was rightly protecting her child.

'There is no need to take that tone, Madam.' The rotund officer blew out his cheeks and slammed shut his notebook. 'We are investigating a very serious and fatal accident.'

Monica watched with mild amusement as the vein in my temple began to throb. She knew what was coming. Pointing at the door, I bellowed, 'GET OUT!'

The officer's cheeks flushed red and without a word the policeman turned on his heels and left the ward, his small counterpart trailing behind him. Monica managed a smile.

'Thanks, Mum.'

'They've got a bloody cheek!' I placed an overflowing carrier bag on the bed. 'I brought you some things from the forecourt.' Monica watched as I removed one thing after another from the bag. She remained silent as she viewed the various items.

'I thought now that your face is beginning to heal you might like some make-up. Help you to feel more like your old self.' I busied myself looking for the cosmetics I'd purchased.

Although I was wearing the red lipstick and heavy eyeliner I always wore, the tiredness that was plainly hanging off me. My hair was flat and limp.

'OK, Mum, thanks.' Monica reached for her make-up. I realised that she had not seen herself in a mirror since before the accident. Above her left eyebrow was a stitched-up gash. The smaller cuts from the glass were now a sprinkling of shrinking scabs. There was no colour in her cheeks and her mouth looked pale and dry.

'I don't recognise myself,' she said as I looked up.

'You are in there. It's going to take some time for you to get back to the old you. But with time, you will get there.'

'I will never be who I was before the accident. Nothing can ever be the same again.'

***

Three weeks later, Monica was able to move around without assistance. Her consultant had given her the good news that her spine had suffered no damage except for the whiplash. Her leg was still in plaster, and now instead of aching, it itched relentlessly. The cuts on her face had healed and the gash above her eye was on the mend. Her ribs still ached but she was assured that they were getting better. She was hobbling about the ward on her crutches, enjoying the freedom she felt. Her mind as well as her body had kept her prisoner in that bed for too long and I could see the escape was giving her the boost she so desperately needed.

That day was a turning point for more than one reason. Monica arranged with Sister Denise to see her son. She had spent a few hours discussing her grief with the hospital counsellor who had kindly paid her a visit. Cathy, a fat woman with a broad Essex accent, had apparently encouraged her to go and say goodbye to her son. It would help with the grieving process. They also gave her a photograph of him. He looked like he was sleeping. A suggestion was made that she give the child a name. After much deliberation, the eight-month-old unborn little boy was named Joshua.

It also occurred to Monica that she could visit Tom's body. She longed to see his face one more time. Without embellishing the details, the counsellor advised that due to the extent of the injuries Tom had suffered it would not be wise for Monica to see him. I remembered how much it had helped me to see Jim hours after he'd died. It made it more final somehow, more realistic. It allows for the reality to slowly drip-feed into one's mind. The fact my girl was not able to benefit from that was a crying shame.

I watched as Monica pushed away the memory of pieces of skull and brain splattered across the smashed windscreen and accepted the advice. It seemed to leave her even sadder than before. The kind bereavement worker had gone on to explain that feelings of guilt, anxiety, depression and post-traumatic stress disorder were common in similar cases. One of the many nurses who had crossed her path had also warned her of PTSD as a potential result of the accident. It seemed grief alone was not enough for my poor darling to have to cope with.

I'd agreed to accompany Monica to see Josh. When I arrived in the ward, she was pacing on her crutches and looking very nervous. I had brought a bunch of yellow lilies and caught myself gripping the stems so tight that I was crushing them. Saying nothing, she sat down on the bed and massaged her temples, as though willing herself to believe that the experience would be cathartic. Then she rose and shuffled towards me. A ginger-haired man in mint-green overalls waited at the door of the ward to lead us to the chapel of rest where the tiny body had been arranged.

'Ready?' she asked.

'Yes, darling. Are you?'

'No, I don't suppose I ever will be.' Monica straightened her head. 'But let's do this.'

With one hand firmly around my daughter's shoulder and the other clasping the bouquet, Monica and I followed the mortician. I could feel Monica tense and shaking.

'Are the flowers for Josh?' Monica's large eyes stared searchingly at the scented petals.

'Yes. They are for my grandson.'

The three of us floated silently down a maze of corridors before reaching the chapel of rest. Monica froze in terror.

'I can't do this. I can't.'

Her breathing became erratic. I turned to my

daughter.

'You can do this and you must. I am with you every step of the way. I know it's incredibly hard, darling but you will regret it for the rest of your life if you don't go through that door. Seeing your father was the most difficult thing I ever had to do but I am so glad I did.'

Monica looked like a rabbit caught in headlights. She closed her eyes and slowly exhaled the air from her lungs, calming herself. When I thought she was ready, I took hold of her hand.

'Come on, my girl, it's time to meet your son.'

CHAPTER 4

I visited Josh every single day that I remained in the hospital. By being in his presence it gave me a feeling of who he was, who he might have been. I could not get over how tiny he was; so small, so pale. They let me pick him up and hold him. He was icy cold and it felt wrong. His little face looked lifeless. People say that the dead look like they are sleeping. It's not true. He looked dead and gone. There was no expression in his small premature face, no sense of life.

Josh had a perfect little heart-shaped mouth. I tried to picture it flooded with pink and not the grey-blue shade that it was now. It broke my heart that I would never know the colour of his eyes. In my imagination they were the same golden brown as Tom's. The mortician, whose name was John, suggested I choose some clothes to dress him in.

After four weeks I was released from hospital. That afternoon I ordered a taxi and took myself straight to Mothercare. Mum had offered to join me but I told her I wanted to go alone. She said she understood. Some things were too personal.

Entering the vast shop with its rails of tiny clothes, shelves packed high with blankets, bottles and various other baby equipment felt horrendous. At home I already had some things I had bought with Tom in preparation for our child's arrival. But it seemed wrong to put him in clothes meant for a sexless child. He was a boy;

my perfect little boy and he deserved a special outfit chosen just for him. When Mum had learnt of my pregnancy she fished out a pair of tiny little white booties that once belonged to me, and told me she had kept them for when I had a child of my own. Remembering them, I realised Josh would never get to wear them.

I fingered through the rows of soft blue clothes. The fabrics felt warm and comforting. It was when I saw a pair of little booties that I began to feel light-headed. Picturing his tiny bare feet made me overcome with sadness. I picked up the minute shoes and held them to my chest. He would have them.

Next I searched for the perfect jumper. I only had one opportunity to get this right. He would only ever need one outfit. I spent my time carefully going through the options. Eventually I came across a blue and white knitted cotton jumper that I liked. It had a small red car in the centre of the front. Although it said newborn on the label, it looked like it would drown him. Then I remembered that he was premature. I hung it back on the rail and started a new search.

I left the shop twenty minutes later holding two bags: one containing a miniature white woollen hat and a pale blue fleecy sleep-suit and the other a soft cream blanket and a small beige beanbag teddy. Although I was able to return home, I opted to return to the hospital to take Josh the things I had just bought for him. After hailing another cab, I was back there in fifteen minutes. On the journey, I stared out at the cold November sky which blanketed the world. Rain threatened the air.

Arriving back at the Whittington, I made my way towards the morgue. Although I had only been gone from the hospital for an hour it felt strange to be back. I hated the uncomfortable familiarity.

When I got to my destination I found John there busily filling out forms. He looked tired and I wondered how he dealt with death every single day of his life. He smiled at me, revealing a set of perfect white teeth. He had a short ginger beard and kind blue eyes.

'Can I see him, please?'

'Yes, Monica. I'll just get him ready for you. Go to the chapel of rest and I'll meet you up there shortly.'

I thanked John, then did as I was told and left the cold morgue clutching tightly onto my shopping bags.

When I reached the chapel I found a large man in his fifties crying. Snot ran down his face. He came out of the room supported by a younger man who was the spitting image of him. Both looked distressed. I heard one of them mutter something about 'Mum' before both slid away down the corridor and out of view. I was reminded of my first visit there and how testing it had been.

Sitting on a hard backed chair outside the chapel, I waited with anticipation for John to appear. A strange sense of excitement had hold of me. I could hardly wait to dress my child for the first time. I pushed away the dreaded knowledge that it would be my one and only opportunity to do so. Knowing that I could have some control over what was going to happen to him made me feel better. Up until that moment everything in my world had been turned upside down. Any drop of hegemony I could get back would be welcomed.

To my surprise I spotted my mother walking briskly towards me. I had expected her to greet me in the discharge lounge.

'What are you doing here?'

'You know I said I'd collect you and take you home, but I arrived too damn late. They told me you'd gone out but that you planned on coming back shortly. I was waiting for you up in the ward when I heard some of the nurses talking. They were saying you were down here. So here I am.'

I didn't want her to come in with me. I wanted to dress him in peace. Mum had been so strong and brilliant for the last few weeks and I didn't know how to tell her that this was something I wanted to do alone.

'Don't worry,' she said, reading my mind the way she often did, 'I won't come in. I'll wait for you out here.' Relief washed over me. I laid my head on her shoulder.

'Thank you.'

Minutes later, John appeared out of the room and told me Josh was ready. I stood up and walked silently into the chapel. I had been there every day for the past three weeks and it felt like home. The room was softly lit and two wreaths of large pure white lilies sat on a long table to the far side of the room. In the centre of it all, on a bed in the middle of the room, lay Josh, resting beneath a white cotton blanket. I kissed his tiny ice-cold head and pulled the bedding back.

Removing one item from the bag at a time, I broke off the tags and laid them out. All the time I spoke to him, talking him through what I was doing. Carefully, I lifted his sparrow-like body up and dressed him in the blue clothes I'd bought. I slipped the little hat onto his head and wrapped him in the brand new blanket. He looked more real than ever. Tears fell out of me. Holding him in my arms, I rocked him back and forth while humming a lullaby I remembered from childhood. It would be the first and last time I felt like a proper mother.

When my time came to an end I laid him back down on the bed in his blanket and snuggled the teddy up close beside him. Stroking his little face, I said my final goodbye. Then quietly I slipped away, pulling the door closed behind me. I knew I would not see him again. I needed to put him to rest. Now that I was better and able to go home it was time to arrange the funerals. At that moment I knew what to do. It suddenly seemed so clear to me. I would bury them together, side by side in the same casket. Neither of them would ever have to be alone again.

Walking away from the chapel for the last time with my mother by my side was one of the hardest things I have ever done. Silently, we found our way to the main entrance and stepped out into sheets of rain. I followed her as she guided me towards her car. My skin was numb and I didn't notice the drops pelting my face. Beneath my feet were large pooling puddles of cold grey water. I sloshed through them, uncaring.

I looked up to see a large black crow watching

me from a window ledge on one of the many hospital buildings, it's eyes glaring at me. I knew it was the same one I had seen on the day of the accident. We stared at each other until I disappeared out of sight bneath the concrete shell of the car park. It felt tomb-like. My world felt void of light and hope as I got into my mum's car and was driven away from all that remained of my husband and son.

***

After the funeral I stood by the side of the grave. Everyone headed off to the wake while I stayed there to be close to my child and husband. Staring down at the coffin in the ground, it felt so far away. I couldn't help thinking how cold and hard the ground looked. It was December so I suppose it wasn't surprising, but I wanted the earth to be warm for Tom and Josh. I pushed away the image of worms and ants eating their way through the soil. It made me shiver.

When I looked up, I saw that Mary had also stayed by the burial site. She was in a wheelchair that Richard had acquired for the day. Although Mary's legs worked perfectly well, she was unable to stand due to her fragile emotional state. The death of her son had taken its toll on her body as well as her mind. She looked so small she resembled a starving child. Her hazel eyes searched the churchyard as though willing her son to appear.

Our watery eyes met. The only thing between us was the hole in the ground that contained the coffin. I felt lost to her and realised that the thing which connected us was now gone. My relationship with Tom's family meant nothing now. But she and I had something in common. We were both mothers who had lost their sons. Wiping the tears away from my eyes, I walked around the grave and squatted down on my heels beside her. She put her cold bony hand on mine. We stayed like that in silence for a long time before Richard appeared and wheeled her off, muttering about the impending rain. I remained alone by the grave.

The world was eerily quiet. There was no wind shaking the naked branches of the trees. No rain, no noise. Time stood still in acknowledgement of death. In my black woollen coat I sat down on the damp cold grass. My leg was only very recently out of its cast and my bones were stiff and ached. I could feel the damp being absorbed by my clothes and it made me feel part of the earth. Part of me wanted to crawl into the hole and lie with the coffin, much as I had done on the day of Dad's funeral. I wished he could have been there to put his large arms around me and tell me everything would be fine. But like Tom and Josh he was gone. The past and the present swirled around my head taking it in turns to batter me. Finally I really understood how my mother must have felt when she buried her husband. It was something we would always share and something I wished we didn't.

Just then I saw a flash in the corner of my eye. I looked up to see a large black crow perched on a headstone very near me. Its shining black eyes stared intently at the hole in which my family lay. The feathers were slick with a green-blue sheen. He was almost beautiful. But beneath his imposing appearance came a darkness that oozed out, poisoning the air around me.

Dumbstruck, I sat looking at the bird that had killed my family. It fluffed its glossy feathers out and tucked its neck in. The dark beak opened and let out a loud harrowing caw. The sound penetrated my soul and I felt as though I had been transported to hell.

Then the creature hopped down from the tombstone and edged closer to the grave. Its powerful charcoal-coloured feet sunk into the wet soil and I saw how sharp its long talons were. I moved backwards on the ground, never taking my eyes off of it. I was scared. The bird stared at me and I knew it wanted me dead too. It had returned to finish the job.

The sky above became unnaturally black and the clouds moved in with ominous purpose. Nature was gathered against me. The crow jumped a few steps closer to the freshly dug grave. I desperately wanted to protect the sacred space. I picked up a mound of dirt and hurled it at the carrion. The bird flinched but stood its ground. Unblinking eyes continued to fix me. I threw another handful. This time it retreated to a low branch of a tree close by. It looked up to the dark heavy sky and let out a long screech. A moment later the heavens opened and buckets of rain started to fall. Instinct told me to find shelter but I refused to leave the bird alone with the grave. I pulled my collar up around my face and remained watching the crow.

Beads of water ran down its slender back and fell to earth. Then, without any warning, the bird stretched out its wings and took off. It flew low, deliberately diving at me and narrowly missing my head before disappearing off into the distance. I fell back onto the wet ground and watched until it was no more than a speck in the distance. It was gone for now but I knew it would be back.

I picked my wet muddy self up off the grass and headed for the church entrance to shelter from the weather. Before turning the corner I looked back at the grave. The rain was causing a small landslide of soil to fall in on top of the coffin. The elements took their turn in burying them.

When I reached the covered entrance to the church I found the vicar standing there alone. He had come out to watch the downpour. I shook the drops off my nose and ruffled my hair.

Reverend George Burnet was of average build with salt and pepper hair that haloed his square face. He had a large strong jaw and round brown eyes. He stood silently holding a Bible in his hands looking out at the churchyard. I was a lapsed Christian and felt uncomfortable being alone with a man of God.

Ickleton is a historic village that lies a few miles to the south of Cambridge and west of the River Granta. Tom's family had lived there for many years and the reverend knew Richard and Mary well. I always enjoyed looking at the pieces of masonry in the walls of some of the houses, which acted as a reminder of its role in the Middle Ages as a Benedictine nunnery.

The Church of St Mary Magdalene was decorated with fresco paintings on the walls that dated back to the twelfth century. Architecturally the church was significant. I had wandered around the building on a few occasions with Tom when we visited his family. Mary and Richard had pleaded to have their son buried in the village he had grown up in. I felt unable to argue and agreed to have the service in Ickleton. Besides, I had also grown up in the area and Tom and I had history there. It seemed as fitting place as any.

Looking at the reverend, I wondered why he wasn't at the wake. I knew he had been invited. We stood side by side looking out at the gloom. I couldn't bear the silence. I needed to tell someone about the crow and it seemed to me at that moment that he might be the right person to confide in. Apart from my outburst in the hospital I had kept quiet about the role the bird had played on the day of the accident.

I told the vicar that I was sure a crow had deliberately caused the crash that had killed my husband and unborn son. He nodded as if what I was telling him seemed perfectly normal. I didn't know if he was humouring me or if he thought I was raving mad. Honestly, I didn't care too much what he thought. I needed to tell someone, to vent about the danger which flew in and around my head.

Telling Reverend Burnet about my experience in the graveyard only moments before caught his interest. He raised one bushy eyebrow as I recounted the attack I had suffered. When I finished telling him my story, he stood still, rubbing his chin with chubby fingers.

'"The eye that mocks a father and scorns to obey a mother will be picked out by the ravens of the valley and eaten by the vultures." Proverbs, verse 30 line 17.'

He stood back to allow the words to sink in but I didn't understand what it meant. I looked down at my mud-caked black leather boots and hoped he would carry on, but he did not speak.

'I'm sorry, but I just don't understand what that means.' I felt like an ignorant schoolgirl caught out by a teacher.

'In many cultures, crows are a bearer of prophecy. In the Old Testament there are many references to them. No other animal in the Bible is treated with such symbolic ambiguity as the crow. Did you know, for example, that the Bible tells us that after their son Abel died, Adam and Eve were at a loss as to what to do with his body? It tells us that a raven killed a fellow bird and buried the body in the ground, showing the man and woman what they should do. God was thankful to the raven and out of gratitude promised to always feed baby birds.' I was impressed by this man's precise knowledge of the Bible. It seemed I had come to the right person.

'As far as I understand it, Monica, ravens and crows are like people continually trying to find their place on God's earth.' He paused and scrunched up his brow. 'I am aware that grief can take many forms. It is possible that this bird has become a tangible representation of the pain you feel. I am sure, in time, you will find comfort in knowing that Tom and your son are at peace in the kingdom of heaven. The Lord is looking after them now.'

Smiling at the pious man, I thanked him for his time and slipped out into the downpour. I felt utterly deflated as I made my way towards the village hall where I knew friends and relatives gathered, eating canapés and sipping wine. It was pointless to think that anyone would comprehend what was happening to me.

CHAPTER 5

I had been staying with my daughter in North London for nearly a month. The cast had been off Monica's leg for some time and any major external injuries had healed, but I worried for her mental health.

Ever since the funeral, Monica had been obsessed with the idea that a crow meant her harm. She told me of her experience in the graveyard and of how she remembered the bird at the site of the accident. I listened patiently to my daughter's rants and tried to offer some common-sense advice.

It seemed likely and unsurprising to me that my daughter was suffering with post-traumatic stress disorder. The doctors had warned us both that it was common after such a horrific accident. Monica seemed frequently on edge and had developed a phobia about crows. She was certain that there was one bird in particular out to get her, and became terrified whenever any crow was nearby. She became increasingly easily startled and anxious about the menacing threat she believed surrounded her.

Most recently, Monica was refusing to get into a car and starting to retreat more and more from normal life. On the few occasions she deemed to venture out into Crouch End, a small area of North London sandwiched between Highgate and Turnpike Lane, she would aimlessly spend time wandering about. Once she was gone for nearly three hours. In a panic, I set out to look for her. I found my daughter standing in the pissing rain staring into a toyshop window like a zombie.

Before the accident, Monica had had a flourishing career as an architect. She'd handed in her notice when she was six months pregnant. She wanted to be a stay-at-home mum. Tom had also been successful and was making enough money to support them both. His income alone was going to allow Monica to be the mother she wanted to be. I was surprised by her giving up the job she loved but said nothing. I was too overjoyed at the prospect of becoming a grandmother.

Now I began to worry endlessly about my daughter's withdrawal from her friends. Monica's friendships had always been so important to her. She had been a social butterfly who flitted between various groups. She was at home with all sorts of people and fitted in anywhere. It was one of the things I so admired about her. Tom occasionally used to complain that he never saw her because of her hectic social schedule. But now all that had changed.

Monica spent hours online looking into crow mythology. She was obsessed with all things crow. It became the only thing she seemed able to think or talk about. She was absolutely certain the bird had deliberately caused the accident.

I have a number of my own kooky superstitions but was unable to get on board with that one. Gently I tried suggesting that I could see no reason why a bird would suddenly decide to cause harm to Monica or her family, but the suggestion was met with anger and resentment. She flew into a rage and screamed at me for not believing her. I had never known her to be so aggressive. It was at that point that I decided I needed to find out about crows myself, to see if I could make any sense of my daughter's wild accusations.

As a child, Monica loved animals. She had even toyed with the idea of becoming a vet. At school she would do sponsored walks to raise money for animal charities and at one point had three rabbits, two guinea pigs, a hamster and a large fish tank that I was regrettably responsible for cleaning on a regular basis. She'd begged for a horse and Jim had even considered allowing it, until I pointed out how costly the hobby would be. This new fear and hatred of a bird seemed so unlike her.

One cold early December afternoon when Monica had gone to visit the grave with Mary and Richard, I sat down on the large stone-coloured linen sofa and opened my laptop. I peered at the Google results. A mother always wants to believe her child but it all sounded so unlikely. Having not really known what it was I was searching for, I typed 'crow attacks' into the search bar.

To my surprise I discovered it was not that uncommon for those birds to attack people. I scrawled through pages of individual stories and immediately started to feel better. Perhaps Monica was right after all. The discovery came as a huge relief.

It was not surprising that after the loss of her husband, child and any future children, Monica could be suffering a kind of breakdown. I was half expecting it. I myself had been severely depressed after the death of my husband and it had taken me months to recover. But what my daughter was going through was much worse. I found it hard to imagine how she got out of bed. On some days she didn't. Reading stories online helped me see how I might help her get over her fear.

Closing the laptop, I sat back into the large soft cushions and looked around my daughter's living room. A large bay window looked out into the quiet street. Striped duck-egg silk curtains hung from the high set wooden rail. A dark mango wood table with carved legs stood pride of place adorned with photo frames. I stared at the once happy faces of my daughter and son-in-law until it became too much to bear. They had only been married for two and a half years.

Oak Avenue was a small quiet residential no through road. It lay moments south of Alexandra Palace and was within walking minutes of Crouch End with its many restaurants and boutique shops. Crouch End had become a very middle class area of London close to Muswell Hill. The streets were bustling with mothers pushing designer prams in and out of the many coffee shops dotted around the streets, much like parts of Cambridge, I supposed. Parochial is the word I'd use to describe it, but its saving grace was the mishmash of people who lived on its doorstep. Turnpike Lane was a stone's throw away with its Asian and Turkish population, and just to the north, Wood Green was a largely West Indian area. One of the things I loved most about London was its diversity.

Number 44 was a large four-bedroom Victorian

semi with a big south-west facing rear garden. It was close to the sprawling green and woodland of Alexandra Park and even closer to Priory Park, which had been important to Tom, who was a regular jogger. It had appealed to Monica who liked animals and wanted to get a puppy, but Tom had made her promise not to get one until the baby was six years old. He said he refused to pick up dog mess as well as having to change nappies. It had seemed to me a strange thing to think since Monica was going to be the one at home while he was out working every day.

My eyes wandered over stripped floorboards which were partially covered with a large pastel-striped rug the couple had bought in Heals. Against one of the white walls stood two art deco brown leather tub chairs. Between them sat a small side table bearing a chrome Anglepoise lamp. On the wall opposite was a larger than average black Victorian fireplace, and above that hung a huge modern mirror that made the room feel even bigger than it was. Monica and Tom had bought the house as a renovation project. It was unrecognisable from the damp, scruffy place it had been three years before. In every detail I could see my daughter's subtle influence.

I admire my daughter's taste although it is entirely different to my own. My house is a mix of brightly coloured pieces of furniture and trinkets I have collected over the years from junk shops. I could see what a lovely home Monica had built for her fledgling family and it seemed like such a waste.

I had an urge for a cup of green tea. I swear it

helps me to think clearly. I got up from the sofa and pottered out of the sitting room into the large hallway, passing a row of neatly hung coats and Tom's study, before entering the kitchen.

It was a large room that had once been small and dark. After receiving planning permission, Monica and Tom had extended the kitchen out into the garden turning it into a big, clean, bright space. Like a lot of people with their taste it was modern and sleek. On the left side was a solid wall of dark wood cupboards, drawers and a very expensive oven. On the opposite wall was a long pale grey marble work surface, featuring a vast double ceramic sink. At the end of that was a state of the art touch-sensitive hob. The long wide room was painted in pure white. The floor was covered with large expensive polished limestone tiles that shone under the artificial lights set high in the ceiling. At the end of the room, looking out over the long garden, was a glass wall with folding doors leading out. Beyond the garden lay Priory Park.

I looked around the room. It was so uncluttered, so clean and tidy. It was a trait I suppose Monica had inherited from her father. Jim had always been very organised and precise, the stark opposite to me. These days, since his death, I live in a happy but chaotic bubble. It was strange because, like mother like daughter, as a child and well into her late teens Monica had been famous for her lack of order. I wondered what had changed.

Looking round, I realised that Monica was still managing to look after the house in the particular way that she now did. I hadn't noticed her cleaning but knew she was suffering from serious insomnia and concluded that was how she must spend her long lonely nights. I was grateful that at least my girl was able to think of something other than the bird, even if it was only to put on some marigolds. It gave me hope for her recovery.

Having made myself a large mug of steaming tea, I moved over to the kitchen table and sat down. Staring out at the winter garden I considered the success my daughter had made of herself. The house alone was evidence of her hard work and determination, and I hoped that the recent tragedy had not permanently killed off that wonderful, capable side of her. It occurred to me that if Monica was going to recover she would need to find something positive and engrossing to take up her time. I realised I should advise Monica to go back to work, when the time was right.

I am a great believer in self-help. After the death of my husband I successfully took up pottery making. There is a small room in my house I have dedicated to the hobby. When I first started, I spent hours in there, moulding clay, painting and creating mugs, vases, plates, urns and pots in bright bold colours and patterns and I even sold some to a small Cambridge shop. It kept me sane and was a healthy outlet for my creativity. I had even made some new friends through the hobby, having taken classes to help me get to grips with the basics.

I fluffed up my hair and went out into the garden. Unlike the house, everything apart from the lawn was wild and unkempt. Monica had never had the green fingers I was blessed with. The borders looked pitiful, partly because of the time of year but also as a result of neglect. I remembered that Tom had planned to arrange for a landscape gardener to come and work some magic with the back garden. My heart felt heavy as I pondered all the things that he had left unfinished.

Rolling up my sleeves I started to dig up weeds that had grown large and stubborn. The ground was very hard and it made the task troublesome, but I was determined to continue and concentrated my attention on the east-facing wall, which was especially overgrown and jungle-like. I felt I needed to do something proactive to help Monica regain some control over her life.

After an hour, the failing light forced me to give up and go inside. My hands were red and cold and my nose and chin tingled in the low freezing mist that had fallen over North London. With my arms loaded carrying small branches I had pruned back and dead plants dug out of the ground, I pushed my way in to the kitchen. My jumper was muddy and twigs clung to the woollen strands. To my surprise I found Monica in there. She was washing up the dirty cup that had contained my green tea. I cursed myself for not remembering to put it in the dishwasher. I didn't want Monica cleaning up after me; it made me feel like a burden and I was supposed to be there making life easier for her.

Dropping the pile of garden clippings onto the kitchen table and dusting off my hands, I asked about her day.

'How were Mary and Richard?'

Monica stood staring into the sink full of glassy bubbles. 'Shocking,' Monica said. It was not the response I was expecting, although it was hardly surprising.

'They asked me to go and spend Christmas with them. I told them I couldn't face it. I can't be there, Mum. It's bad enough being here, surrounded by Tom's things, but there, it's as though he only exists as their son.'

She opened a drawer and pulled out a large garden refuse sack, handing it to me.

'Oh, thanks, darling.'

I set about pushing the awkward cuttings into the sack, trying to avoid getting yet more splinters.

'He was my husband too. It seems they've forgotten that. I mean, of course he was their child. I know that and I know what it's like to lose a child.' Monica's eyes filled with tears. 'But it's as if they are only able to remember him as a child. It's strange, though, because they desperately want me around but when I'm there they talk about him when he was a boy. Richard doesn't say much. He just sits in his armchair with his eyes glued to the paper pretending to read. But Mary has been into the attic and got out all his old toys. It's weird, Mum, and I don't know what to say. She was reminiscing for hours about how he used to play with this toy and that. She kept stroking them as though they were Tom. I had to get out of there. I couldn't stand it.'

I nodded my head.

'I know how impossible this is for you, Mon, but they are grieving too. Everyone has his or her own coping mechanism. That is the way Mary has chosen to remember him, for now. I'm sure it is not meant to hurt you in any way, shape or form. In fact, I bet she would be devastated if she knew how you felt.'

'I feel almost as sad for them as I do myself, but for fuck's sake he was a grown-up. He was going to be a father. I really can't handle their denial.'

At that moment I saw my opportunity to broach the subject I had been waiting for.

'Sweetheart, it's funny that you should mention denial. It's something I have been thinking about. I'm not sure quite how to say this but don't you think maybe you might be suffering from that too?' The gentle tone of my voice unfortunately did not extinguish the impact of my words.

'What do you mean?' Monica was immediately defensive.

'Oh darling, just that I think perhaps all this business about the crow is your way of putting off thinking about what has really happened.'

The words cut through Monica like a knife. I watched the anger rise inside her like a pot about to boil over.

'You think I want this to be happening to me? That I've imagined that fucking bird attacking me?'

'No, no, sweetheart. I just think that you are spending an awful lot of time and energy on worrying about the bird. I worry that in doing so you are not addressing what has really happened to you.'

Monica slumped down onto the floor and hugged her knees up against her chest.

'I really thought you were on my side.'

I went over to my daughter and sat down beside her. I could smell the thin covering of earth on my hands and was reminded of the grave.

'It's not a question of sides, darling. I love you and I'm worried about you. This is all so bloody horrible. I just want you to be all right.'

'I will never be all right, Mum.' Monica fiddled with her platinum wedding ring. 'My life has been ripped away from me. I need to understand why. Can't you see that?'

'Of course you want answers, Mon, but I'm worried that you're searching for them in the wrong place. Life can be shitty, sweetheart, and sometimes you can look for answers that just aren't there.'

'If only I could remember the accident more clearly. It's all there, in my head – I know it is. I just need to remember what made us hit that tree. All I can see is the crow. It's the only thing I recall.'

'But Monica, don't you think it's possible that you just saw a crow? I mean it's not that unusual to see a crow, is it, darling? It doesn't explain why the crash happened. Perhaps it just came to investigate. Maybe its nest was in the tree you collided with. Seeing a crow at the scene doesn't mean that it was responsible.'

Wiping tears away, Monica got up off of the floor and straightened her clothes.

'Well at least I know where you stand now.

Don't worry, I won't talk to you about the crow anymore. The only thing I will discuss with you is that my husband and my baby are dead. Let's concentrate all our efforts on thinking about that happy fact. So where do you want to begin?'

I let out a long frustrated sigh and buried my head in my hands.

'For goodness sake. I am trying my best here. I don't know what to say to you, I don't have all the answers. I just think that spending all your time worrying about a stupid, harmless bird isn't going to get you anywhere.' I immediately regretted my words.

'No Mum, you are right, but thinking about my family lying lifeless in the dirt isn't exactly filling me with hope and light either. Maybe it's best if you go home to Cambridge for a while. I need some space.' And with that, Monica left the room. I listened to my daughter's footsteps on the stairs and wished the conversation had gone differently. Picking myself up I went over to the doors that looked into the garden. It was nearly six o'clock and the blue-black night had laid its blanket over the city.

I closed my eyes and rubbed my temples. My head ached. I had never known Monica be so rude to me. Although it was understandable, given the circumstances, I couldn't help feeling that somehow my daughter had changed. I hoped the accident hadn't killed off who Monica used to be.

Out of nowhere, a loud crash against the glass made me stumble backwards. I didn't know what it was. The evening returned to silence and I peered out into the darkness trying to see what had caused the noise. Reaching for the light switch, I turned on the outdoor light. A yellow glow flooded the garden. Everything was still. I stepped closer to the glass again. Without any warning a large black bird came sweeping into the door. I fell back onto the floor, catching my arm on the corner of the table. The stinging pain travelled through my elbow and I let out a small squeal before looking back over at the door.

To my horror, inches away from the glass door, a large black crow sat on the paving, staring into the house. Its large black eyes fixed me and made my blood run cold. It hopped closer and began pecking at the glass with its strong grey-black beak. The noise was similar to nails down a blackboard, only magnified. I covered my ears with my hands and closed my eyes. Seconds later the noise stopped. I slowly opened my eyes to see that the crow had disappeared. All that remained was one immaculate black feather lying on the cold ground.

CHAPTER 6

Lying on Tom's side of the bed, I gripped the pillow and tried to find his smell. His aftershave was sweet and sickly but I missed it now it was beginning to disappear. I was losing him altogether. Holding the pillow, I walked into the nursery. It was nearly complete; all it was missing was my child. Turning on the light I ran my eye over the cream and yellow toys and furniture. If only I'd known I was going to have a son. I would have painted cars on the walls and planes on the ceiling. The room would have been transformed into a little boy's dream, not this bland space I saw before me. The regret made me want to curl up and die.

Sitting down in the large comfortable nursing chair that would never be used, I thought about the argument I had just had with Mum. I knew she hadn't meant to cause any offence and I silently cursed myself for snapping at her. Where had all this anger come from? It seemed so absurd to be taking it out on her. But on the other hand I wanted her to believe me. She should believe me. I'm not mad. Why couldn't she see that? This wasn't about grief. Something else horrible was happening to me, to my life.

Just as I decided I would return downstairs and make amends, I heard a loud piercing scream coming from the kitchen. I dropped the pillow on the floor and, turning on my heels, ran out of the nursery as fast as I could towards the sound of

Mum wailing.

When I reached the kitchen I found my mother hunched up on the floor with her back against the wall. Her face was ashen and her eyes large and frightened. Crouching down beside her I looked for any signs of injury but found none. She remained there and pointed in the direction of the garden. The doors were closed and I couldn't see any broken glass.

'What is it, Mum?' She stood up gripping my arm tightly.

'There,' she whispered. 'Look.'

I strained to peer through the glass but found nothing.

'You need to explain, Mum. I don't understand. What was it that scared you?' My mother stood glaring through the glass for a long time, refusing to speak. I feared she'd suffered a stroke of some sorts. 'Mum, please.'

Letting go of my hand, she edged closer towards the wall of glass. I could see her face reflected in its surface. I had never seen her like that before. After a few moments I could see her shoulders beginning to relax.

'It's gone.' She turned to face me. 'I need a stiff drink.'

'Mum, seriously, you are scaring me. What's gone on? What are you talking about?'

Reaching into the freezer, she pulled out a frosted bottle of vodka and proceeded to pour herself a large measure. In one large gulp she drained the glass before pouring me one and herself another. I sat down and accepted the drink.

'I saw it. The bird. I saw the crow.'

'What do you mean you saw it?'

'The crow, darling, your crow. It flew at me. It flew at the glass.'

Her hands shook as she lifted the drink to her lips and took a small sip.

'I am so sorry I didn't believe you. You are right. There is something about that bird. Something malevolent. It flew right at the glass, trying to break it. Then it landed on the patio and started violently pecking the glass. It was trying to get in, like a thing possessed. I think it must be mad.'

'Are you serious?'

'Completely.'

'You think it's mad? That's your explanation?'

'Well, I mean, I know it's frightening, darling, but the creature is clearly deranged.'

'Of course it's fucking deranged, but didn't you feel the intent?'

'Intent?'

'Yes Mum, the intent! It's not just mad, it's doing this on purpose. Can't you see that? Didn't you feel it?'

'Now, sweetheart, look, I am sorry I didn't believe you about there being a bird which was attacking you. I was wrong. But it is still just a bird. It can't possibly knowingly mean you any harm. It's just mad. Poor thing.'

I couldn't believe my ears.

'Jesus Christ! You are unbelievable. What is wrong with you?' A ferocious anger was bubbling up inside me.

'Excuse me, Monica, but you need to calm

down. I am not the enemy here...'

'No you're right, that fucking bird is!'

'Look, just sit back down and listen to me. I am not going have a stand-up row with you over a crazy bird.'

I stood with my back to her, staring out at the black night, and spotted the feather on the ground.

'SIT DOWN!' The Rottweiler had returned and suddenly I lost all my steam. I sank down onto a chair and downed my vodka.

'That's better,' she said, pouring herself a third vodka and me my second.

My mother spoke for a long time and I didn't interrupt. She told me how she had done some research online into crow attacks. She said that it happened because the bird had babies or was feeling especially territorial. She had come to the conclusion that the bird might have lived in the hugely tall tree that Tom and I had cut down in the garden. She went on to say that she thought it was a coincidence that I had seen a crow at the scene of the accident. She believed that being dive-bombed at the grave was also unrelated. Mum thought animals had a sixth sense and that the crows were picking up on my fear and reacting to it. She didn't believe there was only one crow responsible for the strange events.

I saw no point in arguing. It was even possible that she had a point. I drank the vodka, numbing the pain in my head with each chilled sip. Fatigue swept over me and I wanted to curl up in bed with the crow gone from my consciousness. I gave my mother a hug, thanked her for being there for me and bid her goodnight.

***

The next morning things looked brighter. I woke up thinking about what had happened to my mum last night. At least now somebody knew I wasn't completely mad. I had an accomplice in my search for answers. Mum was going to help me work out what was going on and how to fix things. No one could bring back Tom or Josh or mend the break in my heart left by their deaths, but the bird would be dealt with somehow.

I got out of bed and felt about on the carpet for my slippers. My cold white feet found the soft fleecy boots and pushed themselves inside. Getting up from the bed I padded over to the window and, yawning, pulled back the curtains. There was a crystal-white frost covering everything. It was the first clear blue day I had seen for some time. The shards of frozen grass glittered in the light and made the garden look magical. The scene was spoilt by the arrival of two large crows. They landed on the lawn and began rummaging for worms. I took a step back and watched them for some time. The birds seemed uninterested in me and I relaxed when I realised neither of them was *that* bird.

I'd never really had any interest in birds until that point. Some people love them, others hate them, but I felt ambiguous about their existence. They had never bothered me and I'd never bothered them. Now it felt as if my life was forever linked to a bird. It had changed everything, seemingly without explanation. I remembered what my mother had said about the possibility of a crow's nest in the large tree that Tom and I had cut down and racked my brains to try and remember if there had been a nest in it. But I was sure that wasn't the reason for the crow's sudden desire to do me harm. And besides, the fact that it had tried to attack Mum last night meant it very unlikely to be related to the felling of the big old tree that had been done more than a year ago.

The first time I became aware of the bird's presence was just after the accident. The answer to this weird mystery was going to be found there. Suddenly I knew what I needed to do. I had to return to the scene.

As I came to that decision I noticed that the birds in the garden below had stopped foraging and were now staring up at my window. I pulled the curtains closed again and went to have a shower.

While I stood beneath the powerful gush of water, I thought about Tom. What was now my past still felt like it was in the present. Although I didn't see him anymore, he remained everywhere. All my actions led back to him. My thoughts were dominated by what he would have thought or said. He was a strong character who had cast a long shadow over my existence. I was exhausted from living with his ghost.

My head took me on a journey through the past. My memory overflowed with things he had said, the way his mouth moved when he spoke. I felt as though I was trapped in a whirlwind of history. Being at home didn't help. Surrounded by things that were his or reminded me of him only kept the images alive.

It wasn't that I wanted to forget, nothing like that, but I wasn't ready to start thinking about him as something from my past. He was always going to be my future and anything else wouldn't do. It made no sense to me. I kept expecting to see him. Round every corner of the house and as I wandered the streets, it was as if he was there with me. But he wasn't, he was gone and the only thing that remained was my memory playing tricks and taunting me.

The bathroom was all his: his soaps and shampoo, his towel on the back of the door, his razor by the sink and our toothbrushes side by side in the tooth mug. It was as though he was everywhere and yet somehow lost to me. I closed my eyes and leant my back against the clouded glass of the shower door. The noise of the water was intolerable. We had made love right there beneath the large chrome head. And now I was alone.

My hand rested lightly on my stomach, feeling the ache of emptiness. Every limb felt heavy. I crouched on the floor of the shower and scrunched my eyes tight. Tom's face was in my head. His reflection was trapped in a circus of hundreds of mirrors. He was smiling and talking. I could see his mouth moving but no words came out. His mouth. I missed his mouth more than anything.

My legs felt wobbly and my mind was spinning. Panic took hold of me and I started to sweat. It was an odd sensation, feeling dirty in the shower. The water was meant to wash all the filth away yet it seemed it only emphasised my horrible, dirty guilt.

Then the penny dropped. I felt guilty. I felt guilty about the accident although I didn't understand why. I felt guilty about the death of my son and my husband, and worst of all, I felt sick to my stomach that I had survived. Why was I here when they were not? I wished I had died with them. As I entertained my morbid thoughts, my body was thrown violently backwards.

I cannot explain what happened. It made no sense. The only way I can describe it is to say it felt as though some unseen force was attacking me. My stomach tightened in response to the feeling of being punched. As I slipped onto the floor of the shower I opened my eyes and searched around for an explanation. The bathroom was empty and quiet except for the thud of the water falling onto the tiles below. Although the glass of the shower walls and door were clouded with steam, I knew I was alone. There were no shadows there. I bent my spine and held my tummy, which still ached. It was as if I was losing Josh all over again.

And then I saw it. Streak of crimson red mingled with the water and whirled around the plug. Blood. Lots of blood. And it was coming from me. I realised it was pouring from my groin. Fresh waves gradually turned the puddle of water I was sitting in pink. Then I started to smell it. A scent like rust rose with the steam. Without warning I began to gag. Breathing seemed impossible.

The water that had once been soothing suddenly began to hurt my skin. It was as though

I was being hammered with icy needles and I could not move. All I wanted to do was to push the door open and escape onto the cold bathroom floor but I was stuck to the spot. Agony and numbness took turns in holding me there. And then I realised the water was rising. The plug wasn't blocked but the water had turned a dark, blackish red and was beginning to fill the shower tray. It felt thick and slimy against my skin. Still I could not move. In a flash, it felt as though I had been transported back to the scene of the accident.

In an attempt to escape the terror surrounding me, I curled my body up into a ball and held my eyes tightly closed. The water went from feeling icy to boiling and I winced away from the flow. When I opened my eyes I could not make sense of what greeted me. Everything had returned to normal.

I was still in the shower but the blood had disappeared. I checked myself all over, looking for evidence. There was none. Closely, I scrutinised my hands and the plug. Nothing. I wiped the condensation from the glass and saw the bathroom was the same as it had always been. Then I was sick. It poured out of me the way that water cascaded from the large showerhead.

Perhaps I was going mad.

I crawled out of the shower on my knees and huddled up on the white-painted floorboards that felt cold and hard against my damp skin. My ebony hair was wrapped around my throat like a noose and my flesh tingled with goose bumps. The white bathroom suddenly seemed very bright. It was shining. A piercing high-pitched scream echoed around my head and I brought my hands up to cover my ears. Then I caught sight of a dark flash. I looked up to see the silhouette of a huge black bird at the window. It was at that point I realised the scream was coming from me.

I put my fist in my mouth to dull the noise escaping from me and the bird took off. I was alone again in a bathroom I recognised, and calm flooded in through the window with the low rays of the winter sun. I felt warm once more. Scrabbling up from the floor, I reached for a large ivory-coloured towel and wrapped it tightly around my shaking frame. Wandering over to the loo, I sat down on the seat and tried to regain my composure. What had just happened to me? I felt sick again but nothing came out. My body was empty of everything.

Then I heard a light knock on the bathroom door. I jumped up and went to crouch down in the far corner, terrified of what might be trying to get in.

'Is everything all right, darling? You've been in there an awful long time.'

The comforting sound of my mother's voice came as a huge relief. My shoulders dropped and I edged closer to the door.

'Just having a good soak, that's all. Be out in a minute.' I wondered if she noticed the quiver in my voice.

'There are some croissants in the oven and a freshly made pot of coffee on the table in the kitchen. Get yourself some breakfast. I've just got to pop out for a bit, the fridge is looking very bare.'

'OK. I might not be here when you get back. I thought I'd go for a wander around Ally Pally.' I listened for a response or the sound of her footsteps going down the stairs but heard nothing. 'Mum?'

'Yes?'

'I'll see you later.'

'OK, Mon. See you later.'

My body had now stopped shaking. What had occurred only moments before suddenly seemed distant from reality. I shook myself off and towel dried my hair. Staring into the bathroom mirror, I realised I hardly recognised myself. I used to look pretty, happy even, but all that remained was a hollow shell of the person I used to be.

I had to somehow find myself again, and instinct told me to start at the beginning. Going back to where the accident took place was going to be hard but I had to begin somewhere. Reaching for a comb, I ran it through my hair, pulling hard at the tangles. For some reason I felt angry. My life had taken a wrong turn and I had lost all control over my own destiny. It was time to get it back.

I marched into my bedroom and flung open my large walk-in wardrobe. Sometimes I was surprised by my own banality. Staring at the neatly lined-up, colour-coded rows of clothes, I wondered why I ever bothered. Fussing about the tidiness of my surroundings suddenly seemed so inane. Tom used to like it though. He said it was a healthy reaction to my mother's charming but chaotic lack of order. I have no doubt he was right.

Gazing at my designer clothes and the numerous expensive bags I'd accumulated now felt worthless. I would have been better off spending the money on building memories with Tom, but hindsight is a cruel thing.

Frustrated by my own yuppie trappings, I searched the rails for my most comfortable sloppy clothes. A pair of green converse high tops, some grey marl jogging bottoms and an old slouchy navy hoodie did the trick. Slipping into my clothes felt good. Then I made my way downstairs. I wasn't hungry so I turned the oven off and put the pastries in the bin. Pouring myself half a cup of filter coffee, I put the plate in the dishwasher and tidied away Mum's crumbs. Some habits are hard to shake.

Getting ready to leave, I put on a large cream beanie then pulled the front door shut behind me. Despite the winter sunshine, the air was nippy and my breath clouded up in front of me as I made my way in the direction of Alexandra Palace Road. Walking along Priory Road, headed in the direction of Muswell Hill, I rubbed my hands together and plunged them into my pockets.

The world was busy with buses, children making their way to school and people trying to get to work. I realised how long it had been since I'd participated in anything as wonderfully perennial. I missed doing the small things in life but everything was such an effort. Being out in the bustling streets of North London made me feel afraid again. The fear I'd felt in the bathroom returned and I began to panic. I suppose it wasn't surprising. I was going back to visit the spot where my husband and child died. It was never going to feel good.

I was determined not to turn around and give up. My mind needed a distraction, and fiddling in my pocket I felt for my iPhone and headphones. Music might be the answer. Walking along the pavement, I flicked through my song library. Most of the tracks I came across reminded me of Tom. He had been part of my life since I was nineteen years old and everything seemed to lead back to him.

Eventually I found an album that was mine and mine alone. I'd always loved Will Young. *Friday's Child* was an album I used to play a lot. It was my guilty pleasure. Whenever Tom was out I'd plug my phone into the speakers and blast it out around our house. Smiling at the safe familiarity of the lyrics, I realised I was almost at the spot where we had crashed.

My stomach knotted and I came to a stop. I couldn't see the tree we had crashed into but I knew that in a few steps, as I turned the corner up the hill, it would come into view. Would there be evidence that a crash had taken place? Was I really ready to face this? My head spun and a strange sensation of vertigo came over me.

A plump man in his mid-twenties was jogging on my side of the road down the hill towards me. He gave me an odd look as he passed me by. I had to steady myself and leant my back up against a tree. The bark felt rough and cold through my clothes and suddenly I didn't want to be there anymore.

Just as I had decided to turn around and go

back, something made me stop. I looked up the hill and listened for a sound. The world seemed eerily silent and strangely deserted. No cars were on the road and it seemed as if all the people had vanished. Something was pulling me up the hill. It was a force that I felt unable to fight. I went with it, wondering what might be waiting for me around the corner. Inexplicably, all the fear I had been feeling melted away as I was pulled towards that fateful spot.

As the large chestnut tree came into view, I pulled the headphones out of my ears. Will Young didn't feel appropriate. I wanted to be alone with my thoughts. Standing just metres away from the place where my husband and child died, I froze. There was no evidence of anything. It was as if the event had been erased or had never happened. Time did not remember what it had done to me, to my family. An unassuming tree stood before me. Only very faint tyre tracks remained on the road where the car had skidded.

Slowly, I edged closer, making sure to keep an eye out for the crow. I could feel its black eyes on me but it remained hidden from sight. What really surprised me was how normal everything looked. In my head the tree was huge and ominous, almost alive with twisting branches and thick gnarled bark. But standing there I could see that it was just a chestnut tree. It looked like all the other trees growing along the wooded road.

Tentatively I approached it and looked up into the naked branches. I searched for signs of the crow but found nothing. Half of me had been expecting to find a nest but the vast sprawling branches were uninhabited. My heart sunk. I had pinned so much on finding answers there. I squatted down onto my heels and picked up a handful of wet dirt and leaves. It felt cold in my hand and I cursed the earth for taking my family from me.

Moments later, a car appeared from nowhere and hurtled past me. It made me jump, and I had to reach out for the trunk to stop myself from falling over into the mud. As my palm made contact with the bark, a stinging image pierced my brain. I saw Tom's face, angry and in pain, looking at me in the car. We hadn't crashed yet but we were speeding down the hill. He was shouting at me, and I was crying. The memory came out of nowhere and hit me like a bullet. I knew it was real but I couldn't remember why he had been so upset. I watched it play out as if it was happening all over again but, like a silent film or a horror movie on mute, no words came from his mouth. I felt frightened and confused again. Somewhere, guilt stirred once more.

As soon as I took my hand off the tree, it stopped, as though the movie suddenly came to an abrupt end. I was back in the present and an elderly woman in a brown coat was standing a few feet away, eyeing me warily. I picked myself up off the ground and started down the hill. Sweat pierced my brow as I ran as fast as my legs would carry me back to the house. My heart thumped in my chest and a knot appeared in my gut. But I pushed through the stitch and kept on running home.

When I reached my red front door I was

panting and dripping with sweat. The combination of fear, confusion and pain mingled together like a tornado around my head. Dizziness stung my eyes and I bent over double trying to catch my breath. Once I'd steadied my nerves, I looked up to see a crow standing on my porch. In its mouth was a small dead mouse. It dropped the fleshy pup onto the doormat and began tearing it apart with its talons. I was horrified.

'Leave me alone!' I screamed. 'What do you want from me?' But the bird became statuesque, looking at me with dead eyes. I stared back at it, hoping to show I was unafraid. Then it looked up to the sky and took off, leaving behind only the mangled carcass of a baby mouse on my doorstep.

CHAPTER 7

As I drove along the M11 in the direction of Cambridge, the rain pelted the windscreen. The radio played softly in the background and in the passenger seat Monica sat staring blankly out of the window. The world was grey and cold and matched the atmosphere inside the Volvo.

The lack of conversation made me feel uncomfortable and I racked my brains for something light to talk about. It was no use. Monica had retreated into herself and I had to accept I'd be wasting my time trying to fill the silence. Besides, I did not want to incur the wrath of my daughter who was often angry these days.

It was two days before Christmas and in a desperate attempt to lift my child out of her despair I'd insisted we both returned to Cambridge to see out the festive period. Monica, who had once loved Christmas, agreed to my request but was unable to muster any signs of enthusiasm. I decided to keep it a very low-key affair and not make much of a fuss. Although I wanted to spoil my daughter, I realised it would neither really help nor be well received. This year, unfortunately, Christmas would pass by unnoticed.

As we ploughed on through the torrent of icy rain I tried to think of things that might help distract Monica from the sadness she was so consumed by. I wished Monica's father had been there to help. Jim would have known what to do. I had never felt so much at a loss, and the pain of my own grief threatened to swallow me whole. My only child felt like a stranger to me.

On the radio a DJ chatted about favourite Christmas songs from days gone by. I could feel Monica's irritation bubbling up and quickly turned the radio off.

'Would you like to go out to supper tonight? I thought I'd treat you. What do you fancy?' I tried to sound jolly.

'I'm not hungry.'

'You don't need to be hungry to eat. Let's go out. Come on, it might be fun.'

Monica turned her head and fixed me with bright green eyes.

'Fun?'

'Yes darling, fun.' I tried hard to temper the twinge of irritation in my voice.

'Fine, but you choose where.' She crossed her arms and returned to staring out of the window.

'OK, good.' I felt better. 'I fancy Chinese. How does that sound?'

'Fine.' Monica remained inanimate.

'Good. Let's go to Charlie Chan's. You used to love it there.'

We continued the drive in silence. The rain had eased to a drizzle now and the Cambridgeshire countryside looked flat and bleak. As we approached the junction that would lead us into Cambridge, Monica turned to me.

'Tom hated Chinese food.'

'Really? I never knew.'

'Yes, he said it was tasteless. I never ate it when he was around. He didn't like the smell. If he went out and I was alone sometimes, then I'd order a takeaway.'

'Oh.'

'I would have to hide the boxes from him though,' Monica said vacantly.

'But hang on, darling, we took him to Charlie Chan's a few years ago, remember? He seemed to enjoy the food.'

'No, Mum. He didn't. He said it made him sick and he banned it from the house after that.'

I was surprised. It seemed like such an out of character thing for Tom to do. He always seemed to me like a laid-back chap, happy to go along with anything and never complaining.

'Well maybe he had a touch of food poisoning. That can really put you off your food. Remember when I had that dodgy oyster? I couldn't be in the same room as one for seven years after that.'

'It wasn't food poisoning.' I noticed she was rubbing the small scar on the back of her right hand and thought I should leave the conversation alone.

As usual, the traffic in Cambridge was horrendous. We crawled along Hills Road at a snail's pace. Normally this would have bothered me, and I would have been impatiently tooting my horn and cursing under my breath, but on that day I enjoyed looking at all the lights and the shoppers on the street. It was the closest thing I'd experience to Christmas that year. While we sat at traffic lights, I watched as three generations of one family crossed the road, wrapped up in hats and scarves, loaded with bags and looking happy. The reminder of what both Monica and I were missing left me feeling miserable. As I swallowed the lump in my throat, I hoped my daughter hadn't noticed them.

It was nearly four o'clock when we pulled into Herbert Street. An indigo sky began to get its grip on the world and Monica hugged herself as she got out of the car. There was a distant hum of traffic, and coming from somewhere we could hear carols being sung. Trying to ignore the jollity, Monica lugged her Louis Vuitton keep-all out of the boot and made her way towards my front door.

My house is a semi-detached Victorian house with a slate roof and chequerboard pathway leading up to the green front door. In the bay window to the left, one of my three cats poked its head around an orange curtain and looked out at us.

'Come on, Mum, its bloody freezing.'

'Coming, coming,' my voice sang as I rummaged about on the back seat retrieving my bags. The long-haired tabby meowed when it recognised the sound of my voice. Just then, a cold sharp breeze blew down the street ruffling the leaves of the evergreen viburnum in the garden next door. Monica gave a little shiver. I could see she was thinking about the crow again. She spun around and searched every rooftop with her eyes. There was, of course, no sign of the bird. Laden with bags, I shuffled my way up to the front door. Fiddling with my keys I finally managed to unlock the door. Pushing it open with my knee I staggered inside. Monica followed me into the house as I stood enjoying the familiar scent of cat's hair and the faint remains of lavender incense.

Since Jim died I'd taken to rescuing strays. Monica preferred dogs but said she was glad I had some company. I was too. It had been impossible for me to imagine trying to meet someone else. Jim was my one and only. There would never be anyone else for me. So instead of trying to find a replacement man, I rescued cats.

The hallway was a mess of coats and shoes. Monica squeezed passed and into the sitting room where, uncharacteristically, she dropped her luggage on the floor. The room was cold and dark. The long-haired tabby jumped down from the windowsill and leapt over in my direction. I stood trying to untangle my orange scarf from my neck while Monica sat down on the sofa in the blackness and looked at the small fireplace adorned with all my ornaments. There were shells and small dusty photograph frames. A carved wooden figure of a cat stood pride of place and next to it was a pair of brass candlesticks. Monica closed her eyes and leant back into the sofa, which I knew also smelt of animal fur. I could see her wondering what she was doing here. It was not her home; she had never lived here.

I had downsized to a smaller house a year after Jim's death. My eclectic taste could be found in every detail, from the large shabby kilim rugs to the faded silk cushion covers. It was homely and warm, even in the darkness, but I knew Monica still felt numb. She looked like a broken woman who did not want colour in her life anymore. She seemed to feel at home in the muted grey spaces of the world.

Monica pulled her knees up under her chin and I said I'd put the kettle on and scuttled off in the direction of the kitchen. I left her alone in the darkness.

I flicked the heating and water timer switch on and listened to the sound of the house coming alive. It was all around, the hum from the boiler kicking into action. I imagined Monica curling up into a small ball in the corner of the sofa, reaching for the woollen blanket that was casually strewn over the back of the couch. As a small child she would pull her favourite blanket up around her body and close her eyes whenever she wanted to go to sleep. I knew her so well. Every movement; the meaning behind each and every sigh.

In the kitchen I clattered about making a cup of tea and sorting through the vast pile of mail that my neighbour had left for me on the kitchen table. Janet Higginson had been a lifesaver and taken care of not only my house but also the cats. I muttered as I pushed aside the bills and opened what looked to be Christmas cards. In the background, the ancient kettle whistled shakily and spurted out a burst of hot steam. As I stood reading the Christmas cards, one of the cats wrapped itself around my ankles.

'Oh, Tinkles, hello!' I bent down and swept the large black cat up into my arms. The feline purred loudly and rubbed its face against my chin with delight. We spent a long time reconnecting. Secretly I was thrilled to be home. I loved my daughter's house normally but since the accident it felt like an empty tomb void of hope. I tried to tell myself warmth would return there one day but worried in case I was wrong.

The kettle screamed that it was boiling, and I set the purring cat back down on the tiled terracotta floor, before removing a pint of milk from a bag of shopping I'd bought back with me. Tinkles resumed wrapping his black tail around my legs.

'Yes, yes, I know. You want some milk. Just wait a moment, fatty.' I poured some of the cold milk into a large ceramic saucer on the floor. Still purring loudly, the cat began to lap up the creamy offering before being barged out of the way by the long-haired tabby. Then I returned to making myself a cup of green tea. Removing one of the large chipped mugs from a cupboard, I called out to Monica, asking if she fancied a cup. When I received no response I yelled out again. Still Monica remained silent.

I carried the steaming mugs back to the sitting room. Walking into the thick blackness I could just make out the small curled-up figure of my daughter on the sofa. I put her tea down on the pine chest coffee table and turned on one of the side lamps. An orange glow flooded the room bringing it instantly to life.

Monica lay sleeping beneath the rug, and tucking her in I sat back to watch her. I was pleased she was asleep. Her nights at home had been so disturbed I was concerned that she was becoming an insomniac. Given the circumstances it was hardly surprising.

Despite being asleep, Monica's face appeared troubled. Her brow was furrowed and her skin pale. I stroked her fringe away from her forehead. Monica stirred and I retracted my hand carefully. Sitting motionless and holding my breath, I wanted my daughter to remain sleeping. After a moment or two, when I felt certain she was in no danger of waking, I got up and went over to the fireplace. Poking about in the hearth I added some coal and firelighters before striking a match and bringing the fire to life. Still on my knees, I watched the little licking flames as they flickered amber and blue.

With a long sigh and cracking knees I got up off the floor and began to arrange the pile of Christmas cards I'd bought in from the kitchen. I stood them on the mantelpiece and slipped them in among books on the shelves. I was grateful for the kind messages I'd received from friends and hoped that Monica might soon be able to reconnect with the friends she had in London. I was sure that with a good support network Monica could get through this.

Then I realised that Monica no longer seemed to have any old friends around her. She used to be so popular. At university she had surrounded herself with a large social group but in the last few years she had seen people less and less. Apart from Tom and I, she had apparently retreated from everyone. It didn't make sense. Where were all her girlfriends? I knew Monica wasn't easy to be around now but surely one of them should want to be there to support her. For example, she hadn't mentioned her dear old friend Simon in months and months and they had been so close. I wondered what had happened to change that? She could do with a friend.

As I stood the last card up among some picture frames, my tired eyes were drawn to a photograph of my daughter on her wedding day. The picture was a portrait photo of the happy couple, surrounded by friends, moments after the ceremony. Both of them were smiling in the sunlight. I had never seen her look so radiant. Reaching out my hand, I touched the glass.

Then I spotted Simon in the background of the picture. He was a good-looking young man, who I'd always liked. He was well mannered and clearly dotty about Monica. He'd been a part of her life as long as Tom had. The three of them all met at UCL and it dawned on me how strange it was that Simon hadn't come to the funeral.

The memory of the funeral came flooding back to me and as my throat began to close up, a loud bang made me jump out of my skin. I spun around to see a large crow standing on the ledge outside the bay window. Stepping back in horror, I knocked the picture over which went crashing to the ground. Glass shattered everywhere and splinters pierced the photograph.

I remained motionless as Monica flinched in her sleep. When I was certain she was not going to wake, I quickly crept over to the window and drew the curtains. In the meantime the bird had flown away but I didn't want it to be able to see us. It was a coincidence, I told myself as I picked up large shattered pieces of glass. Surely the same bird couldn't have followed us from London. Why would it and how could it? Nicking my finger on a piece of glass, drops of blood seeped into the threadbare carpet below, mingling with the orange and red weave. As it merged with the wool, an unwelcome feeling returned to my stomach.

***

I kept my experience with the bird to myself. I was fearful Monica would use it as a further excuse to indulge her new obsession with all things corvid. I'd also hidden the photograph that had been broken during the scene. Upon closer inspection, I realised that most of the pieces of glass were sticking into Monica's face and not that of my son-in-law. Whatever was happening to Monica did seem odd. Although I now believed that a bird had fixated on Monica, I couldn't for the life of me make sense of it.

On Christmas morning, I went into the kitchen to discover Monica sitting drinking a cup of coffee. It was half past eight and the cold winter sunlight poured in through the window. Monica's face looked pale and her dark hair was flat. Yawning, I kissed her, wished her a happy Christmas and turned the kettle on.

'I'm going to visit the grave in a few hours,' Monica said, gazing into her mug of coffee.

'Would you like me to come with you?'

'Actually, that would be great. I've agreed to meet Mary and Richard there. I don't think I can face it alone.'

Rubbing my eyes and running a bony hand through my tangled mass of hair, I yawned again and nodded. I was never normally an early riser but one of the cats had decided it was breakfast time and insisted I got up. Since returning home I'd allowed the cats to all sleep at the end of my bed. I liked the company. Tinkles, Biddy and Bobo platted their way in and out of my legs, meowing and begging for my attention. Monica watched with amusement as I shuffled over to the cupboard and proceeded to knock dry cat food all over the tiled floor.

'Bloody hell,' I muttered.

'Mum, go up and have a wash. I'll deal with the cats.'

I nodded gratefully and sloped off in the direction of the bathroom.

As I left, I saw Monica shove the pushiest cat, Tinkles, out of the way with her foot as she went to fetch the dustpan and brush. The cat stuck its nose in the air and turned its back on her before jumping up onto the work surface. Monica scowled at the cat, which fixed her with a defiant stare.

After she swept up the biscuits on the floor and fed the three felines I heard Monica come upstairs to dress. She went into the spare room and surveyed the mess she had created with her belongings. At home with Tom she'd always been so organised and tidy but here she had reverted to type. Clothes were strewn on the end of the bed frame and on the arm of an old armchair.

I stood in the doorway and watched as Monica picked up a long black Whistles dress. She looked down at the chipped maroon-coloured nail varnish and I remembered how she used to take such pride in her appearance. These days she never went to the salon. It had always been important to Tom that she looked her best. I could see her wondering what he would think if he could see her now.

Monica let the black dress fall down over her head. I could smell her fabric softener from the doorway and it reminded me of springtime. Monica had discovered she was pregnant in April. Tom had been so happy, so looking forward to starting a family and becoming a father. A hollow feeling returned to my belly and I ached for my daughter.

I remained watching as Monica went over to the mirror and applied some make-up. The cuts to her face had disappeared and no evidence of the trauma remained, at least on the outside.

Rubbing some blush onto her cheeks I could see she was dreading the day ahead. Being around Richard and Mary should have been a comfort but it had the opposite effect. She was trying hard not to think about Tom or Josh but when in the company of her in-laws it was inescapable.

Monica called over her shoulder that she would keep the visit short. She couldn't handle anyone else's doom and gloom, she was struggling enough coping with her own. I agreed and disappeared off to dress myself.

After a slice of toast and a hot cup of tea, Monica and I left Herbert Street and drove out of Cambridge. The city was strangely quiet even for Christmas Day. Hardly any cars were on the road. As I drove I couldn't help imagining families happily in their homes sitting round the tree awaiting a plump goose. I still wasn't sure that ignoring Christmas was the right thing to do, but since Monica had shown no enthusiasm for it I was left with little choice. But in my heart I felt sadder than I could ever admit to myself. A long shadow had been cast by the untimely deaths of my grandson and son-in-law, a shadow that covered everything in my daughter's life, leaving it void of warmth and light. It was a cold black shadow.

I pulled up the car and parked near the Ickleton church. Monica said she felt sick. The colour drained from her face, and reaching out to take her hand, I saw the look of terror in her eyes.

'I … I … I didn't get him a Christmas present.' Monica's eyes brimmed with tears. I immediately understood that she was talking about Josh.

'Sshh, sweetheart. It's OK. Josh doesn't need anything. He's got his father and his grandfather with him.'

Thankfully my words seemed to sooth her somewhat. Wiping her eyes, she nodded and opened the car door.

Although the sun was shining, the bitter cold made us catch our breath. The air clouded in a warm fog with each breath we took. The village looked chocolate-box pretty but I could tell Monica was beginning to feel spooked. Even to me, the church appeared larger and more daunting than it had done previously. I couldn't help notice its tall spire jutting into the sky, blocking out the sun in defiance.

Infected by Monica's sense of foreboding, I looked around for the bird. All I discovered was a robin sitting on the fence. With that, a Christmas feeling returned and I started to feel better. But I could see Monica did not. She looked like a startled deer frozen in fear by the knowledge that something threatening was around the corner.

We tentatively stepped into the churchyard and made our way towards the unmarked graves. The stone had yet to be laid. Cold grass crunched beneath our feet as we wound in and out of gravestones. Monica felt in her coat pocket for her gloves. She couldn't stop her hands from shaking.

When we got to the spot where Tom and Josh were buried, my eyes filled with tears. I'd promised myself I would be strong for her but the sadness overwhelmed me. I brushed away the tears quickly so Monica wouldn't see, but Monica was too wrapped up in her own dread to notice my pain.

She stared down at the mound of dirt, as did I. In my memory it seemed bigger somehow. I'd imagined a huge mountainous pile of mud, crawling with bugs. Standing there, I realised that there was only dirt, nothing living, and it made me hurt for everyone who was left behind to grieve.

We stood silently side by side in the Christmas sunlight and sent warm thoughts out to the bodies buried below our feet. I could feel Monica was concentrating all her thoughts on Josh and trying to hold on to the memory of what the little boy looked like. The image of a small boy running through a garden full of flowers flashed across my consciousness like a shooting star.

I also focused on Tom's parents who were due

to arrive any moment and how sad it was for them to have lost a child. I was sure it would help Monica to spend time grieving with Mary, Tom's mother. The two women should have been able to help each other through the tragedy they shared. Although I had lost my son-in-law and grandson, I felt as though I remained on the periphery of the event, unable to show my sadness or feelings for fear of appearing self-indulgent. My thoughts led me to memories of my own husband and how much I missed him. Christmas had never been the same since his death.

Something made Monica jump and she fell back against me. I steadied myself.

'What is it?'

Monica pointed a gloved finger in the direction of a black cat that stalked through the graveyard like a ghost.

'Oh for goodness sake, Mon, it's just a cat. You scared the life out of me.'

Monica's face remained pale and her eyes wide and staring. She huddled close to me as she watched the animal sloped off into a hedgerow. While she stared at the privet waiting for the cat to reappear, she failed to notice the arrival of Richard, Mary and their daughter Jenny.

Mary, like Monica, was also dressed entirely in black. As the trio came closer I saw Mary was clutching a small blue teddy bear. Richard stared down at the ground as they approached. Only Jenny managed to offer a friendly smile. I was thankful for her efforts and reciprocated.

When Monica felt the presence of her in-laws, she turned to greet them. Jenny immediately approached and embraced her sister-in-law. The two women had not known one another well but the death of Tom provided them with a bond.

Jenny was a free-spirited creature who loved to travel. While Tom had been at university she had been adventuring around the world, leaving behind her a string of broken hearts. She was unnaturally beautiful and it was obvious that most younger women would be intimidated by her looks. It had been no different for Monica.

Long blonde hair framed the heart-shaped face with its prominent cheekbones and sparkling bright blue eyes. Jenny's mouth was pink and soft and men swooned whenever they were near her. Despite her beauty, she was neither arrogant nor self-conscious. She floated through life seemingly unaware of the effect she had on people, which only added to her attraction.

Monica had always worried that Jenny thought she was uptight, but standing in the graveyard they were finally on even ground. She fought back tears and Jenny wrapped her arm around her shoulder and gave it a gentle squeeze. The five of us remained quiet and stood for a moment peering down at the grave.

Richard looked skinny and gaunt. His face was the colour of putty. I had always pictured him as a round man until that moment. My heart hurt for everyone standing there. I wanted to speak but did not know what to say. What was there to say? Stepping back, I allowed Mary to get closer to the grave. There was a noticeable physical distance between the husband and wife. The pain engrained on Richard's furrowed brow told of a man who struggled to express his feelings.

Mary knelt down on the frosty ground. Her skeletal fingers with their swollen knuckles clung to the small blue bear. Jenny approached and put a hand on her mother's shoulder. Mary sobbed quietly. No one said anything. When the sobbing had subsided, Mary gently placed the stuffed toy down on the ground.

'For you, my darling boy. Happy Christmas.' There was a tremor in her voice.

'Happy Christmas, you two,' Jenny spoke quietly.

Monica, Richard and I said nothing. We did not see the point. Being there was enough for us.

After a few more moments' reflection at the graveside, the five of us made our way back towards Richard and Mary's home nearby. Ickleton was silent, clean and cold beneath the winter sun. Monica pushed the churchyard gate open and thanked Mary for Josh's present.

'Josh would have loved the bear, I'm sure. It was very kind of you.'

Mary stopped and a confused look crossed her face.

'Oh no, the bear wasn't for Josh, it was for Tom. He loves cuddly toys.'

Everyone except Mary felt the flush of anger rise up in Monica.

'What do you mean, he *loves* cuddly toys?' she spat.

'I would get him a new bear every Christmas,' Mary spoke proudly.

I darted towards my daughter to try and temper her but it was too late.

'What the fuck are you talking about?' Everyone froze. 'I know you got him a bear every Christmas, but he was a grown man, for Christ's sake. He didn't love cuddly toys. He liked rugby and whisky and expensive cars.'

'Now, Monica…' Richard stepped forward.

'Really, what is wrong with you people? You act like he was an innocent little boy. He was an adult, a father, a husband.'

Jenny, normally a placid person, moved closer to her mother and glared at Monica coldly.

'Don't look at me like that, Jenny, you know I'm right. All this bullshit about their perfect little boy, it makes me sick. What about *my* little boy? What about their grandson, for fuck sake?'

'Enough!' Richard barked.

'No, I'm not done yet. You will hear what I have to say.'

I looked at my daughter, pleading for her to stop, but it was no use.

'He was a grown-up married man. I cannot have you pretending that he was a child and that Josh didn't exist. It's wrong. I know we are all hurting but I can't do this. I can't pretend for you people. I won't.'

It was around her mother that Jenny now put her arm.

'Come on, Mum, let's go home,' she said, leading her away.

'Oh great, run away, pretend I don't exist! Do you know what? Fuck you! Fuck all of you!' Monica roared.

By that point, Mary, Richard and Jenny were already halfway down the street. None of them turned to look at Monica, who stood fuming on the spot. In desperation I followed them.

'Mary, Richard, please…' I was gaining ground.

'Ingrid.' Richard turned around. 'I have never in my life been spoken to like that. I won't have it. She needs help. That girl needs help.'

'I'm sorry.' I was out of breath. 'I'm so sorry. She isn't herself. She hasn't been since the accident. It's all too much for her. She can't cope. I'm sure she didn't mean it. Just give her some time. Let me talk to her.'

Jenny spun round to face me.

'I suggest that for the moment she stays away from us. My brother is dead. My mother and father have lost their son and we don't need your daughter ranting at us in a churchyard, of all places, because she can't cope with her grief. What about us? We don't deserve that. Get her some help, Ingrid. Just keep her away from my family and get her some bloody help.'

The trio left me standing alone, watching them walk away.

I blamed myself for the incident. I should never have brought Monica to see the grave knowing that Tom's family would be there too. I knew my daughter was on the edge but up until that point hadn't realised how bad things had become. Letting out a long sigh, I turned around and headed back to where she was waiting by the car.

'Well, I hope you are proud of yourself,' I said as I fiddled about in my bag for my car keys.

'Don't, Mum. Just don't'

'Now look here, I know you are hurting, but they are good people, they didn't deserve that.'

'And I deserve it, do I?'

'No, of course not.' We got into the car.

'It's insane what she's doing. Pretending he was a child. It's sick.'

'It's Christmas Day, sweetheart. If you had to say anything you might have done it more gently.'

'Why?' Monica asked. 'Why should I dance around them? They clearly don't give a fuck about my feelings.'

'I'm sure that's not true. Mary is dealing with things in her own way. I know it must be difficult for you—'

'Difficult?' Monica's words were gaining speed as she interrupted. 'Difficult doesn't even start! I lost everything in that crash. Everything.'

I inserted the keys into the ignition. The car spluttered into life. It was pointless trying to reason with my daughter in the state she was in. We drove back to Cambridge in silence. I knew that if I said anything it would only make things worse. Monica was still seething in the passenger seat.

When we reached Herbert Street, Monica got out of the car and slammed the door closed behind her. By that point, I too was beginning to feel angry. I had done everything I could to placate my daughter but Monica was refusing to see things from anyone else's point of view. As I opened the front door I thought about Mary's behaviour at the churchyard and started to feel defensive on my daughter's behalf. It had been very tactless of Mary to take the bloody bear for Tom. Silly woman.

Monica stormed into the house and pushed

passed me as I hung my coat up on one of the hooks in the entrance hall. Monica stomped up the stairs as I called out to her.

'Would you like a coffee?' There was no response.

Flooded with exhaustion, I pottered into the kitchen and turned the kettle on. Once I'd sat down at the table with my green tea, the ginger tomcat jumped onto my lap and curled up in a ball, purring. I stroked his long velvet coat and he nuzzled up closer to me. He was the nicest of all of my rescues and I was grateful for his warm affection.

Moments later, Monica appeared in the doorway gripping her holdall.

'Where are you going?'

'I can't stay here, Mum. I need to be my own for a while. I'm going back to London. You don't need to worry. I'll be fine. We'll speak soon.' She turned on her heels and headed for the front door.

'But darling, it's Christmas Day. How will you get home?'

My words were wasted. The door had already slammed shut.

CHAPTER 8

The journey home was difficult. No buses or normal trains were running on Christmas Day, so I walked in the cold towards the centre of Cambridge phoning various cab companies. It took quite a while to find one to drive me to Stansted Airport where I had established there were a few trains running to Liverpool Street. From there I then took another very expensive taxi to my front door. I didn't mind though. I needed to get away from everything. Home was the only place I could be myself, even if I didn't feel safe there. The crow was with me wherever I went, but at least in my own house I felt in control, sort of.

As I stepped into the hallway, I noticed how cold the house felt. I had been planning to stay with Mum for a while and had turned the heating off. Now I regretted that decision. The house also felt very lonely, but I was pleased to be back. Dropping my bag to the floor, I shrugged my coat off and hung it up on the chrome coat rack Tom had chosen. I'd never really liked it but he had, so that had been that.

I turned on the heating before going into the sitting room, where I perched on the edge of the sofa and looked around my home. In the reflective mood I was in, my eyes wandered over all the things in the room that I had worked so hard to get. Everything was designer and expensive. When had status become so important to me?

Inside, I envied how my mother lived. Her house was a home. Mine looked like the cover of a glossy magazine. It was empty of real life; it was all for show. Tom had wanted it that way and I had allowed it. Now I was cross with myself for letting him dominate how the house looked. As the woman I should have been the nest maker but he had insisted on implementing his style and taste.

I decided I needed to inject some colour into my world and promised myself I would go shopping for some new things for the house. Then I remembered it was Christmas time. I had calmed down after my outburst at Mary, and although I now accepted it could have been delivered more gently, I didn't feel guilty about having made my point. I was angry with her for her behaviour and I was angry with Richard and Jenny for allowing it. Mum was disappointed in me though, and I regretted that. I should never have left her house under a cloud, but I had to get away from everyone. Since Tom and Josh's death I had barely had any time to myself, and although the house was painfully empty, it was going to do me some good.

Getting up from the sofa I wandered over to fireplace. It had never been used. Tom hated the smell of dying embers. But he wasn't there anymore and I was cold, so I decided to go for a walk around the park to look for suitable bits of wood to burn.

After spending some time searching for something suitable to put the wood in, I fished out a large wicker basket, put my coat back on and left the house.

It was three o'clock and the sun had stopped shining. London was under a blanket of grey cloud. The temperature had dropped considerably since I had left the taxi. Crouch End was eerily still. It was so strange to see the streets abandoned.

I went into Priory Park and headed straight to Philosophers' Corner to look for appropriate logs. A few families had ventured out to the playground with their small children. The only other people I saw were dedicated dog walkers. A small black poodle jumped around its owner's feet yapping and I wished the woman would silence the hyperactive mutt.

The light was fading fast. I scrabbled around in hedgerows looking for wood to burn. Because of the size of the fireplace, I only needed to find a few logs. It was strange looking in a park, in London, for logs. I felt like a camper who had taken a wrong turn.

After unearthing a couple of hefty fallen branches I left the Philosophers' Corner and went to search elsewhere. By then the sky was a muted black-blue and the street lamps had just come on. After a few more minutes scavenging I felt I had collected just enough firewood. I pulled my coat collar up around my neck and made my way back through the park towards home. The basket was heavy and I had to keep changing hands. The twisted wicker handle rubbed against my cold palm.

When I reached the park entrance I almost collided with a couple coming through. The pair held onto one another and I dropped my bundle all over the pavement. Bending down to pick them up, I looked up and recognised the faces staring down at me.

'Monica!' The lady bent down to help me retrieve my sticks. 'What are you doing out here?'

Erin was a woman I had met during a yoga class. She lived a few streets away with her husband Alex, who stood puffing a cigarette and rubbing his hands together in the cold. I felt self-conscious scrabbling about grabbing at sticks.

'Just getting a bit of firewood.' My cheeks flushed and I couldn't look her in the eye.

'I'm sorry we haven't seen you recently. How are you?' Her pity filled me with sadness.

'Oh you know, surviving. How are the twins?'

'Very well, you know, exhausting but lovely. Alex and I have left them with his parents while we take ourselves off to the pub for a well-deserved tipple.' I could hear the embarrassment in her voice. 'Why don't you join us?' I felt Alex flash her a disapproving look.

'Oh, that's very kind but I've got to get back. Mum is staying with me.'

The lie rolled off my tongue with surprising ease.

'Of course,' Erin said, putting the last stick back in my basket.

'Come on, Hun.' Alex rubbed his hands harder. 'It's bloody freezing.'

'Well, it was nice to see you again. We'll get a date in the diary. Do something in the New Year maybe.'

'Maybe yes, that might be good.' But I knew I wouldn't hear from her. People who had children had been avoiding me ever since the accident. It was as though they felt guilty about still having their darlings when I had lost mine. I didn't understand it but then at that time very few things made sense.

'Happy Christmas, Mon.' Erin linked arms with her husband.

'You, too.' I watched them walk off. I was alone again.

As I walked back to the house, I thought about my absent friends. It was true that some of them had tried to see me but on the whole people were too scared to face me. They couldn't deal with what had happened and shied away from addressing it. Things had been especially quiet since the funeral. Up until that point people hadn't left me alone. But once it was all done and Tom and Josh were in the ground, it was as though that was the end of it. Content to forget, they got on with their lives. I could do neither of those things and feared I never would.

By the time I reached the front door, I felt angry. Erin and Alex had made me feel like a leper. I didn't deserve that. So what if it was difficult for them? They should have tried harder. Tom had never liked Alex and had little time for Erin. He said they were too nice. I had wanted us all to be friends and thought it would have been nice to meet a couple we could spend time with. Tom had dismissed the idea and banned me from inviting them over to the house when he was around. I now wondered if he had seen something I hadn't.

The house was still icy and I set about building

a fire. I collected old newspaper, scrunched it up and stuffed it in between the sticks. After a few failed attempts I eventually managed to get a steady flame going. Hypnotised, I sat on the floor in the dark watching the fire lick around the wood, eating the paper. The heat coming from the hearth was comforting. I felt at home without the lights on and with only the glow of the flames.

My stomach began to rumble and I realised I hadn't had a thing to eat since breakfast. I got up and went into the kitchen. The electric light felt very bright. Opening the fridge I inspected the sparse contents. My options were limited so I decided to have cheese and crackers. To accompany my humble meal, and since it was Christmas Day, I opened an expensive bottle of Bordeaux and poured myself a large glass.

I returned to the sitting room, pulled an armchair close to the fire and tucked in to the food and drink. The wine was fruity and warmed me from the inside. At last my shoulders began to drop. The fire enveloped the piled wood and roared. I had never made a fire before and was pleased with my efforts. For the first time since the accident I didn't feel scared. I could look after myself. I somehow knew that I was going to be all right. In the end, life must carry on.

With my new-found hope, I celebrated with another large glass of wine. By the time the night had crept up and the embers had died I had finished that bottle and was halfway through another. The intoxication felt good and I found freedom in it.

Tom used to forbid me from drinking too much.

He said it was not ladylike. I probably hadn't been drunk since my university days. I wanted to lose myself, and the wine was the perfect partner in crime. The more I swallowed down, the better I felt. It coursed through my veins, numbing my conscious pain. I got up out of the armchair and realised my head was spinning. I tottered over to Tom's drinks cabinet. From it, I removed a bottle of Scotch and took a long swig. The alcohol burnt my throat and warmed my belly. I did it again. I felt like a teenager misbehaving, stealing alcohol from my parents' supply. But Tom had been my husband. The strange feeling sat awkwardly in my stomach and sloshed about with the wine and whisky.

I went over to the sofa and collapsed, feeling sick and dizzy. Just then, my mobile phone beeped. There was a voice mail from my mother. I deleted it halfway through listening. Her concern for me was irritating. Suddenly I felt angry again and painfully alone.

Out of nowhere I thought of Simon. It felt as if a light switch had been turned on in my head. I had to talk to him so badly, to hear the sound of his voice. In my drunken state I fumbled with my phone for some time before eventually accessing his number. My heart was beating hard in my chest while I held my breath and waited for him to answer. But the phone just rang and rang. He wasn't at home. My heart sank, but then I remembered I had his mobile number.

Gingerly, I steadied myself on my feet and went carefully up the stairs to my office. It was at the top of the house. It was the only room that we had decorated according my taste, thanks to Tom giving me the freedom to do so. But I hadn't been in there for weeks. There had been no need.

As I approached my Victorian walnut desk I noticed my hands were shaking. I couldn't be sure if it was the chill in the room or nervous anticipation. In the corner of the room I could make out the industrial theatre spotlight. I fiddled for the switch. The room flooded with a bright white light. My eyes took some time to adjust. I looked around my office at my things. It had been my private place, my sanctuary. It was the room in the house I was most proud of.

When Tom and I had bought the house he had agreed to let me have an office of my own. His was on the first floor sandwiched between our bedroom and the spare room. He had said he didn't want all my crap cluttering up his workspace. After inspecting the attic, I deemed we could renovate and turn it into an office space for me. He was so busy concentrating on making his workroom perfect, it gave me some space to do as I wished with mine.

I had painted the walls in a soft duck-egg blue and hung vintage framed French posters on the walls. In the corner was a large pine bookcase stuffed full of all my favourite authors. On top of the bookcase were big cream candles and a cascading fuchsia orchid in a pot. Beside the shelves was my club armchair upholstered in bright green velvet. A low chest coffee table was nearby on which a number of design magazines were strewn. The floor was stripped oak and a huge sheepskin rug lay in the middle of the room.

In the sloping roof on one side was a small skylight that had a pull-down roller blind in a similar green to the velvet of my chair. On the opposite side we had incorporated a pair of French doors that led out onto a minute balcony that surveyed the garden below and the park beyond that.

As I stood swaying, looking at my things, I realised I'd forgotten why I had gone into my office. I felt like a tourist in my own life. I was existing but only in a parallel universe where everything was wrong. Then I remembered that I wanted to call Simon. I went over to my desk and from the secret compartment removed a mobile phone. Anxiety gripped me as I dialled his number. The phone rang a number of times before going to answerphone.

'Hi, Simon here, I can't get to the phone now but if you leave a message I might just call you back.' Beep. I panicked and hung up. This was silly, I told myself. I am a grown woman, for goodness sake. I dialled the number again. Again it went to answerphone. The tone of his voice was as smooth as his coffee-coloured skin.

Simon and I met at university and had been close friends ever since. He was an exotic-looking man. His mum was a glamorous Indian and his father a dark-haired, blue-eyed Irishman. The combination of the two resulted in Simon: a dark-skinned, broad-shouldered, tall man with striking blue-green eyes.

'Hi, Simon. Hi, it's me. Please call me. Please, I really want to talk to you. I need to talk to you. Please, just when you get this, call me. We need to talk. So much has happened. I need you. Please I ... I miss you. Call me when you get this, OK?'

I hung up the phone and collapsed on the floor in a gibbering mess. Snot ran down my face, as did tears. It was the first time I had allowed myself to think about him since the accident. Tom's death changed what had been before. My reality had been altered in so many ways. I couldn't face thinking about what I'd done. The guilt was excruciating. Then I was sick. Vomit poured out of me onto the sheepskin rug. When I got up, white spots danced in front of my eyes and I had to steady myself. Staring down at the puddle of red-wine-stained sick, it smelt disgusting, but for some reason I started to laugh. I laughed because I knew that if Tom had been alive and had seen me in that state he would have flipped. I was glad to be able to make a mistake and not have anyone to answer to. Then the feeling of guilt returned.

I knelt down and bundled up the vomit-stained rug. It was beyond saving and would need to be thrown away. I went over to the light and turned it off. The room filled with darkness and the feeling of sadness returned. What was I doing there? It had been a mistake to call Simon and I wished I could take the message back. Leaving the room, I felt worse than ever.

***

When I woke up the next morning I had a bitter hangover. My mouth tasted like vinegar and my tongue felt furry. I remembered why I didn't drink very often. I rolled over in bed, still dressed in yesterday's clothes, and pulled the pillow over my thumping head. It was Boxing Day and I was completely alone. Boxing Day with Tom used to be lovely. We would stay in our PJs all day, picking at leftovers and watching television curled up together. But there were no leftovers this year.

With my head still aching, I dragged myself off the bed and went in search of aspirin. The medicine cabinet failed me so I took myself downstairs to get some breakfast, hoping that food might soak up some of the alcohol I had continued to drink after being sick the previous night.

I went into the kitchen and was shocked by the state of it. There were dirty glasses and empty bottles on the table. A half-eaten packet of crisps lay open, its contents spilling out. Tom would have been furious, but at that moment I didn't care. I padded over to the fridge in search of nourishment. As I pulled the door open, a waft of strong cheese hit me. I scowled at the piece of Stilton that sat alone on the shelf. Apart from that, the fridge was more or less empty and I realised that what I fancied more than anything in the world was curry. I removed a bottle of milk and closed the door. Tea was needed before I could think about doing anything.

After boiling the kettle and making myself a huge mug of hot tea, I went over to the kitchen table and sat down. The world outside looked grey and cold.

Then it appeared. The crow. It flew down onto the patio and stood looking at me. It was such a deliberate act that I was taken back. For a little while I had managed to forget my troubles, but now, sitting in the kitchen in the daylight, everything returned to me. I stared back at it. Our eyes never blinked. It felt as though it was gazing into my soul and I knew if I kept looking at it I would lose myself completely. I broke my gaze and got up from my chair. For some reason it seemed like a good idea to approach the glass door. I was scared but I edged closer. Still the bird did not flinch.

'Please leave me alone.' There was a tremor in my voice as I spoke directly to the bird.

'I don't know what I've done, but please, just leave me alone. I'm a good person. I don't deserve this. I'm begging you, stop. I don't understand what you want. I don't have anything else. It's gone. It's all gone. Please leave me in peace. Just go back to being a bird and let me get on with my life.'

Very casually, the bird began preening its feathers. It was as though I didn't exist. My shoulders dropped a little and I started to believe my words had worked. A few moments later the bird took off and disappeared. Maybe things were going to get better. I returned to my seat and sat sipping the tea.

Then out of nowhere came a loud crash. Something black had come at the glass in the kitchen door. Shaking, I got up and went closer to inspect. There was nothing there. I looked around warily, expecting to see the crow. The garden was uninhabited. I edged closer still until my nose was inches away from the glass. Then it came again. I ducked. It was a silly thing to do but instinct just took over. Curled up in a ball on the floor, I lifted my head to find the crow back on the patio staring at me again. On my hands and knees I crawled out of the kitchen and went into the sitting room. In there the curtains were still drawn and I scrambled onto the sofa and curled up. Hugging my knees to my chest, I closed my eyes and prayed my torment would stop.

Earlier, I'd decided I would walk to Turnpike Lane to pick up an Indian takeaway but my latest meeting with the crow put an end to that idea. It was out there, waiting for me. I could feel it. I listened for the sound of the bird banging on the glass. There was silence. My heart was in my mouth and I felt fear tighten its grip on me. I was a prisoner in my own house. Then out of nowhere I had a eureka moment. I knew what I needed to do. I ran out of the sitting room and up the stairs. In the spare room was a large built-in cupboard that contained excess bed linen. In my frantic search I pulled down pillowcases and duvet covers. Right at the back of the cupboard I found a thick blanket. Standing on tiptoes I managed to reach it with my fingertips and eased it forward. I tucked the tartan picnic blanket under my arm and went downstairs. In our storage cupboard in the hall I found what I was looking for. I picked up Tom's toolbox and marched into the kitchen. The crow had gone but it made no difference.

I put the blanket and toolbox down on the kitchen table before dragging a chair over to the door. Then I returned to the toolbox and opened it. It was neatly organised, just like everything else had to be in Tom's world. I found some nails and a hammer. Returning to the chair with the blanket, the nails and hammer, I got up onto it and began to hang the blanket over the door. The wall above the door was rock hard and did not take kindly to having nails bashed into it. Nonetheless, I managed to screen off the garden. I got down off the chair and stood back to admire my handiwork. I saw that there was still some glass visible and looked around desperately trying to find something suitable. Newspaper would have been perfect, I thought, but there was none. Then I had the idea to tape tinfoil to the window. I knew it wouldn't look great but it would do the job.

By the time I had finished there was no natural light getting into the kitchen. I had covered every chink. Satisfied, I said aloud, 'There, try scaring me now.'

I took myself upstairs, still armed with the tinfoil, to secure all the windows up there too. When I reached my bedroom I collapsed onto the floor. A sudden pain dug into my belly, rendering me helpless. I felt as if I had been stabbed. My ribs ached as though they'd been broken and my stomach tightened and pulsed. I was in agony. I called out in pain.

'Help me, please, someone...'

And then I saw the blood. My hands were covered in it. I stood staring down at the thick red liquid oozing out of my tummy. Horrified, I lay back on the ground pleading for it to stop. I could feel a huge hole in my body where my stomach should have been. And then came the stabbing pain again. I reeled in agony and using my arms dragged my body out onto the landing. The daylight was pouring in and I thought I might pass out. My legs went numb as the piercing pain in my gut increased. My eyes searched for an explanation but found none. Why was this happening to me? What was doing this?

As I dragged myself closer to the top of the stairs I thought I might be sick. My hands were soaked in blood and my body was wet with it. I was convinced I was dying. My head felt as if it was in a clamp. A splitting pain ran through my brain and I had to close my eyes, it hurt so badly. It was as if electricity was being passed through my skull.

Then it stopped. All of a sudden, the pain disappeared. I opened my eyes and looked at my stomach. It was back to normal. There was no evidence of blood anywhere. Shaking, I got up off the floor and looked for signs of what had just happened. There were none, only a feeling of foolishness combined with intense fear. I was too frightened to carry on securing the windows. Returning to my bedroom, I crawled under the bedcovers where I started to sob.

CHAPTER 9

I had been worrying for days. I hadn't heard from Monica since she had stormed out on Christmas morning. I called her a number of times and left messages. What happened by the graves had stuck with me. It was so unlike Monica to verbally attack anyone. I feared for the wellbeing of my girl. Monica was a kind person, a gentle soul who would never deliberately hurt someone. Yet she was behaving so out of character and had done so ever since the accident. I understood that Monica wanted time alone but not to answer the phone was just strange. Then I began to wonder if Monica had taken herself off somewhere. It seemed unlikely but it would explain the lack of contact.

For the third time that day I called Monica's house. The phone rang and rang and eventually went to answer machine. Again I felt a pull of sadness as I listened to Tom's voice echo down the line. It had taken me months to pluck up the courage to erase Jim's voice from our answerphone and I wondered if Monica would ever manage it herself.

Ever since the accident I had cursed myself for not having a mobile phone. Now I decided to go into Cambridge town centre and buy myself one. I wanted to be contactable all of the time. Just in case.

I grabbed my worn leather handbag and left the house. A bitter wind greeted me when I stepped out onto the street. It blew along the pavement forcing a discarded piece of rubbish to dance. Pulling my scarf up over my mouth, I pushed on through the cold.

It only took ten minutes to get to the phone shop in the middle of town. I walked over the river, through the wet grass of Midsummer Common and came into the centre via Thompson's Lane. I loved that part of Cambridge. No cars were allowed and people walked lazily through the streets enjoying the historic surroundings.

The town was busy with post-Christmas sale shoppers in search of a bargain. I kept my head down and wove in and out of the crowds, feeling flustered. The wind whipped up a strange feeling in me. I couldn't explain it but I sensed Monica was in trouble. I had always felt a psychic connection with my daughter. I tried to shake the feeling but it sat in the pit of my stomach like a stone, tormenting me. My sixth sense when it came to Monica always told me when something was wrong but could never explain why.

I left the Orange shop with a shiny new iPhone in my hand. The gawky young shop assistant had been very helpful and patiently taught me how to use it. Having once scoffed at such technology, I now felt good having a phone in my pocket. As I walked back towards the house I tried calling Monica again. Still there was no answer and I was beginning to get frantic.

'For goodness sake, Monica, just call me please. I'm worried. I know you are angry with me but just let me know you are all right. I just want to hear that you are safe. *Please* call me. I've bought myself a mobile phone and 07486 529487 is the number you can reach me on if I'm not at home. I know it will annoy you but I'm worried. Put me out of my misery darling, *please.*'

When I got home, Bobo made a huge fuss in demanding some food. As I ripped open the foil sachet and emptied the fishy contents into the bowl, the other two cats appeared, pushing and shoving each other out of the way trying to share the food. I am sure they can hear meal time from miles away.

As I sat down at the kitchen table with my newspaper, I tried to push away the feelings of loneliness. Although I didn't want to admit it, having someone else to worry about felt good. Monica had given me a purpose again. I missed the company as well as the responsibility. I had plenty of friends but many of them were married and had busy lives. Sometimes I felt like a third wheel when I was in the company of my married friends. For a while I entertained the idea of Internet dating but after a number of disastrous dates I gave up on trying to find a man. No one would ever replace Jim but companionship would have been better than nothing.

In the spur of the moment I found my address book and looked up my brother's phone number. Ralph Bayer was my older brother and only sibling. He lived near Cheltenham with his wife Susan. They had grown-up twin sons, Michael and Peter. Unlike me, Ralph was a very conventional person. He had made a huge amount of money in the city as a banker and now lived a rarefied life, spending his time having drinks parties in his multimillion pound residence in the rolling countryside around Cheltenham. Susan was the perfect rich man's wife, who always looked immaculate and was a consummate hostess.

Ralph and I had a deep fondness for one another but as a result of living such different lives and travelling in alien circles to one another we did not see each other very often. Nonetheless, Ralph was a good brother and a dependable one. He had always been there to help me out financially and was very generous with his wealth. We were chalk and cheese but that hadn't got in the way of us having a close relationship as children. I knew Ralph would always be there for me and he knew the same applied to him.

Our parents had moved to England from the Netherlands during World War two. In 1940 the Germans had occupied Holland and started their extermination of the Jews. The Dutch had hoped to stay neutral when the war broke out but their desire for peace was ignored. After the bombing of Rotterdam the Dutch forces surrendered and the Nazis occupied the country from then on. A huge number of Jews were exterminated in Holland during the Holocaust, the largest number in any single country. Scared of what was happening in their country, my parents, Erik and Gerarda Bayer, decided to leave everything behind. After a difficult and dangerous journey, they arrived in England in 1943, bringing with them their only child at the time, Ralph. We had relatives in the UK and were quickly able to settle and build a new life. In 1950, I had been born.

Ralph had few memories of being in Holland as he had been three when they had left the country so he had grown up feeling British. Ralph had embraced everything English and his lifestyle reflected that. He loved to hunt, was an avid royalist, a churchgoer and respected pillar of his community. Jim used to say Ralph was more British than the British.

Picking up the house phone, I dialled my brother's home number.

'Hello, Susan speaking.' A delicate voice resonated down the line.

'Susan, it's Ingrid. Happy Christmas.'

'Oh, Ingrid darling,' the words purred, 'how marvellous to hear from you. How are you?'

'Holding up, thank you. Have you had a nice Christmas?'

'Oh it's been the best. We've had the boys and their families here.' Her words froze as guilt reminded her of my recent troubles. She cleared her throat. 'I am so sorry. That was very tactless of me. How are you really? And Monica?'

'Oh you know me, I'm a tough old bird, but I'll be honest, Monica isn't great. That's why I called. I wonder if I could have a word with that brother of mine. Is he there?'

'Oh yes, of course. He's just in the office. I'll fetch him for you.' There was a long pause. 'I do hope you'll come and see us soon. Perhaps bring Monica to stay for a few days? We could arrange a get-together, to jolly her up a bit. A party always cheers me up.'

'Perhaps, yes. Thank you.' I did my best not to sound irritated.

'Well, Merry Christmas, Ingrid darling, and a Happy New Year.'

'To you, too.' Then there was the sound of footsteps scurrying off. A moment later, a man's voice boomed down the line.

'Ingrid! How lovely of you to call. How are you?' A lump formed in my throat when I heard the sound of his voice.

'Hello, Rara.' (As a small child I had been unable to pronounce Ralph, and the nickname had stuck ever since.)

'Is everything OK, old girl?'

'No, not really. I was wondering if you were free next week?'

'Free as a bird, apart from the hunt on New Year's Day, and then a party in the evening.' I smiled to myself and stifled a giggle.

'Could we meet for lunch? I'd like some advice.'

'Of course, of course! You say when and I'll be there.'

I flicked through my calendar.

'Does next Wednesday suit you? January 4th?'

'I'm certain I am free but you know what Susan is like, such a social animal. I better just check with her first, hold on.' I listened to my brother's voice bellowing to his wife in the distance.

'Susan? Susan!' A pause. 'Am I busy on January 4th?' Another pause. 'Good, make a note that I am going to have lunch with In. Yes, on the fourth. Good girl.' Ralph cleared his throat. 'In? Hello? Yes that's fine. London or Oxford? You choose.'

'Oh, not London. Oxford is better for me.'

'Fine, fine. Choose a restaurant and I'll meet

you there at one.'

'Perfect. See you then. And Rara ... thanks.'

'Don't mention it. I always have time for my little sister. See you on the fourth,' and he hung up.

Having spoken to Ralph, I felt better. I didn't know what use it would be to see him and share my concerns but I needed to offload to someone. He may not have been the world's most intelligent man but he had a heart of gold and would always listen to my rants. His advice was always practical and it was possible that he may come up with a way to lift Monica out of her gloom.

I replaced the receiver and went into the sitting room where I searched the bookshelves for a particular book, before finding it, removing it and curling up on the sofa to read. Placing my new mobile on the coffee table in front of me, I willed Monica to ring.

***

I sat at a table in Brasserie Blanc, examining the menu. The restaurant was on Walton Street, a stone's throw from Oxford College. I'd eaten there on many previous occasions with Ralph. The familiarity of the place, with its clean white linen tablecloths and wooden floor, was good. Waiting for my brother to arrive, I nursed a vodka and tonic and checked my wristwatch a few times. Ralph was always guaranteed to be late. That day was no different.

Eventually, at twenty past one, he bustled into the restaurant carrying a Harrods bag. When he spotted me sitting at a table on the far side of the room he waved enthusiastically and called out.

'Bloody traffic.' He unwound a bright red cashmere scarf from his neck.

Ralph was a tall skinny man with a pointy nose, small blue eyes and white receding hair. His clothes spoke of money, as did his accent. After removing his navy Burberry mac, he revealed a pair of burgundy corduroy trousers, a lemon yellow V-neck sweater and a pale blue and white checked shirt. I couldn't help a smirk as I noticed his bright green socks sticking out of his shiny leather loafers. As a child he had never dressed in such outfits but after marrying Susan his wardrobe had changed dramatically. 'Susan loves colour,' he would always say by way of an explanation.

I watched as a young couple raised their eyebrows at his appearance. He looked absurd but thankfully he didn't realise and that was his saving grace.

Ralph bent down and kissed me on the forehead before he pulled up a chair and placed the bag down onto the table.

'Christmas presents from Susan for you.' His cheeks and nose were flushed pink from the cold. 'Sorry I'm late. Bloody traffic, I tell you.'

'I haven't been here long. No need to worry.' I sipped my drink.

Ralph searched about in his coat pocket for his glasses before removing them and exploring the a la carte menu and then the wine list.

'All looks good.' Ralph smiled.

'So', he said, 'how are you?'

At the vital moment, the waitress re-emerged to ask for our order. She turned to me and waited for my choices. I felt flustered and had yet to decide.

'I will have the snails, followed by boeuf bourguignon.' Always a decisive man, Ralph handed the menu to the blonde young waitress dressed in black.

'Can I have the pumpkin and kirsch soup followed by the turbot?' I made a snap choice and suddenly started to feel hungry.

'Certainly, Madam. Would you like any side orders?'

'Some French beans, and perhaps some olives while we wait?'

Ralph's eyes sparkled at the thought of food. Although he was skinny, he was also known for having a bottomless appetite. The waitress smiled, revealing a perfect row of pearly whites.

'And have you decided on the wine, sir?'

'I'll have a bottle of Chateau des Bardes, please.' It was a Grand Cru, and the most expensive red on the menu. 'And how about a bottle of Crozes-Hermitage Blanc for you, In?'

I inwardly gasped at the extravagance of both his purse and his knowledge of wine.

It was a foregone conclusion that Ralph would pay as he was a very great deal better off than I. He always did and I didn't even pretend to offer to go halves.

'Sounds wonderful, but I don't think I'll manage a whole bottle!'

'Oh, don't worry about that. Drink what you can.' He turned back to the waitress whose huge smile seemed to imply she had hit the jackpot, which, in a way, she had. She bustled off to fetch the order.

'Good. Pretty girl.' He leant back in his chair.

'Sorry In, where were we?' Ralph remembered why we were there.

I leant my head in my hands, took a deep breath and told him all about Monica's obsessive behaviour. I barely stopped when the waitress arrived with the bottles and opened them in front of us. I couldn't check my emotions that poured out in a spate of verbal diarrhoea even with Ralph breaking to taste the freshly opened bottle of wine at the waitress's request.

When I came to the end, I noticed how furrowed my brother's brow had become.

'So what am I supposed to do?' Ralph swirled the wine around in his glass.

'I need help, Ra. She's a total mess and I can't get through to her.'

'Well, I mean it must be terribly hard for her. She just needs a lot of time. Ghastly what's happened to her and all that she's been through but she's a bright girl. She'll bounce back, mark my words.'

'You would have been right before, but something has changed, something inside her just isn't the same anymore. She's so angry all the time. The way she spoke to Tom's parents on Christmas Day ... Honestly Rara, it was almost cruel.'

'Hmm.' Ralph had one eye on the doors into the kitchen.

'If it was one of the boys, what would you do?'

'Well I…' He looked flummoxed. 'You know I'm not very good at all this psychology business. Maybe you could speak to Susan, she always knows exactly how to deal with difficult situations. She's a very clever woman.'

I had to bite my tongue. The only difficult situation Susan had ever had to face was deciding which Designers Guild fabric to have her curtains made from and how many canapés to order from Waitrose.

The olives were delivered to the table. I'd hoped Ralph might have some answers, but felt as if I'd come up against another brick wall. My heart sank as I watched my brother stuff green and black olives into his mouth as he spoke.

'What about her friends? Maybe one of them might be able to do something.'

'Yes, well that might work, if only she would see and speak to any of them. She's become so reclusive. She won't even answer my calls for Christ's sake.'

Ralph wriggled in his seat. He could see how unhappy I was, and I could tell he felt powerless to help me.

'There must be someone she trusts. If not a friend, maybe she needs a doctor?'

'She's had enough doctors lately to last her a lifetime. Besides, she's developed a new stubborn streak and doesn't listen to my advice.'

'Well, it was just an idea.'

Bits of black olive were stuck between Ralph's teeth.

Very soon our starters were delivered to the table. A plate of steaming hot snails sat in front of

Ralph, who licked his lips and laid a napkin across his lap. When the soup was put down in front of me, although it smelt delicious, I realised I no longer had an appetite. I had so hoped Ralph might be able to make me feel better or to come up with a plan to help Monica. Disappointment mingled with the heavy odour of garlic.

'All I'm saying is that maybe the girl could do with a friend at the moment. You are telling me that she is unwilling to allow you in, so maybe someone else could get through to her. I mean, I would try but...'

A dribble of butter ran down Ralph's chin as he chewed on a snail.

'Thanks Ra but I don't think you are the person.'

'Well maybe Susan could talk to her?'

I shifted in my seat. 'I think you have a point about someone outside of the family being the best person for her to confide in. Clearly I keep saying the wrong things.'

I took a spoonful of the creamy orange soup to my lips and wavered.

Lowering the spoon again, Ralph watched as the cogs of my mind set about working. A twinkle appeared in my eye that I saw he recognised. There was a spark of hope.

'You know,' I said, feeling my lips curl into a smile, 'I think there is someone.'

CHAPTER 10

I was scared. I was really scared. Black birds had surrounded my house and were trying to get in. I heard them scratching at the window, pecking at the door, trying to get me. Although all the windows had been covered, I knew they were there.

It was best that I stayed inside for the time being. I'd taken to living in the sitting room and kitchen. There was no need for me to go upstairs. It was easier staying downstairs, near the doors, in case I needed to leave in a hurry. Although I was scared, I was fairly sure I'd made the house safe. I didn't think they could get in. I burnt a fire in the hearth night and day just in case they tried to come in down the chimney. They were very clever. Especially that crow. The one that sat out there, waiting.

To begin with I was worried about how I'd survive. There was no way I was going to leave the house. But the Internet had been my saviour. I had everything I needed delivered to my door. I hadn't left the house for nearly three weeks but thankfully anything I wanted could be ordered online.

The phone kept ringing so I unplugged it. I'd spoken to my mother a while before. She'd said she thought I should get away and go and visit a friend. I told her I was too busy but that everything was fine. She seemed to believe me and stopped bugging me. I just wanted to be left alone. No one knew what I was going through. They could never understand what was happening to me. Even I was struggling to understand it.

If I ever required some company I put on the television or played some music. It had been good spending time alone. I'd been able to think properly about Tom and Josh and about everything that had happened. It was clear to me. I was being punished. Losing everything was my punishment. The crow was there to make sure I got what I deserved. It watched my every move and made sure I didn't escape my fate.

My denial was futile. Now that I could see why this had happened I felt more at peace. I was a bad person, a horrid nasty woman who did not deserve to have a family. Losing my womb was nature's guarantee that I could not pass on my poison to a child. Josh was lucky, I suppose. That was what the crow thought. It killed him to protect him from me. The bird wasn't a demon. It was a protector. It wanted to protect Tom too.

I had come to accept this as the truth. I got what I deserved and now that everything I loved had been ripped away from me. I had nothing left, nothing except self-hatred and fear for my own pathetic life. Why didn't it just kill *me?* Why end *their* lives? *I* should have died in that car, not them.

I'd done lots of research. I was now an expert on crow mythology. I knew all about them. To overcome one's enemy one needs to familiarise oneself with it. I had done that and discovered some amazing things.

Many legends across the world suggest that crows were once white. Thus, crows have always featured in the fight of good versus evil. That fact alone only helped to prove my suspicions. Jewish law considered the raven to be unclean and the Egyptians believed that crows represented monogamy, since they are monogamous birds. To see a single crow is therefore meant to be a bad omen, as I well know.

Crows seem to have crept into language too. Crow's feet, meaning the signs of age, are commonly used, and then of course there is the term crow's nest. Although it is reported that the term came into use because crows build their nests at the top of trees, I learnt that it was also likely that the term referred to the observation tower as a clairvoyant's position. Again, that fact suggested that the birds were connected with prophecy. But what was the bird trying to tell me? It appeared to me after the accident. What could it possibly be trying to warn me of now? The worst had already happened.

I also read that crows were considered notorious thieves. They would steal meat left as offerings to the gods and eat the bodies of the dead left behind after battles. They seemed to be linked with death throughout history. I learnt that ravens would peck out the eyes of dead soldiers and then remove the brains from the socket holes. The thought of this made me shudder.

During the Great Fire of London, it was reported that flocks of crows and ravens came to London to feast on the burnt bodies. The people at the time were frightened, and with the blessing of the king set about killing huge numbers of them and destroying their nests. The more I read, the more my head spun. Superstition seemed to follow crows around.

The bodies of the poor souls left hanging on the gallows were famous for attracting crows. 'Ravenstone' became known as the name of the block that criminals were beheaded on. The more I learnt, the more I feared for my safety. But what I came to realise is that although corvids often foretold tragedy, they were never the cause of it. This left me wondering.

In Native American folklore the crow was a shape shifter. Supposing they were right, could it have been Josh trying to communicate with me somehow?

Then I was distracted from my train of thought. Oh shit, what was that noise? Scrabbling outside the front of the house. I could hear it getting closer. I needed to protect myself. I wasn't safe. I ran into the kitchen and grabbed a knife, the biggest one I could find. The noise was still there. I could hear it right by the front door. Whatever it was, it sounded large. My heart was racing; I could hear the blood pumping in my ears. My hand shook as I clutched the knife that glinted under the electric light. I had my back to the wall and I slowly edged closer as I waited for something to come bursting through the wood. Curiosity had a hold of me as I carefully peeled away some newspaper from the glass in the front door. BANG, BANG, BANG! I jumped out of my skin. I fell to the floor and dropped the knife. It wasn't the bird. It couldn't be. I could see the silhouette of a man at the door. I recognised the blue coat. It was my postman. Gingerly, I got up. My hip was sore. I unlocked the three bolts I'd had put on the front door and opened it up just enough to be able to receive my post. The postman looked at me strangely.

'You need to sign for this.'

He handed over a long package. My hand was still shaking as I signed on the electronic pad. Then I moved back into the house, closed the door behind me and fastened the locks again. My heart was still racing but I felt safer. I took some deep breaths and steadied my nerves. Then I moved into the kitchen and put the package down on the table.

If I hadn't opened the door I would not know it was light outside, I'd grown so accustomed to living in the darkness. Electricity and the fire provide me with the light I needed. I had come to realise what it must be like to live in Alaska. Daylight isn't something I missed. I liked the cocoon of the darkness.

I wished I could stop shaking. Suddenly I felt I needed a drink. I went into the sitting room and poured a large brandy into a crystal tumbler. Drink had become my friend – It soothed and helped me pass the hours. Tom would have strongly disapproved but I was beyond redemption. He cannot judge me anymore. Only the crow can do that.

The drink was warm and sweet. I held it in my mouth and allowed the flavour to penetrate my gums. It was helping to calm me. Then I remembered the package and went back into the kitchen.

A long slim shape lay on the table wrapped neatly in brown paper. My hands only trembled a little and I could undo the packaging. When I got into it, I could see what it was. It had arrived sooner than I anticipated. I'd only ordered it the previous morning. I realised I was excited as I removed it. It was lighter than it looked. I held it in my hands. The walnut and metal were almost beautiful. Then I raised it and pointed it at the clock on the wall. I pulled the trigger but nothing happened. The gun was not loaded.

CHAPTER 11

January came to an end and Cambridge was covered in a thick layer of crisp white snow. I awoke one morning to discover my garden had transformed into a land of diamonds overnight. The sky was clear and blue. The ground sparkled beneath the light, and naked tree branches glistened with the cold. The only sign of life was the trail of small neat cat's footprints that wound a path through the garden and disappeared over a wall.

I stood in my dressing gown absorbing the winter scene outside. It reminded me of years gone by, when Monica was a child. How she used to love to play in the snow. I had a sudden memory of Jim pulling an old-fashioned sledge along a winding country road, a small figure of a girl clinging to it, her hat bobbing with the movement. I smiled to myself with the recollection and thanked my lucky stars I was lucky enough to have such wonderful memories of family life. I ached for Monica's lack thereof. The only things she had to cling to were sadness and regret for what might have been.

We had not spoken in weeks. I kept calling and sending messages but got no response. It was as if Monica had just disappeared off the face of the planet. I hoped she had taken my advice and gone to visit a friend. My daughter was an adult, I kept reminding myself, and free to go wherever and do whatever she chose. Yet a strong maternal intuition told me all was very far from well. This feeling had been lingering for days, weeks, and the lack of contact only exacerbated it.

I watched out of the kitchen window as an icicle that had formed on the gutter slowly began to thaw in the gentle sunlight. Each drop fell in slow motion before sinking into the snow below. It was as hypnotic as watching flames in a fire. Then and there I made a decision. I would get in the car and go to London. I needed to know my daughter was all right. Common sense told me that I would likely arrive to find the house empty but that in itself would at least tell me something. As far as I was concerned it was a necessary risk.

Turning away from the garden, I surveyed the kitchen. The surfaces were cluttered and the sink needed emptying. Shrugging at the mess with little interest, I went upstairs to get dressed. All that really worried me was that the cat's food and water bowls were well stocked, which they were.

As I pushed open the pine door into my bedroom, the hinges creaked. Every time this happened I made a mental note to oil them, but that had been ongoing for years. Out of sight was out of mind as far as my memory was concerned about menial matters. Jim had been the practical one, and ever since his death I bucked against changing my ways. If I oiled the door it would mean he was no longer needed, or missed. My friends laughed at me when I made such remarks but it was how I felt. I wanted reminders of him everywhere I went, even in the creak of a rusty door hinge. I pictured him smiling every time the door squeaked and it brought me closer to him.

I threw my tatty faded towelling gown over the back of a chair and began to dress. On the bed the ginger cat lay curled up, watching me with one eye open.

'Hello lazy bones,' I muttered in the direction of the ginger tom as I pulled a chunky brown cowl-neck jumper down over my peroxide head of hair. Then I slipped into a pair of skinny, bleached jeans and went over to the mirror to inspect my face.

The woman looking back at me had aged. The skin around my eyes was dark and lined. Little grey-blue eyes searched my face. I needed to find some strength again, for my daughter's sake. I examined my wiry uncontrollable hair, noticed that the silver roots needed retouching and wondered when I had become so old.

Reaching for my make-up, I roughly rubbed foundation onto my face before applying charcoal eyeliner and a thick layer of mascara. I felt better already. Moving over to the bed, I carefully pushed the cat off the vintage patchwork quilt and straightened the sheets, before pulling a small holdall down from the chaotic cupboard and packing a few clothes. I had no idea if Monica was at home or not and if she was whether I would need to stay but felt I should go prepared, just in case. I was unable to shake the inkling that something was terribly wrong.

When I returned downstairs I had to push my way past the ginger cat that now sat halfway up the stairs, refusing to move and sharpening his claws on the carpet.

'I know you don't like it when I go away but I'm afraid that's tough,' I spoke over my shoulder to the cat, who paid no attention. 'But I'll be back by tomorrow, I should think. You've got plenty of food in your bowl.' The tom sat licking a long paw while I put the luggage down by the front door. 'You'll be fine.'

I shrugged on a camelhair coat over my slender frame and slipped my feet into a pair of black suede boots.

Suddenly the cat appeared to realise what was happening and jumped down the stairs to bid farewell to me as I wrapped an orange pashmina tightly around my neck in preparation for the cold that would greet me when I stepped outside.

'Be good,' I instructed, walking out into the winter sunlight and pulling the front door closed behind me.

Out on the street a few children who lived a couple of doors down skidded around in the road hocking snowballs at one another. The boy, who was no older than eleven, gave me a cheeky smile as he rolled a ball of snow in his small-gloved hands.

'Don't you even think about it, young man.' I smiled, and with my sleeve I wiped the layer of snow covering my windscreen onto the road. As I turned my back I felt fairly sure the boy stuck out his tongue. I got into the cold car and turned the engine on. The Volvo spluttered into life with a groan while I watched the kid hurl the snowball at his younger sister, who was busily building a snowman.

The sun was low and large in the sky and it

made me wince. Fiddling around in my handbag, I searched for my sunglasses. I had a sudden memory of skiing. It had not been something at which I'd been very good, but Jim, who loved all sporting pastimes, had insisted one year that the family went. Monica and I had spent most of our time sitting drinking hot chocolate while we watched Jim ski effortlessly down the slopes. I began to wonder whether it might be an idea to try and take Monica away on holiday. As I pulled out of Herbert Street I pictured she and I trekking in Australia, and the thought put a smile on my face. I was sure Monica could be happy again. It was just a case of riding out the storm.

***

The traffic up to London was hellish. The snow made the drive painfully slow, and by the time I pulled up outside my daughter's house I was not in the best mood. I usually liked to drive like a bat out of hell, and being forced to crawl behind a string of cars did not suit me at all.

It was mid-morning and already a lot of the snow had begun to thaw. The roads through Wood Green had been a grey icy slush. I muttered to myself as I got out of the car and put my boot down into a cold puddle of mush. This was not turning out to have been such a good idea after all.

As I approached the front door I noticed the windows of Monica's house. The curtains were all closed which seemed strange. The front door, which had a panel of leaded glass in it, was also blacked out. There was no way to see inside. My heart jumped up into my throat as I warily knocked on the door and listened for a response. There was none. I knocked again, more loudly, and craned my ear to the door. Still there was no reply.

Taking a few steps back, I arched my neck to look up at the house. There were no signs of life, yet something told me to persist. I returned to the door and banged for a third time.

'Monica? Are you in there, darling? It's Mum.' Then out the corner of my eye I spotted a large terracotta urn and remembered Monica kept a key in it for emergencies. I reached into the glossy leaves of the camellia and felt about in the damp cold earth for the metal set of keys. My fingers hit the jackpot and I discovered the icy cold set at the back of the plant. Examining the bunch, I racked my brains to remember which key did what before trying one in the lock. It was the wrong one so I tried another. The key turned and I heard the click of a bolt. Stepping forward, I tried to push the door open but it would not budge. I put the key back into the lock and tried again. The same thing happened. Then I heard a noise coming from inside the house.

'Monica, sweetheart, it's me, it's Mum.' I listened for a response.

'What are you doing here?'

I barely recognised my daughter's voice. The words were faint and timid.

'I wanted to see you. You haven't been answering your phone. I was worried. Is everything all right? Can I come in?'

'I'm fine.'

'Can I come in, darling? It's freezing out here.' I listened to the silence, then after a moment or two heard a click, followed by two bolts being unlocked.

I stepped back from the door, holding my breath. I did not know what to expect but feared for what I might find. Slowly the door edged open and from a gap only a few inches wide Monica's face appeared. She looked skinnier than she ever had and her face was white and blotchy. Red circled her eyes and her hair was greasy and flat. The skin around her mouth was pale and cracked and her eyes darted wildly around checking the sky. Then I was hit with a strong waft of alcohol. I was horrified but did my best to disguise the shock.

'Hello, darling,' I spoke softly. 'How lovely to see you.'

I edged closer to the door, and as I did, Monica retreated like an animal under attack.

'Can I come in, sweetheart?'

Monica's bony fingers clung tightly to the door while she considered the question.

'It's a bit of a mess. I've been busy.' She couldn't look at me as she spoke. Her eyes still frantically searched the sky.

'It's me, Mon, you know I don't mind. Hardly the patron saint of organisation, now am I?' The words hung flatly in the air. I felt it was best not to be pushy but was determined to get into that house.

'I'm bursting for the loo. Come on, let me in.' I moved closer still. Monica finally relented and opened the door.

'Quickly, quickly.' Monica sounded frantic and swiftly closed the door behind me, locking it again, and I realised why I'd had no luck getting in. She had added two new locks to the door.

The hallway was dark and it took some time before my eyes adjusted to the lack of light. I hardly recognised the house. It smelt stale and felt cold. From the hallway I saw there was a light on in the kitchen and decided to follow the beacon.

The kitchen was utter chaos. Dirty bowls, cups and plates lay strewn across the table and work surfaces. Rubbish overflowed from the bin and a vast pile of empty wine bottles stood bunched together in a far corner. The room smelt of Chinese food. Then I noticed it – the gun lying on the table. I stood in the doorway too nervous to enter as Monica pushed passed me and ran into the room. She lurched over the mess on the table and grabbed the gun. She held the barrel close to her chest and looked at me with wild crazed fear.

'Monica!' I was flabbergasted.

'It's fine. It's not what it looks like. It's for protection.'

'What on earth from?'

No answer was forthcoming as Monica sat down at one of the kitchen chairs and pulled her knees up under her chin, all the while clutching the gun tightly in her hands. She looked like a frightened little mouse and I felt my heart breaking. Then I noticed the blacked-out windows. It was a thought that I had walked into a crack den. The only thing missing was graffiti and the smell of urine.

I lowered my bag onto the floor and tucked my

hands deep into my pockets. My fingernails dug into my palms. I felt uneasy and didn't know what to say or do. Honestly, I felt totally unsafe.

'Monica, you don't need the gun now. Put it down, sweetheart. Go on.' Monica looked as if she hadn't slept in days. She examined the gun she was clutching and decided after a moment to do as I asked. She put the air rifle down on the table but kept it within reaching distance.

'There, that's better.' My heart was beating fast. Monica remained curled up in the chair. She'd lost so much weight she looked like a skeleton. Her clothes hung from her bones. I was horrified by how pathetic she looked but marginally relieved when she relinquished the gun. I cautiously took a few steps closer, almost able to smell my daughter's fragility.

'The traffic here was a nightmare. I could murder a cup of tea.'

Monica looked blankly at me before signalling over to the kettle with one hand. I accepted the invitation and removed two mugs from a cupboard.

'No, no, Mum. I don't want one.' Monica picked up a half glass of white wine and took a long gulp. My natural instincts were to say something, but, since none of what I was seeing was normal, I decided to bite my tongue. I struggled to get the thought of that gun out of my mind.

Monica held the glass up to her lips and kept it rested there. I could smell the wine. She took another sip. It was obvious she had been in a drunken blur for days. As she downed the remaining wine from her glass, I could see her speculating about what I was doing there. She wore confusion like a mask. It was as though she was racking her brains to try and remember something. Maybe she was wondering if she had invited me. Resentment began to build as she watched me make a cup of tea. You could have cut the atmosphere with a knife.

'What are you doing here?' Monica's speech was slurred, which I'd failed to notice previously.

'I just wanted to come and see you, darling.' I attempted to sound light-hearted and Monica's bloodshot eyes narrowed.

'You're spying on me.' She reached for the open bottle of wine. 'I know that's why you're here. To spy on me.'

I looked at my daughter, who was drinking wine at half past eleven on a Tuesday morning.

'I just wanted to see if you are all right.' The statement sounded ludicrous given the circumstances.

'Well, now you know I am.' Monica's hand shook as she held the glass. I could feel a frustrated rage bubble up inside me but did my best to temper my words.

'I'm not entirely sure that's true, now is it?'

'What's that supposed to mean?' she spat.

'Mon, I've never known you to drink much, let alone at this time in the morning.'

'That was the old me.'

'Oh I see. And this is the new you?'

'Yes.'

'A stinking drunk who lives in a filthy pit?' The words left my mouth before I even realised I had thought them. Monica sat looking at me dumbfounded.

'Why thank you. I appreciate your kindness and honesty.' She took another long drink. 'You can leave now.' She slammed the glass down on the table.

I was so full of anger that I forgot about the gun on the table. Picking up the bottle of wine on the table I threw it onto the stone floor. Monica shrunk into herself as the glass shattered into a thousand pieces.

'If your father could see you now!' I bellowed. 'This is a disgrace. You can *not* behave like this! How would Tom feel? And Josh?'

'They can't see me, any of them, because they're dead. They're all fucking dead!' Monica shook in her seat. I spotted the gun again and felt my daughter's desperation. So I decided to calmly sit down.

'Yes they are and it's horrific. It's the worst possible thing that could have happened, but Monica, you are not dead. You are alive and you have to keep fighting.' I reached over to take hold of her hand but Monica pulled away as though I had leprosy.

'Darling, please.'

'Well, perhaps I don't want to live anymore.' She got up out of her seat and went over to the fridge where she removed another bottle of wine.

It was the most painful statement I had ever heard her speak and watched helplessly as she searched for a corkscrew.

'Did you ever think of that?' she continued, 'Maybe I don't want to live. Not here. Not like this. This is hell I am living in. My life is fucked.'

'I know that's how you feel at the moment, sweetheart,'

Then in horror I looked at the table.

'Is that what the gun is for?'

Monica's laugh was unexpected.

'No. No yet, anyway.' She unscrewed the cork. My shoulders dropped a little bit. 'It's for that bird, that fucking devil bird.' My head dropped to my chest.

'Not the bird again, Monica, for Christ's sake.'

'Just leave, Mum. Go. I don't want you here. You aren't welcome.' I looked coolly at my daughter's face, so full of hatred and pain.

'No, Monica, I will not leave.'

'I am asking that you do. Get out. This is the last time I will ask nicely.'

I jumped out of the chair and marched over to Monica.

'You can speak to me like that if you think it helps,' I hissed. 'But let me tell you, my girl, that all of this is insane. You need help. Serious help, and I intend to make sure you get it. Shout at me all you like but I'm not going anywhere.'

We were face to face and only inches apart. I could smell the alcohol on Monica's breath.

'Well, if you really want to help, you can get rid of that bird! Get rid of all of them!' she screamed. 'In fact, you can kill them. Kill them all!'

CHAPTER 12

After a lot of shouting and crying I finally relented and let Mum stay. It took a few days for everything to calm down. I was a mess. We talked for hours and she listened, actually properly listened to me for the first time. Having been so dismissive about the crow, she decided to take on board what I was saying. I was surprised by how supportive she was. I'd felt so very alone in the house, locked up away from the world.

At the time it had felt it was the best and only thing for me. I couldn't imagine that anyone might be able to help. But then she had arrived. She had shocked me by just turning up like that. I wasn't prepared to have to deal with anyone. Loneliness had become my home and she shattered it and for that I am grateful. I feel much better now.

I realise it must have been a shock for her seeing me like that. I barely recognised myself. She was brilliant. She took control of the situation, control of me. She ran me a bath and made me take a long soak. I couldn't remember the last time I'd had a wash. It felt good. Then she slowly started to arrange the house. I wouldn't let her take the blackout down; I was ready for an argument about it but instead she said she would go and buy some fabric to hang up in place of the paper and foil. I hadn't expected Mum to be so understanding and felt guilty for prejudging her.

She came back from John Lewis with some pretty paisley fabric in soft blues and greens. I have to admit it looked much better. The house started to feel like a home again, and with that came a sense of calm.

Mum also put a stop to me drinking so much. I wouldn't say I had become an alcoholic, nothing so dramatic, but I was binge drinking and it needed to stop. After spending a day or two sober I could think more clearly. Suddenly the urge to lock myself away from the outside world seemed less of a necessity.

When she told me she had called my doctor, I was annoyed. It wasn't her place. She told me it was the only thing she could think to do. Actually, when he arrived, a good-looking man in his early forties, he was kind and decent. He prescribed me some sleeping pills and a low dose of valium, just to help me get through what he called 'a difficult period'.

When the pills kicked in, twinned with a few nights' adequate sleep, I began to get back to normal. I tidied the house and remembered I wanted to make some changes to it. The place needed a feminine touch. So Mum and I ventured out to do some shopping.

My first experience back in the real world was bizarre. Nothing looked the way I had been imagining it. My thoughts had become so dark they had twisted my perception of the world. It was a relief to discover monsters weren't lurking around every corner, and as we walked along Park Road, I felt a spring return to my step. We passed a new house being built and I experienced the renewed interest of my out-of-use architect's eye as I scanned it for details.

The February cold tussled my hair and blew my green cashmere scarf as we walked. A low grey sky overhead hinted at rain. I pulled the scarf up over my nose and mouth, put my head down and continued along the pavement. Suddenly it dawned on me that every sign of Christmas had disappeared. It was as if I had missed it altogether. I should have felt sad but I didn't, and as we got closer to our destination I started to imagine that I might be able to enjoy next Christmas. It was a thought I'd been unable to entertain for weeks but the return of hope went a long way to lift my mood.

As my mother and I entered the furniture shop, a tinge of excitement ran through me. It was the familiar buzz of shopping joy. Silently, I walked around running my fingers along the various smooth, painted, limed and waxed pieces of furniture. The style of every piece was shabby chic meets contemporary classic. Wardrobes, chairs, tables and benches were light neutral colours and everything looked clean. I wanted to buy it all.

Mum was drawn to a set of four bentwood chairs painted in soft dove-grey.

'Aren't these stylish.'

She sat herself down and smiled. Tom would have hated them. He only liked modern furniture. But he was gone now and I had to get on with my life somehow. I decided to buy the set there and then. Not to spite him really but to regain some control over my rocky existence. They were only chairs but it felt like a good starting point.

Then I spotted it. It sat proudly against one wall beckoning for me to go over. A large white-painted French Louis XV bed. It was the kind of bed I had always wanted and there it was right in front of me. As I sunk down into the soft mattress I knew I had to have it. My mother watched me from the other side of the shop and smiled.

'Treat yourself, darling,' she said, beaming.

'It's lovely, isn't it?' I said, imagining it in my bedroom. 'But it feels wrong.'

Mum approached and sat on the bed beside me. 'Wrong, how?'

'Well, I mean getting rid of the bed Tom and I shared. It feels too soon.'

'Oh darling, you're not erasing the memory of Tom from your life by buying some new things. He'd want you to be happy, I'm sure.'

I felt my face furrow into a frown. He wouldn't have liked it at all. But something inside of me said to hell with it. He was gone and I was the one who had to keep on living. Mum continued, 'Surrounding yourself with things you like can't possibly be a bad thing, sweetheart.'

'You're right.' I got up and approached the till.

'I would like to buy that bed,' I said, pointing over at it, 'and the set of four pale grey chairs you've got in the window.'

The portly gentleman behind the desk suddenly came to life. His eyes glinted as if he'd won the jackpot.

'Why of course, Madam.' He scurried over to the furniture and proudly hung sold tags onto them. Returning to the counter, he asked, 'Would you like me to arrange delivery for you?'

'Yes, I would, please.'

'Our delivery fee is sixty pounds. Would that be all right for you, Madam?'

'That's not a problem.' I reached into my Mulberry bag to retrieve my wallet and fished out my gold Visa.

'We have a lovely pair of bedside tables that complement the bed beautifully. Would you like to see them?' Still his round piggy eyes glowed with pound signs.

'No, no thank you,' I said, handing over my credit card. He rang the numbers in and then told me to insert my card. By then Mum had joined us over by the till.

'Do you ever paint any of your furniture in brighter colours?' she asked.

'We will paint any of our furniture according to your specification, Madam.'

'Oh, how marvellous,' my mother said.

I looked at the large sum due on the small hand-held machine and proceeded to enter my pin. Spending money felt good.

The fat man in the argyll sweater handed my card back over to me, then took my home address and arranged a delivery date. I left the shop feeling as though I hadn't missed out on Christmas after all. Mum then suggested we stop and have a bite to eat somewhere. She had been checking her watch all morning. I hadn't had any breakfast and the shopping had left me with an appetite so I led her in the direction of my favourite gastro pub in Crouch End, The Maynard Arms.

The moment we stepped into the pub, I regretted the decision. Sitting at one of the tables was Alex, Erin and a couple I recognised but whose names I couldn't remember. They smiled over at me but stayed in their seats. I could feel my ears burning as I approached the bar. Mum sensed the change in my mood and linked arms with me.

'That was fun.' She peered at the menu written in chalk above the bar.

A young woman wearing a black jumper and beanie and a silver piercing in her nose approached us with a relaxed smile.

'What can I get you?'

'Vodka and tonic, please. Double. With ice and lemon.' I needed something strong.

'I'll have the same.' Mum squeezed my arm.

'Coming up,' the girl said, sliding down the bar to get us our drinks.

'Darling, where are the loos? I'm bursting.' My mother was hopping on the spot. I signalled to some double doors on the far side of the room. She rushed off, leaving me standing alone at the bar.

I could feel the eyes of my friends burning into the back of my head. Butterflies danced around my stomach. The unwelcome sense of dizziness made my hands began to tremble with dread. Nausea swirled in my stomach as I felt a hand come from behind and touch my shoulder. I turned around to find Erin and the woman whose name I couldn't remember standing there.

'Hi Erin.' As I kissed her cheek, I wished I'd never left the house. 'How are you?'

'Very well, Mon. How are you?'

The look of pity in her eyes made me want to curl up and die.

'Just out for a spot of lunch with my mum. Did you enjoy the rest of your Christmas?' I was determined to keep the conversation short and light.

'Oh yes, we had a lovely time.'

Erin looked embarrassed and I felt the familiar swell of anger returning. Just then, the girl from behind the bar arrived with our drinks.

'Well, it's lovely seeing you but I'd better get back to ordering my lunch.'

Then the woman whose name I couldn't remember spoke.

'I just wanted to say how sorry I am to hear what happened.'

Her tone suggested to me a love of gossip and drama. I could feel myself stiffen.

'Thank you.'

'I mean to lose your child as well, it just doesn't bear thinking about.'

Erin shuffled on the spot and looked down at the ground. Then Mum reappeared just in time to hear, 'You know, my cat was run over last year. Terrible it was. So I know what it is you're going through.'

I was speechless. I looked at her with disbelief.

'Sorry, who are you?'

'It's Clare. We met at Erin's fundraiser last year, remember?'

'No, I'm afraid I don't remember,' I said, lying. 'But thank you for your kind words.' The sarcasm dripped from the sentence, and with that I turned back to the bar to pay for the drinks. Erin and

Clare lingered for a second, unsure whether the conversation had ended. I remained with my back to them until they finally got the message and sloped off back over to their table.

'Who on earth was that?' My mother was eyeballing Clare fiercely.

'Just some busybody.'

My blood was boiling and the nausea felt stronger than ever.

'Can we just go and sit down, please.'

We left the bar and went to find a table as far away from my so-called friends as possible.

When we found a suitable table out of sight, I sunk down into a chair holding my head in my hands.

'Who was that silly woman?' Mum asked again, grappling with her coat.

'No one of any consequence.'

My hands still shook and my legs felt like jelly so I was glad to be seated. 'Let's just order, please, can we?'

I reached for the typewritten menu on our table.

'The food here is good.' Mum realised I wanted to change the subject but couldn't let it go.

'Who needs friends like that, anyway?' she muttered as I focused my attention on the list of starters. My head was swimming and I had lost my appetite. But I refused to leave just because of a stupid woman's thoughtless comment.

'But you know, Mon, I've been thinking. Friends are really important at a time like this. You need your friends around you. Not idiots like that woman but proper friends.'

I ignored her and carried on looking at the menu, trying to lose myself in the thought of food. Inside I was cursing myself for being so schizophrenic. How could I go from being so happy one minute to feeling so miserable and panicky the next? When would my feelings start behaving themselves again?

'My friends were so helpful to me when your father died.' She seemed oblivious to my internal turmoil.

'Mum, please. Just drop it, OK? We came to have lunch, so let's do that.'

She immediately shut up and turned her attention back to squinting at the specials board.

***

When we got back to the house, I felt inexplicably exhausted and had to excuse myself for a nap. Lying in my marital bed, it occurred to me how strange it would be to sleep in a new one soon. For a while I lay enjoying the silence with my eyes closed. But then my head began to race. My mind was flooded with flashbacks of the accident. They came out of nowhere. Images of shattered glass and contorted metal spun around my head. I could see myself looking at my own hands in disbelief and turning to see Tom. He was motionless; his head flopped over to one side and a large dark wet patch on his skull was growing slowly like a fungus.

Until that moment, I hadn't remembered seeing him dead. Clearly I'd blocked it out. The memory returned with a vengeance and I lay frozen on the bed, reliving the horror. It was as though I was back in the car. I could smell the blood and oil and smoke that poured out of the bonnet. The panic I had felt then returned and took over once more. It felt so real. I felt scared and numb and confused, just as I had before.

My body wouldn't move. I was a prisoner on the bed, and it felt as if an invisible force was holding me down, forcing me to relive the worst day of my life. I tried to scream but no sound came out. My head filled with visions of blood. I saw images of shattered bone protruding out of flesh like spikes and began to feel sick. When I opened my eyes the sight remained vivid as I stared down at my body in disbelief. There was a large hole in my stomach where my womb should have been. The white sheets on which I lay were soaked in dark red blood, which oozed from my gaping wounds. I was lying in a warm puddle, unable to escape. Drops of blood snaked their way down my face and into my eyes. Blinded, I wriggled on the spot trying to free myself from the terror. All I could see was red.

Then, just as I had done on the day, my body started to go into shock. My skin felt cool and clammy and my mouth felt dry. My heart was pounding fast in my chest. I felt extraordinarily weak. My bones felt like cast iron and I couldn't lift my arms. As my heart rate raced, I could feel the blood in my body moving around my veins. I was sure I was dying. My whole body started to shake as an icy coldness fell over me and the smell of burning rubber choked my throat and nostrils.

Then out of nowhere I heard a distant sound. Something was tapping on glass and as quickly as the terrifying vision had occurred, it disappeared, leaving me frozen with fear. My eyes searched my body first and then the room for evidence of what had happened to me. But the room was still and clean, just as it always had been. Then the tapping came again. I sat bolt upright, suddenly able to move, and looked over in the direction the sound came from. I stared at the window. The sage green damask curtains were closed. I heard it again, only this time it sounded like nails travelling down a chalkboard, and I realised it was the crow. It had returned for the first time in weeks. My heart sank and fear got a grip on me. I pulled the white bedsheets up around myself and leant against the leather bedhead. The fabric was cold and smooth against my back and I shivered. The room felt like a prison I was unable to leave. The sound came again, only this time louder. I put my hands up over my ears and sunk down beneath the duvet.

I lay like that for a long time. It felt like hours had gone by. My breath was hot beneath the duvet. I was cocooned in my terror. Pealing my hands away from my ears, I listened for the sound. The world was silent but I refused to move. I knew how clever the bird was. It would wait until I felt safe before returning again to send shock waves through my brain.

After a long while I began to believe it had gone. I slowly removed the hot covers and looked around the room. On top of the modern walnut chest of draws was a picture of Tom and me on a beach. It had been taken on our honeymoon. We were sun-kissed and happy but that was not why I noticed it. The mirrored frame was cracked, and out of the cracks seeped deep-red blood. It slowly snaked down the glass, covering our faces and turning the idyllic image into one of horror.

I knew that what I was seeing wasn't real but I found little solace in that fact. Instead I was left wondering if I was going mad. I scrabbled out of the bed and ran out of the bedroom on to the landing. The house was as quiet as a tomb. I didn't know whether to go outside and risk an attack from the crow or whether I was better off staying inside for the next horrendous vision to present itself.

As I pondered my options, I heard a noise coming from the kitchen. There was someone in my house. I could hear them banging about and I ran up to the office on the second floor and pushed the green velvet chair up against the door. The room felt so cold. I half expected to see Tom's ghost or find a flock of crows waiting for me. But I was alone. I didn't know what my next move was going to be. I had unwittingly trapped myself in a room at the top of the house and I didn't know how I was going to get out. I moved over to the far wall and stood with my back against it. Think, I kept telling myself, think. But my mind was blank.

On the wall opposite, something moved. I turned my head and gazed at a poster on the wall. It was a French art nouveau print of a peacock. He had a long tail that curled around the text that read 'Bienvenue au cirque'. The colours were rich and vibrant, and I stared as they started to swirl around. The blues, yellows and reds gradually merged as the bird came to life.

I watched transfixed as his talons began to uncurl. The long feathers on his head ruffled and seemed to move with a breeze. His black eye was looking at me, staring into my soul, and I felt a shiver run up and down my spine. Then, slowly, he arched his head back, opened his beak and let out a bloodcurdling scream. I fell to my knees as a sudden stabbing pain ran through my head. It felt like electricity being passed through my body. White spots danced in front of my eyes as the bird let out another horrifying screech. On my hands and knees, and hardly able to see, I crawled towards the door and pulled the heavy velvet-covered chair out of my way. Unable to stand, I reached for the door handle and turned it. A blinding white light greeted me as I pulled open the door. The light felt hot and burning. It was as if I was staring at the sun. My eyes began to pour and I wiped the tears away, trying to retrieve my sight. But when I looked down at my hands I saw red. I was not crying tears. I was crying blood.

I had nowhere to turn. Wherever I went, terror was waiting for me. I had to decide then which was worse. Did I stay in the burning light or did I return to face the bird? I could feel my skin blistering and the smell of burning hair was thick in the air. On my bottom I edged away from the heat and retreated back into the office. With my left foot I managed to push the door shut and suddenly my world returned to normal. The poster was static once more. I touched my face with my hands, feeling for evidence of the blistered skin and the rivers of blood that had cascaded down my cheeks. There was nothing there. My face was cold and smooth once more.

I could not explain it but somehow I knew it was over. The demons had gone for the time being. Alone once again in my office, I pulled the sheepskin rug towards me and wrapped it around my trembling body. With a great effort, I hoisted myself up into the armchair and collapsed in a fit of tears.

CHAPTER 13

I had been in Monica's kitchen cleaning for some time. I was trying to do my best to help her keep things in order. The domestic goddess role was not one I was used to or comfortable with and having bleached the work surfaces, wiped down the cupboards, cleaned the oven and hob until the metal was gleaming, I sat down at the table with a steaming cup of green tea, pleased with my efforts.

The tiles gleamed and the room smelt of lemon. I had pulled back the fabric that had been hung over the windows and doors, shutting out all the natural light. The room needed some fresh air and daylight. I hoped Monica would understand and not freak out. As I sipped the tea I looked at the clock on the wall. It was nearly five in the afternoon and still there was no sign of my daughter.

Getting up from the chair, I stretched my stiff back and went through into the hall. At the bottom of the stairs I stood listening for signs of life. There was no sound of Monica stirring. I decided to go and check on her and as I did there was a strange change in atmosphere. All of a sudden the house felt alive and threatening around me.

Upstairs, I found the door to my daughter's bedroom ajar. Monica was nowhere to be seen. I had a surge of panic as I went from room to room looking for my child. I called out to her, wondering if it was possible she had left the house without my knowledge. Just as I dismissed the idea, I heard the creek of floorboards above me. She was in the office at the top of the house. I felt better knowing she had not disappeared and made my way to the narrow staircase that led to the second floor. When I was halfway up I heard a loud crash from the office. Leaping up the steps a few at a time, I burst in to see what had caused the noise.

I was shocked to discover Monica ripping up a large picture of a peacock. On the floor all around my daughter's feet were large shards of glass and a broken pine picture frame. Monica was behaving like a wild animal, doing her best to kill the inanimate object.

'What on earth is going on?' She was like a stranger to me. She didn't reply, just kept tearing the paper into the smallest possible pieces. 'Monica, please stop. Whatever's the matter?'

Monica froze and looked at me. Clearly, she had been unaware of my presence until that moment. A look of fear tinged with embarrassment fell across her face. The poor darling looked down at her hands and the chaos of glass and splintered wood that lay around her feet. She didn't know what to say to me or how to explain her behaviour. She knew the truth sounded laughable. As she racked her brains to come up with a sane explanation, a torrent of tears fell from her exhausted green eyes.

Carefully, I stepped over the mess and moved towards her.

'It's OK, sweetheart. Everything's OK.' I

rubbed my daughter's back.

'No, Mum, it's not. It's not fucking OK. It's very far from being OK.'

Monica dropped the remains of the picture, which fell silently to the floor. Smudged mascara streaked down her cheeks and her bottom lip quivered. I had dared to hope that she had got past that stage and despaired to see my daughter in that fragile state once again. Guiding Monica over to the armchair, I sat her down. Monica looked over at the mess she had created and put her hands over her face.

'I never liked that picture, anyway,' I said as I started to collect pieces of glass off the floor. Monica sniffed and watched me tidy up. Eventually her tears stemmed and she spoke.

'I did like it. But...' She couldn't think of a reasonable justification for her wild outburst.

'You know,' I spoke softly, 'when your father died, I was so angry, so sad, that one day for no real reason I broke one of my favourite pots. It was just sitting on a shelf and I saw it, picked it up and hurled it at a wall. I don't know why I did it, but watching it smash made me feel better. It's a bit like screaming into a pillow, I suppose. Cathartic somehow.'

Monica seemed to doubt that the story was true, which in fact it was, but grateful to me for telling it. Since I had entered the study, the atmosphere had changed again. It was as if I carried something positive with me that counteracted whatever was haunting Monica. The room no longer felt like a gateway to hell. It was just an ordinary office again. The only evidence of anything being out of the ordinary was the destroyed picture on the floor.

'I can't go on like this, Mum.' Monica got out of the chair and steadied her fragile frame by holding on to the edge of the door. 'I can't live like this.'

I stopped picking up the wood and glass and faced my daughter.

'You are right. You need help, darling. I thought I could get you through this but I'm not the right person. I've tried my best but it's not working. You're not making the progress you should be.' The sentence hung in the air with unpleasant clarity.

'So, what now?' Monica appeared light-headed.

'Honestly Mon, I'm not sure. The doctor has seen you and done all he can. Perhaps you need counselling. Something more than just pills.'

Monica watched as the cogs of my mind clicked into motion. Whenever I think hard about something, I rub my temples with my index fingers and close my eyes. I could sense Monica had a sudden urge to leave the room. She couldn't bear looking at the destruction she had caused and who could blame her. It was tangible evidence of her instability.

'I need a bath, Mum.' She spoke with urgency. 'Please stop cleaning. I'll do it later. It's my mess. I have to sort it out.'

Was Monica referring to the broken picture or something greater, I wondered.

'OK, good idea. Go and have a nice long soak.'

As Monica disappeared down the stairs I knew what I had to do. Removing my mobile phone from my pocket I dialled Directory Enquiries.

***

After an early supper of baked potatoes, salad and ham, Monica and I went into the sitting room to indulge in some terrestrial pleasures. We sat curled up on the sofa while the fire roared in the hearth, watching a rerun of a David Attenborough programme about insects. I love all things related to nature and was fascinated by what I learnt about centipedes. Monica didn't pay much attention to what was being said. She stared at the screen while the images melted into one another. Her mind looked blank and her soul seemed empty.

The night grew thick around the house and Monica said she had a headache. That did not surprise me as the poor love was tired from the dreadful day she had had, but when I suggested she went to bed she said she was scared to return to her bedroom. Her tension radiated around the room. In a decisive move I turned the television off and turned to face her.

'I think you need to talk about this. Maybe I am not the ideal person but right now I'm all you've got and I'm here for you. Tell me what happened up there earlier. I promise to try and understand. You can be honest with me, darling. I'm your mother and I love you.'

Monica immediately welled up. She wanted to speak but she couldn't. A thick heavy veil had fallen over her mind that would not allow it. Seeing the pain on my daughter's face, I edged over on the sofa and wiped the hair away from her brow. Monica looked smaller than she had ever done. All I wanted to do was wrap her up and take her away somewhere where she would feel safe.

'I'm sorry, Mum. I can't do this now. My head hurts. I just need to sleep.'

But Monica did not move from the sofa. She was too scared to go upstairs.

'I'm going to get a blanket and hope I drift off down here in front of the box.'

I told Monica to make herself comfortable while I fetched her a blanket. Monica did as she was told and rolled herself up in a small ball in the corner of the large soft sofa. I was reminded of nursing my teenage daughter years ago when she returned home after her first experience with cider, although she had not looked as ill and as beaten then as she did now.

When I returned with a huge herringbone woollen rug and the duvet off my bed, I tucked up my darling, who was already beginning to drift off into a dreamless sleep.

'Tomorrow will be different. You'll see. I've got a good feeling about it.' Stroking Monica's silky hair, I held tightly onto the foreign feeling of hope that stirred in my stomach. 'I'm going to sleep in here with you.'

Monica blinked her eyes half-open to let me know she had heard. I slipped off my jeans and top and settled myself down on the other sofa. I was not going to leave her alone in the state she was in.

***

The next day things seemed to return to normal. The odious feeling that had hung over the place had dissipated. Monica appeared brighter than I expected she would be and I was very grateful for it.

We ate boiled eggs for breakfast and Monica revealed her plans to switch bedrooms.

'It feels wrong being there now. I don't know why. I don't like it anymore. And since the new bed is being delivered today, I might as well seize this opportunity to make a proper change. I've always liked the back spare room. It's got such a nice view over the garden.'

I nodded encouragingly but wondered how easy Monica would find clearing the room that had been intended for Josh's nursery. As though reading my mind, she said, 'There is no point holding onto those baby things. I'm going to call the Salvation Army and see if they want to take them away. Someone will be able to make use of them, they're brand new.'

'And you feel ready for that?' Doubt crept into my voice.

'Well, Mum, no, not really. But I can't imagine a time I'll ever be OK with the fact my child is dead and so are my chances of having any more.' Monica cupped a mug in her hands and looked down into the beige liquid. 'I need to keep busy.'

'I think you are very brave and I'm so proud of you.' I spoke with my mouth full of toast. 'Do you think repainting the room might help?'

'Actually yes, I think that's a great idea.'

'I could help. Let's go and buy some paint this morning. No time like the present.'

'Good idea, Mum.' Monica stared out of the kitchen window at a large black crow on the grass that was fighting to pull a worm out of the cold ground. She did not comment that the curtains had been pulled down. I watched my daughter watching the crow and waited with bated breath for a reaction. But Monica got up out of her seat, tidied away the breakfast things and excused herself upstairs for a shower. I gave a relieved sigh and then returned to the spare room to dress.

I had been sharing Mon's clothes for some time. I'd only intended to stay one night but upon discovering my daughter in that state I'd refused to return home until she was better. I didn't want to leave her alone for even a few hours so I could go back to Cambridge and fetch my own clothes. We had been sharing a wardrobe.

Luckily we had a similar physique. The only difference was that I was more like an ironing board, with no bust and small hips. Monica, although slender, did have a bit of bust, something she had inherited from her father's family. His mum had been amply endowed. In the past, Monica had been the larger of us two but since the accident she had lost so much weight she was now as skinny as me. The clothes hung off us but we agreed it was better than having to squeeze into garments that were too small. Even in times of serious tragedy a woman is able to appreciate losing weight.

As I pulled a cream Nicole Farhi jumper down over my head, I noticed the smell of Monica's fabric softener. It smelt of lavender and I realised how removed from my own life I had become. I was living in my daughter's house, wearing her clothes and was utterly consumed with everything that went along with that. Walking over to the long modern mirror that hung on the wall, I looked at myself and felt my own identity slipping away. Cream wasn't even my colour. It made me look washed out. I suddenly missed my own clothes and colour in my life.

I looked around the room I had called home on and off since October. It was clean and bright. The bed was cast iron and had pinstriped pillowcases and duvet cover in white and lime green. A tall mango wood wardrobe stood in the corner of the room, and on the wall above the bed was a large modernist painting of the London skyline. The brushstrokes were in thick black oil. It was coarse and lacked subtlety. Like the rest of the room it was crying out for warmth. I stood examining it for some time and came to the conclusion that I didn't like it.

After a moment or two it dawned on me that I could see no sign of my daughter in the room. It was missing a female touch and I was surprised by the realisation. Then I started to see that most of the house shared the same lack of personality. I thought back to the days when Monica had been a university student. She had always surrounded herself with warm colours and bright objects. The house in Crouch End reminded me of a magazine photograph, too manicured to be real.

As I closed the bedroom door behind me, I called out.

'I'm ready when you are, darling.'

'Be with you in a minute,' Monica replied from behind her bedroom door.

I went up into the office on the second floor and looked around. The mess was cleared away, the Hoover having sucked up any evidence of the chaos. I looked at the colours in the room, hoping to find inspiration, wanting to help Monica choose a bright, jolly colour to paint her new bedroom in. I am a great believer that colour can help to lift one's mood. Within seconds my eyes were drawn to the beautiful orchid on the bookshelf. It was a pure rose pink with a bright cerise centre. I went over to the flower and touched it lightly. As I did so it fell from the stem and landed on the floorboards below. I bent over and picked it up.

'You'll do nicely.' I cupped the flower in my hands and carried it back downstairs.

We returned from the DIY store just after one o'clock and immediately set about masking the doorframe, skirting board and windows. Monica found an ancient radio and plugged it in. Music filled the room and we worked happily, singing along to the golden oldies that floated in the air around us.

When we had finished the masking, I left to make tea while Monica started to box up the various baby related items that scattered the room. She collected together a changing mat, a number of soft blankets still in their packaging, muslins, unopened newborn baby-grows, a plastic baby bath and a nappy bin and piled them all out on the landing along with a brand new Moses basket and its rocker.

I appeared behind my daughter, who stood in the doorway staring at the pile of belongings.

'I can take them to a charity shop for you if you like?'

'Yes, Mum, thanks. That would be great.'

Monica was relieved not to have to be the one who physically gave the things away.

'How about I make us some food?' I said, looking at my watch.

'Sounds good. I'll do a bit more up here and then come down and join you.' I gathered as many of the baby things I could carry and made my way downstairs, leaving Monica in her new empty bedroom busily laying down dustsheets.

After we ate Brie and rocket baguettes, I packed the car up with all the baby related effects and set off, armed with Monica's directions, to find a suitable charity shop that would take them. Monica returned upstairs to begin painting the walls.

The colour she had chosen was bold and unlike anything else in the house. Inspired by my offering of the orchid, Monica had decided that pink was exactly the colour she should get. Having spent a long time looking at colour cards in the shop she had eventually decided to go with a colour called Cherry Blush. It was a true pink but soft enough not to be overwhelming. She hoped it would be the statement she needed. I also persuaded Monica to buy some scatter cushions for her new bed that complimented the colour scheme.

While I was out, as Monica opened the tin of paint and dunked her brush into the thick silky liquid, she heard a knock at the door. Huffing, she wiped the brush and rested it in a tray. She later told me she was irritated that I never seemed to remember to take the set of keys she had given me. Monica bounced down the stairs, dressed in a pair of jogging bottoms and an old T-shirt of Tom's. Her hair was tied back in a messy bun.

'Coming, coming!' Monica was irritable as she opened the door. But the person standing on the other side wasn't me. It was a surprise I'd arranged for her.

CHAPTER 14

A tall man stood on the doorstep with his back to me. He turned around, a big, warm smile on his face.

'Simon!' I couldn't hide my shock. 'What are you doing here?'

He leant forward, lingered, and then planted a gentle kiss on my cheek. His short dark beard felt soft against my face.

'Aren't you going to invite me in?' His blue-grey eyes seemed to look into me. I stood motionless for a moment, allowing the shock time to sink in.

'Now is really not a good time. I ... I can't let you in. I've got my mother staying.'

'Yes, I know.' He pushed his hands into his jean pockets. 'She was the one who called me.'

He watched as confusion fell across my face. She hadn't warned me to expect him. I suspect she knew that if I had known I might have flown off the handle and chastise her for interfering.

'She called you?' My pitch was noticeably higher than normal.

'Yes, Mon, and if you let me in, I can explain.'

I opened the door further and stepped aside.

'You had better come in then.' A small smile was beginning to form as I spoke. 'Go through into the sitting room,' I said, gesturing, 'it's in there.'

Simon left the hallway and went through into the sitting room as instructed. He was a tall man of over six foot with broad shoulders and short dark hair. He seemed unsure of himself as he stood lingering near the sofa, not sure whether to sit down or not.

I also felt uneasy. It had been nearly a year since I'd last seen him. Simon looked around the sitting room at the furniture and belongings scattered about.

'Nice place.' He had always been polite.

'What are you doing here, Si? My mum will be back any minute.'

His facial expression changed and softened as he took a few steps towards me.

'Your mum has told me everything. Jesus, Mon, I am just so sorry.'

Simon wrapped his arms around me and held on. It was the first time I had felt safe in a long while. Nuzzling into his chest I inhaled the smell of his aftershave. It had been ages since I had been this close to a man.

'Why didn't you call me? I would have come, if I'd known.'

'Would you?' Stepping back, I looked up into his eyes.

'You know I would.' I knew Simon would never lie about something so important.

'Well, after everything that happened, I thought I'd be the last person you'd want to speak to.' Crossing my arms, I moved over to look out of the window. 'I wanted to speak to you. I tried to call.'

Simon sat down on the sofa and put his head in his hands.

'When I got the phone call from your mum, I was completely thrown. She told me you could do with a friend. Can you believe that? And then she explained about the accident and the baby.' He removed his car keys from his pocket and started to play with them. 'I had to come. What was I supposed to do? Ignore her request for help?'

I turned to look at him. His coffee-coloured skin looked warm, and I found myself wishing I could be close to it again.

'I think this is a really bad idea.'

Simon looked up.

'So am I just supposed to leave now and pretend that nothing has happened?'

'It's probably for the best. I can't deal with this right now. Mum's staying here, you know. The last thing I need is to be in this house with the two of you together.'

'It's OK. I'd sleep in the spare room.'

'No, Mum's in there.'

'OK, I'll take the couch then. Or do you really expect me to drive all the way back to Cornwall?'

Just then I heard a car pull up outside. Mum had returned from the charity shops.

'Fuck,' I muttered under my breath, 'Mum's back.'

'She knew I was coming today. It was her idea, remember.' Simon stood up and began to shift awkwardly.

'I wish she wouldn't interfere. If she knew what she'd done, well, she would never have called you.'

'But she did, Mon. And now I'm here.'

I left the sitting room and went to open the front door. It had begun to rain and Mum shook drops off her hair and coat as she entered the hall.

'It's done,' she said. 'They were very grateful for the donation.'

'Simon is here.' I stood with my hands on my hips and eyeballed my mother.

'Oh, marvellous!' She ignored my look of disdain and pushed past me into the sitting room.

'Simon, darling!'

I listened to Mum greet him and felt out of sync. It was not a situation I'd been expecting or knew how to cope with.

'I'm going to put the kettle on.' Calling out, I made my way into the kitchen to escape the awkwardness I was soon going to have to face.

***

When I woke up the next morning my stomach was in knots. I had spent the previous afternoon with Mum and Simon, when all I had wanted to do was hide beneath my bedcovers. How could she have called him without telling me? Of all the people. But I suppose she didn't know what she was doing. She was trying to be helpful. I get that. There's no point in being angry with her. But she'd made my life more complicated than she could ever know.

Simon was in my house. The house I once shared with Tom. It felt so wrong. It made me feel dirty. I needed to push those feelings away and felt forced to pretend that everything was all right and my life was normal. The truth was that it was far from that.

I made a bed up for Simon on the sofa downstairs. He was right, I couldn't send him back to Cornwall straight away but I couldn't believe he was happy to stay. It was all so surreal.

My mind was all over the place. Part of me felt happy to see him but with that came a stabbing guilt. He would have to go. He couldn't stay any longer. I slipped out from under the covers and ducked into the bathroom to have a much-needed shower.

I immersed myself in the warm gushing water and tried to prepare myself for a difficult morning ahead. Simon had to go. I dabbed my skin with a soapy sponge and let the suds slide down my body and into the plughole. I felt relaxed in the steamy glass box. The water pelted my shoulders and I hung my head down letting my neck soak in the heat. It felt good and as I stood beneath the cascade, and it dawned on me that I had learnt that Simon now lived in Cornwall. No wonder I hadn't been able to reach him. I wondered when he'd moved. Then very quickly the penny dropped. I knew the answer to that question.

When I finished my shower I dried myself with a white fluffy towel, warm from the heated towel rack, and stepped out onto the landing and was surprised to find my mother standing there with a small suitcase by her feet.

'Morning.' She bent down to pick up the bag. 'I have been waiting for you to get up. I don't want any arguments now, but I'm going back to Cambridge for a few days. I think it will be good for you to spend some time with your old friend without your mother cramping your style. I've told Simon to stay here with you until I return on Saturday.'

'But Mum…' I stood shivering on the landing.

'No arguments, you hear? We've been in each

other's pockets for far too long. I daren't leave you alone at the moment but I'm tired, Mon. You know I'll do anything for you but these last few months have been a strain on me too. I need to go home and connect with my life for a little while.'

I was speechless. Without realising it she was doing exactly what I wanted her to do. Practically dropping the towel that was wrapped around my naked body, I hugged my mother and thanked her.

'This was not the reaction I was expecting, I thought you might be cross. Well, have a lovely time with Simon. He's such a nice man.' Mum walked down the stairs until, halfway, she stopped and turned. 'I'm on the end of the phone. Any time, Monica, remember that. I love you and I'll see you on Saturday.'

I blew her a kiss as she disappeared out of sight and I went back into my bedroom to dress.

It had been some time since I'd taken any pride in my appearance but after pulling on a pair of skinny Joseph jeans, a grass-green cashmere sweater and my Ugg boots, I went over to my dressing table and sat down to apply some make-up. I brushed black mascara onto my lashes and rubbed some rouge into my cheeks. With my index finger I lightly applied some rose-coloured lip tint and then sat back to look at myself.

My hair looked good. It was clean, straight and shining. The make-up had put some colour back on my face. I looked good. It was a refreshing feeling. I stood up and went over to the window and opened the curtains. It was something I had not done in a long time and I enjoyed it when the soft morning light flooded the room. Then I sprayed on a little scent and went downstairs to make breakfast for my guest.

I went into the kitchen to find Simon sitting at the table nursing a cup of coffee. Although I was expecting to see him, it was strange to find him in my kitchen. He looked so out of place in my home. I had to keep reminding myself that this was his first visit to the house.

He smiled when he saw me and immediately stood up.

'I made you a coffee. Just how you like it.' He pushed a cup over towards me.

'Thanks.' I took a sip. 'Perfect.'

We stood in silence while I slowly drank my coffee. Neither of us knew what to say. There was so much we needed to discuss. It was overwhelming and difficult to know where to begin. I could feel his unease as clearly as he could feel mine.

Breaking the long silence, he said, 'Is it OK if I have a shower?' He was wearing the same clothes as he'd arrived in the day before.

'Sure. I'll show you where the guest bathroom is and get you a fresh towel.' I lead the way upstairs.

Walking up them with him behind me gave me a sense of déjà vu. As I poked about in the airing cupboard I did my best to push it from my mind.

'Here you are.' I handed him a large cream towel. 'You can use that bathroom.' I indicated to the one next to the room my mother had been using.

'Thanks.' He was looking into the room that

was going to have been the nursery.

'I'm going to the shop at the end of the road. I should be back before you're out of the shower, but if not, feel free to make yourself some toast.' Simon nodded and went into the bathroom, closing the door gently behind him. I felt my heart skip a beat as I turned and walked away from him.

Wrapping myself up in my thick black coat, I left the house. Outside, the February sun was trying to break through the thick grey cloud that blanketed London. The street was busy with traffic and people making their way to work. At the traffic lights I had to wait for a long time before the green man gave me the go-ahead to cross. I felt impatient. I wanted to get back to Simon.

In the Turkish shop I grabbed some eggs, sausages, tomatoes and mushrooms. I also picked up a copy of *The Times* for Simon. I remembered that he liked that newspaper. When I reached the counter I asked the friendly man with the pudgy face for one of the more expensive bottles of Rioja. He did so smiling and handed over my change. I thanked him, dashed out of the shop and hurried back to the house.

I got in to find Simon sitting on the sofa. He looked uncomfortable as he got up and offered to take the shopping bag off my hands.

'I got you a paper,' I said, placing it on a small table next to an armchair.

'*The Times*. You remembered.' He looked pleased.

'I remember everything.' My cheeks flushed

red. 'Do you want something to eat?' I changed the subject.

'Sure, why not?' Simon knew my barriers had come up again and I could hear the disappointment in his voice. 'Whatever you're having is fine.'

He picked up the newspaper, tucked it under his arm and carried the loaded blue carrier bag into the kitchen. I followed nervously. The butterflies had returned. He put the shopping down near the hob and went over to the table where he sat and unfolded the paper.

Simon paid no attention to me as I started to prepare breakfast. He was irritated and I could feel it oozing from him. I put the sausages under the grill and started to chop up the tomatoes and mushrooms. Out of the corner of my eye I could see him staring at the paper but I knew he wasn't reading. He didn't turn a page the whole time I was cooking.

'Scrambled or fried?' I asked, stirring butter into the mushrooms which sizzled in a saucepan.

'You decide.'

He put the paper down, folded his arms and stared out of the window. His irritation with me was growing. I couldn't face a confrontation so fried the eggs silently, pretending to be unaware of his frustration. Then I smelt the toast starting to burn. It was not going to be an easy day.

After an uncomfortable breakfast we went into the sitting room. He took his paper with him and continued to pretend to read. I sat at my laptop in the armchair for want of a better thing to do. The atmosphere was icy and I hated the silence. I couldn't understand why he had come all the way from Cornwall if all he planned on doing was ignoring me. There were things that needed to be said and I decided to bite the bullet. I closed my laptop and looked over at him. He glared harder at the paper. I was in no hurry. I would wait until he was ready to talk. I continued looking at him for a few moments before he finally relented and put the newspaper down on the coffee table.

'I can tell you're angry. I'm not stupid. Whatever you need to say I think it's for the best if you just come out and say it.' I tried not to sound aggressive but was unsuccessful.

'From your tone, I gather I'm not the only one who's angry.'

'Well, what do you expect? Turning up here unannounced without any warning.'

'I came because your mother asked me to.'

'You've seen me now. You've done your duty. There's no reason to hang around.' I hissed with more venom than intended. Simon put his head in his hands and looked down at the floor. I felt terrible. The last thing I wanted was an argument. I got up out of the armchair and went and joined him on the sofa. 'I'm sorry. I just don't know what to say to you.'

He looked at me.

'Why don't we start again?' He offered a small smile. It melted my heart. 'This is more fucked up than either of us could have predicted but the only way to sort through it is to talk. Don't you think?'

I nodded and let him continue.

'The last time I saw you things were messy.

You told me you needed time and that I had to back off. It was hard for me but I respected your wishes. After spending weeks waiting for you to get in touch, hoping that you would call or write, I started to lose hope. I thought perhaps you'd decided to give the marriage another go. Since you were pregnant I did what I believed was the noble thing and left you alone. You will never know how fucking difficult that was for me, Mon. I loved you. I loved you so much, and for a while I believed that you loved me too, that we could make a fresh start.'

His eyes were filled with a pain I had not seen before. I felt all the colour drain out of my face and a feeling of sickness take over.

'Then, last week, out of the blue, I get a call from your mum telling me about the accident. She begged me to come and see you. Does she know about us?'

'NO! Jesus Christ, no! It was just a coincidence. She knows we've been friends for years. I suppose she just thought I'd like to see you. That it would do me some good.'

'I thought as much but I needed to check.' Simon put his hands on his knees and leant back into the sofa.

'So this is the house you shared with him. I have to say I never thought I'd come here.'

'Me too. It feels wrong, doesn't it?' A shiver ran down my spine.

'Do you want me to leave? Is that what you want?' His words were filled with sadness.

'Honestly, Si, I really don't know.' There was a long silence. 'Do you think that I haven't thought about you? The guilt inside me has been unbearable. I never in a million years thought I'd be the type of woman to have an affair. But it happened. I fell in love with you all over again.' I could feel the tears burning my eyes. 'I was so confused. I was expecting a baby. I was married. I had a life here with Tom. You wanted me to leave everything behind, my entire life, and start again as if nothing had happened. I needed time to think, to work out what I wanted.'

'So you said you needed space...'

'Yes exactly. I thought if I didn't see you for a little while it would be easier for me to work out what I really wanted. You were in my head and I needed the decision to come from me. Not you or Tom, but me.'

'OK, I respect that. But then days turned into weeks and still you didn't call.'

'Because of the accident! It changed everything. Suddenly my husband and my baby were dead. What was I meant to do? Jump straight into your arms like they never existed? Everything I had worked for, this house, my marriage, a family, suddenly it was all ripped away from me. Don't you get that?'

'Of course I do!' he bellowed. 'But all you had to do was call. I would have been here for you. I could have helped.'

'No, you couldn't, you would have made things worse. I had to go through it alone. It was my grief, my heartache. Having you around would have made me feel a million times worse. I felt guilty enough already.'

My hands were shaking. Simon sighed, got up

from the sofa and walked over to the window. He stood looking out and I stared at his strong back, broad shoulders, long legs and short, dark, wavy espresso hair. He was so handsome and I wanted to hold him. But I didn't move; there was so much more that we needed to say first.

'All right, all right. I get it. But you could have called me, you know.'

Simon spun around to face me.

'But I didn't know about the accident, did I? You said you wanted a break. The first I heard of it was last week.'

'I left messages on your phone.'

'Since we were over, I stopped using that mobile. I didn't see the point in keeping it anymore. Yours was the only number on it anyway.'

'Oh.' I felt foolish. Simon came back over to the sofa and sat down close to me. Our legs were touching.

'I need to ask you something, Mon, and I need you to be truthful with me.'

'OK.' My stomach knotted.

'The baby, was it mine?'

Time froze.

'What good will it do?' I felt hopeless.

'Monica, I have a right to know.'

I wriggled in my seat. The truth was terrible.

'Honestly, I don't know.' He looked crestfallen. 'I did all the dates. I went over them hundreds of times. Tom and I hadn't been sleeping together much. I couldn't bear him touching me ... We used condoms on the few occasions that we did have sex.'

I stopped myself from continuing. I'd said enough already.

'So he was...' Simon sat back and let it sink in.

'In all probability, yes, Josh was your son.'

'I feel sick.' Simon dashed out of the room. I heard him vomiting in the downstairs loo and regretted telling him the truth. I should have protected him from the horror of it all. The moment he'd shown up on the doorstep I'd known I'd be faced with that question and had been dreading it ever since.

Now the truth was out, I felt dirtier than ever. I pictured the body of my little boy wrapped up next to Tom in the coffin and I too started to feel sick. I had done a terrible thing and the bird was punishing me. At last I started to understand what was happening.

Simon came out of the bathroom looking ashen; any of the Indian blood that coloured his skin had temporarily vanished. For the first time he looked like a fragile man.

'Why didn't you tell me?' He kept his distance.

'How could I? That's why I sent you away. I had to work out what I should do.' He was too tired and beaten down to argue back.

'I need to get out of this house,' Simon said, looking around him. 'I can't have this conversation here.' He made a move towards the door. 'Come on, we're going out.'

'Where?' I asked, following and reaching for my coat.

'Anywhere but here.'

***

We spent the entire day out of the house. Having walked around Alexandra Palace for hours, we went into a nearby pub and sat down to talk more. It was exhausting. By the evening we were both emotionally drained. We sat at the kitchen table nursing a glass of Rioja, each unable to say anymore. My head was spinning. Guilt and relief swirled around taking it in turns to batter me.

Simon reached into his jeans pocket and removed a pouch of grass, some tobacco and rolling papers.

'I need this,' he said, licking the gum on the paper and pressing it down. He had smoked pot for as long as I had known him. It went along with his creativity.

I sat looking at the man I had loved. He was so different from Tom. He was relaxed, calm and easy-going. I remembered watching him play his guitar in bed one afternoon after we'd snuck off to a hotel together. It should have felt sordid but it didn't. We really loved each other. He was my soul mate. When I was with him I felt like myself. We were good for each other and always had been. He was the man I should have married.

I met Simon at university. We were in the same dorm. Back then he used to have dreadlocks and wore his jeans loose around his bum. That memory always makes me smile.

Rarely seen without his guitar slung over his shoulder, Simon was studying music and played with various indie bands he met through friends and people in his class. He had known he wanted to be a musician since he was four years old. I admired his ambition and dedication to his craft. A few times, I'd been to his gigs. He was always the quiet one in the background with his head down, playing as if his life depended on it, totally absorbed by the music.

We had been good friends for some time before I started a relationship with Tom. One day, Simon had come to me and told me he was in love with me. It had come as a huge shock. I'd had no idea. For want of anything else to say, I told him I loved him as a friend. He accepted that and we remained close, much to the disapproval of Tom, for whom the connection we shared was clear to see. It bothered him and he did his best to discourage the friendship, but we were solid. Simon was always going to be a part of my life and Tom had no choice but to accept it.

After university we had stopped seeing so much of one another. We had fallen into different worlds. He had his music and I had Tom and my job as an architect. We kept in touch but rarely saw one another. Then Tom proposed to me. It was on holiday in Greece. I remember it so well. We were sitting on a beach on the south coast of Rhodes, the sun beating down on our shoulders. I was reading a book when Tom told me he wanted me to be his wife. There was no ring, no bended knee. It was a statement rather than a question but I happily accepted.

He never did get me an engagement ring. To this day I wear only a platinum band on my wedding finger. My mother used to tut but I dismissed her mutterings saying I didn't need diamonds. Secretly, I wished he had produced a ring. It would have shown me he was serious enough to put some effort in, to put his hand in his pocket and prove I really was what he wanted. I suppose I never really forgave him for that. I used to look at other women's engagement rings with envy. Second-hand would have been fine. I didn't need Tiffany's or Cartier, just something simple would have made me so happy. At the time money was tight but a few years later we were doing well. When we had plenty of money, he still never thought to produce a ring.

I spent some time planning our wedding. Tom was busy with work and uninterested in the finer details so I had attempted to organise the perfect day. I looked forward to the opportunity to stand up in a room surrounded by people I cared about and declare my love for that man.

Since neither of us were religious we had opted to have the ceremony at Islington Town Hall. It was a small service with only close friends and limited family. Afterwards, we went to a venue in Soho where we had a long luxurious lunch, followed by an afternoon of sipping champagne and chatting with the guests. The night ended with a band playing and we had danced into the small hours. Ironically, that was the day I reconnected with Simon. Looking back, it seems so inappropriate but that was just the way it happened. So we rekindled our friendship, called one another from time to time and met for occasional lunches. I didn't hide the fact from Tom, although he was very discouraging. The affair did not start until six months later.

As soon as Tom and I had been married, there

had been a stark change in his behaviour. He began to nit-pick about the house, about the way I cleaned it, about the clothes I wore, about the people I associated with. I began to feel unhappy in the marriage. Then, one evening when Tom was out with friends, I had arranged to meet Simon for dinner. He'd been in my head for weeks and the mention of his name had caused my stomach to do summersaults. Gradually, it had dawned on me that I'd fallen in love with him. I knew I should have stayed away but it had been impossible. We were drawn together as though we were magnets.

That night at dinner Simon had been nervous. I couldn't understand what was the matter with him. He was behaving so strangely. After two glasses of wine, he had looked over the table at me and told me that he was in love with me. My heart had jumped and I had known that this was the beginning of the end of my marriage to Tom.

We had found a small hotel where we had made love. Simon had been so shaky with nerves that the sex wasn't very successful but that had not mattered. I had told him that I loved him too and our affair had begun. Once or twice a week we would meet somewhere in London, usually south of the river, close to where he lived in Clapham. There we could be together away from prying eyes. We created our own private world. A place where only we existed and nothing else mattered. It was hopelessly romantic but equally unhealthy.

With the passing of each month, Tom grew more and more controlling. I vented my fears and frustrations to Simon, who encouraged me to leave him. He begged me to run away with him and I nearly did. But there was an incident with Tom that changed everything.

One evening after work, Tom came home in a foul mood. He threw his keys onto the glass kitchen table and stood seething on the spot. I knew better than to ask what was wrong. He poured himself a large whisky and sat down. I stood by the sink, washing up, and concentrated on my task. After a long noxious silence he revealed that a colleague at work had quit, leaving the rest of the team with mounds of extra work to do. I listened patiently to him ranting about responsibility and the selfishness of his co-worker's actions. Tom had gone on to say that the reason John had resigned was because his wife had discovered he was having an affair and had thrown him out. Like a dog with its tail between its legs, John had sloped off to Derbyshire to hide from his wife with his mistress, leaving the company up shit creek. I remember feeling my own guilt plastered across my face and had quickly turned back to the washing-up in an attempt to hide it.

After another triple whisky, Tom sat in the chair watching me. I could feel his eyes burning into my back and I did my best to stop my hands from shaking. He said he thought John got off lightly and warned me that if he ever discovered I was having an affair, he would go to the ends of the earth to make me pay.

I knew that if I left with Simon, Tom would find me. He would have never given up. He did not like being made a fool of. He would have hunted us until he breathed his last breath. So I had told Simon I couldn't leave Tom and the affair had continued.

A few months later I had discovered I was pregnant. I knew it was Simon's child I was carrying. I didn't want to share the news of the pregnancy with Tom and put the pregnancy test that had confirmed it in our bathroom bin under some tissue paper. As luck would have it, Tom had found the discarded test and confronted me. I had had to embellish my lies further. In order to explain why I had thrown it away without telling him, I told Tom that I had planned to go to the doctors to confirm it before I told him. Luckily, he had seemed to accept that. The next day the two of us had gone to the GP's surgery to take another test. My doctor had confirmed that I was six weeks pregnant.

Naturally the situation had been complicated by my news. For as long as possible, I had kept my pregnancy from Simon. I had been trapped in my marriage unable to leave while knowing another man's baby was growing in my belly. When eventually I had come clean with Simon, it had broken him. I never said that the child wasn't his but had made sure not to confirm it either. I'd had to buy myself some time. Making a decision of such magnitude was never going to be easy and I put it off for as long as I could. Simon had struggled though. He had kept begging me to run away with him, even claiming he would happily raise the child as his own, (not knowing it was his anyway.) When it had all become too much for me,

I had asked Simon to let me have some breathing space. He had been gutted but kindly respected my decision. Then the accident had happened.

Sitting opposite Simon now, I so wished my life had turned out differently. When I looked back at the young woman on holiday with her boyfriend in Rhodes, I wished I could scream at her to listen to the alarm bells that were ringing. But hindsight is a fool's game. My life had taken the path it had and that was that.

Simon was inhaling long breaths of the hazy smoke and holding them down in his lungs before slowly letting it escape from the small parting between his smooth lips. I got up from my chair and went over to him. He handed the joint over to me and I took a puff. It went straight to my head. I hadn't smoked dope for some time. The taste was bitter and hit the back of my throat but I held it down, letting the drug take its effect.

'Now what?' he said, stubbing out the spliff.

'Now we go to bed.' I felt the blood pumping in my lungs and the dope coursing through my body. Simon looked at me as if he had known what I was going to say. He stood up, took my hand in his, led me out of the kitchen and up the stairs.

I followed silently, my heart thumping. I had not made love for nearly a year and as I went into my new bedroom I realised I had thought I would never make love in that house again. I switched on the light and turned to face Simon. His lids were low over his eyes, like hoods to hide his feeling.

Without saying a word, I pulled my jumper up over my head and dropped it casually on to the floor. As I stood there in my bra and trousers, the hairs on my arms stood up. I don't know if it was the cold or the excitement. Simon moved over to me and slid his hands around my waist, linking them behind my back, and pulled me in to his chest. He opened his mouth slightly and brought it down towards mine. His lips were comforting and familiar as his tongue travelled around my mouth. He lifted me up onto the bed and removed his top, lay down on top of me and kissed my breasts before moving down my stomach and unbuttoning my jeans. With a playful tug he removed my trousers and then my lace knickers, which he dropped onto the floor.

Simon lay beside me examining my body for some time. I was perfectly still as his hands worked their way over my breasts, down my cold flat stomach and towards my pubic hair. My body tingled with elation as he brought his mouth down to my groin. The pleasure lasted for a long while as his tongue reacquainted itself with my body. I shook with pleasure and groaned with each new wave of ecstasy. Finally he raised his head, wiped his mouth with the back of his hand, pulled down his own trousers and entered me. The sex was slow and rhythmic to begin with but our passions grew with each thrust. Afterwards, we lay in the dark staring up at the ceiling sharing another joint.

I didn't know what it meant but I knew that I was happy for the first time in ages. I was where I was meant to be and felt totally at peace with myself. Simon stroked his fingers up and down my forearm and rested his head on the pillow.

There was nothing for us to say. Neither of us dared ruin the moment. Eventually, when he began to softly snore, I cuddled up against him and closed my eyes. I was going to sleep well that night, safe in the knowledge that I would wake up and find Simon in bed beside me in the morning. Suddenly my life had direction again.

CHAPTER 15

When I woke up the next day I found Monica sleeping peacefully beside me. Despite this, I felt out of sync and didn't recognise the room I was in. It took a few seconds for my eyes to adjust before I remembered where I was. Sitting up in bed, I stretched my arms out and looked down at her, noticing how skinny she was. I moved the dark silky hair away from her face to see how beautiful she was and lightly ran my finger down the pale skin on her naked back. She flinched for a second and returned to her dream world. I didn't want to wake her but missed her when she was asleep.

I never did understand why she ended up with Tom. He was never going to be right for her. At university, Monica was popular. She could have had her pick of the men. It was unsurprising. Her clever brain, artistic streak, sensitive nature and good looks made her a real catch. It was mysterious that she chose Tom. He was a lucky sod who wore her on his arm with pride but I always got the impression she was just a prize to him.

I lay silently next to her in the strange room for a long time. My mind was on a merry-go-round. Everything I had learnt the day before spiralled around my head. I'd had a son. The woman I loved had been unable to share her grief and had had to face it all alone. On top of that, she had lost him in a terrifying accident that had badly injured her both physically and mentally. She had also had to deal with a crushing guilt with no one she could talk to about it. No wonder her nerves were in a bad way. The sadness returned again. Monica was returning from her sleep. I ached for us both, for the pain and loss we would share for the rest of our lives. Josh. The name would forever be engraved on my mind.

As she stirred, I found myself wondering what the future held for us both and whether in fact we could have a future together at all. For a long time that was all I had ever wanted but not at the expense of the life of our child. Would we ever be able to get over what had happened? I really hoped so but couldn't help doubting it. It seemed too big a thing to move on from. Whatever happened, we would both need time to work through it. I envied her for having the head start. I wish I could have met our son, held him and then said goodbye. That had been stolen from me and I felt a sudden surge of anger rise up. What right did she have to keep me from my son? But then I remembered Tom and all the complications that came with the accident. Nothing is ever clear-cut. I was torn between pity and sorrow for her and the same for myself.

I got up quietly and went over to the window to peer through the curtains. There was a sprinkling of dew on the ground that glistened in the early spring light. Glancing at my wristwatch I realised it was early in the morning. The sun was low in the sky. In contrast to how I felt inside I could see it was going to be a beautiful day.

Watching some sparrows hop about on the

lawn, I felt numb and dreaded the day ahead. I picked up my boxer shorts that lay discarded on the ground, left the bedroom and went into the bathroom to splash some water onto my face. The wine and weed from the night before left a fog hanging over me. There was only one thing for it – coffee and another joint.

I returned to the bedroom and pulled my trousers on just as Monica woke. She sat up in bed and I could tell she was conscious of her nakedness. It felt odd being in the house she had shared with Tom. I think we both wondered if we were bad people. While she rubbed the sleep out of her eyes, her thoughts looked heavy and she seemed unready to face the day.

'Morning.'

I sounded as awkward as she looked. She offered me a small smile as she readjusted the sheet around her chest.

'I'm going to make some coffee. Do you want anything?'

I didn't know whether to behave like a guest or the man of the house.

'Not at the moment, thanks. I'll jump in the shower first.' I moved towards the window to open the curtains.

'No!' Monica sounded frantic. 'Sorry, I just mean not yet. I'll do it later.' Nodding, I decided to leave Monica alone, as she seemed to have woken up in a peculiar state.

As I left the room she hunched her knees up to her chest and rubbed her eyes again. Last night's events clung to her like an unwelcome odour. She looked as though she needed to wash them away and I heard her dash into the guest bathroom.

I guess Monica couldn't face using the bathroom she shared with Tom anymore than she wished to sleep in what had been their marital bedroom. I knew her mind was reliving the infidelity and that she was torturing herself for it. My thoughts followed a similar path.

From the kitchen below, I heard her flush the loo before turning on the shower. Downstairs, I made some real coffee and sat at the table rolling a spliff. Usually I'm only a light smoker, but unable to deal with what had happened, I craved the soft haze that pot offers. It helps distance me from the world. I'm able to see more clearly with the marijuana than without it. I always have. It is my thing, my crutch. Everyone has one. Some people have a few.

Gentle sunlight flooded into the clinical kitchen and I started to picture Tom in the house. I knew, of course, that this was his home but had been trying not to imagine him in it. As I did, the pangs of guilt grew stronger. Looking around the kitchen, I realised it was all Tom. There was no sign of Mon anywhere. It was modern, cold and spotless and I fought a sudden desire to trash it. I wanted to smash all the square plates on the ground and rip the cupboard doors off of their hinges. Maybe it was grief kicking in. I am normally not a violent man.

My anger with Tom was as alive as it had ever been. I had always hated the way he used to squash who Monica really was. Everything unique and wonderful about her was slowly crushed by his desires and personality. Standing in his kitchen I wondered if the man had ever known what love really meant. Then I came to a stark realisation; I still wanted to be with Monica, perhaps more now than ever before. But we couldn't be together in that house. Sitting in the sunlight, I began to consider plans for a future together. She could return with me to Cornwall, and we could start a new life by the sea. Mon had always loved the coast. I wanted her life to be full of the things she loved.

I'd moved to Cornwall only four months earlier. Believing the relationship with Monica was over and unable to face the thought of seeing her with Tom and the baby I had decided to get away from London. My sister and her husband lived in Cornwall and I knew it had a decent music scene so without a second thought I gave notice to my landlord, upped and left. I never told Monica I was leaving.

When the affair had begun we had invested in mobile phones to use specifically for the purpose of contacting each other. Monica was terrified that Tom would see a condemning message if she used her normal phone. Unbeknown to Monica, I had thrown my mobile into a bin when I thought she had made her choice to stay with Tom.

Ingrid had cannily contacted Jay, a mutual friend of ours, to ask for my phone number. He had given her my number and told her I'd gone to Cornwall. She had been surprised to learn I had recently moved there. Without a second thought Ingrid had called and asked for my help. She knew that we were close friends and thought I might be able to get through to Monica. Had she known I was the true father of the baby and that we had been having an affair, I'm sure she would never have picked up the phone. But fate could not be avoided. There was a tragic comfort that came with the acceptance. It seemed life was telling me I was meant to be with her again.

When Monica came into the kitchen the room was thick with heady smoke. It floated like a transparent sheet in the air.

'Bloody hell!' she exclaimed, fanning her hand. 'A bit early, isn't it, Si?'

I flashed her a defiant look, grinned and took a long hard drag.

'So what do you want to do today?' Monica ignored my insolence as I stubbed the glowing end out into a small pot and got up out of my seat.

'I am going to make us some breakfast and then we are going to go and spend the rest of the day on the sofa.'

'But I need to start painting my room. I've put it off long enough.' She stirred some sugar into her coffee.

'Fine, then I'll help you.' I put my hands on her skinny shoulders and began to massage them.

'I need to make this house my own. Painting the walls is a good place to start.'

'I agree.' I was thoughtful. 'Do you plan on staying here?' Monica spun round to look at me.

'What do you mean?'

'Well I was wondering if you'd considered selling it. You know, starting somewhere new. Leaving all the ghosts behind.'

'There are no ghosts here.' Monica sounded prickly. 'Only the living haunt me.'

My head cocked to one side.

'What are you talking about?'

'Didn't Mum mention it to you on the phone? The crow? I'm talking about the crow.'

'What crow?' I was puzzled.

'You'd better sit down. There are still some things you need to hear.'

***

When we went up to bed that night we did not make love. Monica curled up in my arms and listened to the sound of my heart beating. She lay like that until she drifted off into a light sleep. I stroked her hair and held her close. She felt so slight in my arms, so fragile.

I was rocked by her beliefs about the crow and never imagined she could entertain something so unlikely. Ingrid had told me that Monica was on the verge of a breakdown but I had not been prepared for the level of insanity I now faced. When recounting her episodes with the crow Monica seemed convinced of the malevolence of the bird. I tried gently to imply that it sounded implausible but Monica had flown into a rage and accused me of doubting her.

Lying in bed in the darkness, I wondered how best to help put her mind at rest. It suddenly occurred to me that her fear was the reason she had behaved oddly when I'd suggested opening the curtains. Holding onto her more tightly, I whispered to the sleeping girl that I would never let anything bad happen to her again.

Unable to sleep, I got out of bed and wandered

over to the window. It's a habit of mine. I find looking at the world beyond helps me to think. Pulling back the thick white curtain, I stood flooded in the moonlight, looking up at the canopy of stars that pierced the blue night. The garden was still and the trees and plants below were shades of silver and black. It reminded me of a Monet painting.

As I stared out of the window, for a long time I thought about what would be best for Monica. She needed help. I now understood that. What surprised me most was how together she appeared most of the time. The only inkling that all was not well was when she had opened up and shared her paranoid fears about a crow. I felt sure that the best thing for her was going to be a fresh start. It was not surprising that she felt tormented living in that house, especially alone. I knew that if I could convince her to come with me to Cornwall, everything would be better. There, she'd be free from Tom and her past. It wasn't a crow that was tormenting her but the ghost of her dead husband. I knew it would take some convincing but there was a plan brewing in my mind, a plan that involved Ingrid.

Ingrid could help persuade Monica to move out of London. I knew she might buck against the idea since it meant her daughter moving to the other side of the country, but I was confident that she'd be inspired to do right by Mon. It wasn't going to be easy for her to hear, but it was time Ingrid learnt the truth about Tom and the affair.

As I slipped back under the covers, I looked at Monica who lay sleeping soundly with her mouth slightly ajar. Planting a kiss on her forehead I made her a silent promise that everything was going to be all right. Along with her and me, it was time the past was put to bed and with that comforting thought I began to nod off.

CHAPTER 16

By Saturday morning, Simon and I had come to some decisions. He wanted to tell my mum about our affair and get everything out in the open. It had taken a lot of persuading to convince him to keep the secret to himself. I couldn't see what help it would do, her knowing. She would have been disappointed and confused. She'd loved Tom, even if she hadn't known the real him, and I didn't want to strip that away from her.

To begin with, Simon couldn't understand my reasons. He was sure she'd be grateful when she saw the whole picture, but he didn't know her like I did. I knew she would never understand. The loyalty my parents had shared was something she held dear. In the thirty years they had been married, neither of them had ever strayed.

It was hard for Simon to accept that we had to put off telling the world about our relationship, but he said he'd wait forever if he had to. That was one of the reasons I loved him so much; he was so kind and understanding. He never asked me to do anything I felt uncomfortable with.

I rushed around upstairs hiding all the evidence that Simon had been sharing my bed. I wasn't expecting Mum to start snooping around the minute she arrived, but she was canny and had a nose for that kind of thing. It was important that nothing was rushed. If Simon and I were going to make a go of it, we needed to do it properly. We would never stand a chance if people knew we'd cheated on Tom. Not only that, but people would start to wonder about Josh and I couldn't face those sorts of questions. It was a private matter and should remain so.

As I picked up his boxer shorts from the floor and shoved a pair of jeans and a couple of T-shirts into a plastic bag, I had a flashback of being a teenager and hiding a boy from my parents. The memory brought a smile to my face. It disappeared the moment I heard the doorbell. Mum had arrived.

I rushed down the stairs carrying the bag, which I threw over to Simon who was sitting casually on the sofa with his feet up on the coffee table. He was wearing odd socks and reading the paper. He caught the bag and shoved it down beside him. I noticed the smirk on his face and had to stop myself from bursting into laughter as I opened the door and greeted my mum.

As always, she arrived laden with bags. Mum could never travel light. She stood on the doorstep for a moment or two looking at me with bemusement.

'What's got you so flustered?' She raised an eyebrow.

'Oh just been rushing around this morning. Come in, Mum, come in.' In the corner of my eye I spotted the dark silhouette of a bird flying low in the sky. As she stepped inside I slammed the door hard behind her and she jumped, dropping one of her bags to the floor with a thud. Smiling nervously, I herded her into the sitting room. Simon was already standing up waiting to greet her. They shared a hug and I enjoyed watching the two people I loved most in the world connect.

'Right. Tea, Mum?' I could hear the brightness in my own voice.

'Hang on, hang on, let me sit down first!' She was as exuberant as ever.

I could see the time spent away from me had done her good. She'd been to the hairdresser where her neglected roots had been given the attention they deserved. She looked fresher than she had for a while and I was pleased. It occurred to me what a burden I must have been over the last few months. Then and there I felt as though I had turned a corner and would no longer need the kind of exhausting support she had provided. I was an independent grown-up once more.

The three of us sat down in the living room. Soft rays of light crept through a gap in the curtains, creating a kaleidoscopic pattern on the cream carpet. It was beautiful and I lost myself in the pictures I saw in the shapes of light. The conversation between my Mum and Simon floated above me like an aeroplane flying high overhead. Suddenly I felt like a stranger in my own house. Everything looked foreign to me and I didn't recognise my surroundings. I could feel the presence of the crow nearby. I tried to shake it off and concentrate on the words being said but a shroud of darkness had fallen over me and my head felt muddied.

Disappointment flooded me. Since Simon had arrived I'd felt safe and back to my old self again. Although I'd always known that the crow might return, I presumed his presence would make me stronger and more able to deal with it. But my legs started to feel like jelly and my stomach ached with a horrendous sickness. I closed my eyes and sat back in the chair, hoping the feeling would disappear.

Suddenly I felt warm breath against my face. It was Simon's voice.

'Are you OK, Mon?'

'Monica, sweetheart, you're as white as a sheet, what is it? What's wrong?' Mum's voice sounded miles away.

'Mon, talk to me...'

'Simon, fetch her a glass of water and a blanket. Quickly!'

I could feel my brow suddenly littered with icy beads of sweat and I started to shiver. My teeth chattered so violently that I was unable to speak. Mum and Simon buzzed around me and the world was a speeding blur.

When Simon returned with the water, in the place of his face I saw the image of a bird's head. The eyes were dark and empty. Its feathers glimmered with a blue-green sheen like crude oil and its beak was mouthing words I could not hear. Then I noticed the blood. It streamed in a drizzle from the bird's beak. More and more came, as the carrion face grew closer. Then out of nowhere another crow's head appeared. It inched closer to me, getting larger by the second. It was as though I had been plunged into a masquerade nightmare. The birds seemed to be in cahoots and I could feel their hateful thoughts infecting the air. The eyes stared into me sending an instant stinging pain through my brain. My head was in a vice tight around my cranium. My skull would surely explode. I tried to call out but don't think I made a sound. Was I there? Was it really happening? I shook my head, trying to free myself from the horror. The beaks kept coming, closer and closer until they were millimetres from my eyeballs.

They intended to peck out my eyes. I was being treated like a corpse by the flesh-eating birds. After the accident I had felt dead inside, but the arrival of Simon had changed that. He had brought me back to life. I needed to fight this somehow. Surely I'd paid for my mistakes? Was the life of my child and the loss of my womb not enough to satisfy karma?

I squirmed and begged for Mum and Simon to help me. Then suddenly everything returned to normal. I was sitting in the chair again facing my mother and Simon, who were crouched either side of the chair looking at me in horror. Maybe I had fallen asleep for a moment and was having a bad dream. Looking at their faces I knew that wasn't the case. They had seen me tumble into a hallucination and it scared them senseless.

Adjusting myself in my seat and trying to regain some composure, I apologised for my turn and explained that I'd been struck by an instant agonising migraine. They looked at me knowing I was lying and the only thing I could do was gaze at the floor. How could I admit what was happening to me? I felt my mum flash Simon a concerned look before sitting back down on the sofa.

I felt exhausted, as if I'd completed a

marathon, and I excused myself to bed. Simon stood up holding my elbow for support. I could see he thought I was going to collapse any moment. The worry on his face was heartbreaking. I was destroying everyone around me. His pity made me feel more helpless than I had done during the vision. I pulled my arm away from his hand and walked out of the room. My head was still spinning when I made it to the bottom of the staircase.

The memory of the images I had seen reminded me of a terrifying film. It was almost wonderful had it not been for the dark oozing blood. I balanced myself again before facing the mountain of stairs ahead of me. In the background I heard voices.

'You see, I told you, she's not well.' My mother could never keep her voice to a whisper.

'She seemed fine until just now. What the hell was that?' Alarm rang out in Simon's words like church bells. My happiness, it seemed, was short-lived.

***

After an uncomfortable sleep I got up and went down to see Mum and Simon. I felt so foolish and worried that they thought I was mad. It was the kind of shame you feel after you have behaved badly at a party and drunk far too much. My head pounded as though I was suffering a terrible hangover, so when I got into the kitchen I headed straight to a drawer where there was a packet of Cocodamol. I could feel their eyes burning into my back. No one said anything as I popped two pills into my mouth and drank a large gulp of tepid water.

Simon was sitting at the table with his hands folded together. His look was intense. My eyes met his and his mouth curled into a small smile.

'Better?' he asked.

'I hope so.' I sat down opposite him.

'So are you going to tell us what that was?' His words were kind and non-accusing. My head still pounded. I didn't want to think about what I'd experienced. I wanted it to sink down deep into my subconscious and remain forever locked away.

'I can't talk about it now. I'm sorry. I know you want answers but I don't have the strength.' There was a tremble in my voice. I sounded as weak as I felt.

'Do you think it might be wise to visit the doctor again?' My mother spoke softly.

'You think I'm mad, don't you?' Anger rose with each word.

'No, no, of course not. I just think that maybe you could do with some help.' She looked over at Simon, who was nodding in agreement.

'Pills aren't going to do a bloody thing. It's that bird. I'm being haunted. An exorcist would be more appropriate. Or pest control.' Simon grinned and I glared at him. 'It's not a fucking joke. You haven't been here. You haven't seen what's been happening to me.'

'I am not psychic, Monica.' Simon looked offended and immediately I started to soften.

'I know. I didn't mean to snap.'

My mother remained silent, twiddling the large

silver topaz ring on her middle finger.

'So what do you think needs to be done?' Simon leant forward and I got a waft of his aftershave. It made my knees feel weak. I wanted him to hold me.

'If I knew that…' I hung my head.

'What about some sort of bird psychologist?' my mother chipped in sounding hopeful. I looked at Simon whose expression stung with disapproval.

'I'm not sure that is the answer, Ingrid.' He folded his arms across his chest and sat back in his chair.

'No, Mum, Simon's right. It's not the bird that needs help, it's me.'

'I think the only thing to do is kill it.'

Mum and Simon shared a glance before turning to look at me as if I'd just suggested genocide.

'Look at me like that all you want but if you want proof that it's the bird and not me that is crazy, it needs to be illustrated.'

My mother raised her hand to her mouth and gasped.

'OK, so we kill the bird, then what?' Simon sounded tired.

'Well, then everything can get back to normal. I know it will.'

'Monica, I really think…' My mother leant forward and put her hand on my arm.

'Don't, Mum. Can't we just try? Look, I promise if things don't improve after it's gone, I'll go and see the doctor. I will.'

'OK.'

She sounded defeated. There was a long

silence. The death sentence hung in the air as if it were toxic fumes.

After some time, Simon spoke. 'I'll do it.' He was stepping up to the role. 'It won't be much fun killing it, and you shouldn't have to go through that.' I knew how much he liked animals and understood what a difficult offer it must have been.

'No, Simon. I need to do this myself. It's okay, I'm a big girl. This is between me and the bird. I have to be the one to finish this.'

Suddenly, my mother stood up.

'I really don't think I want to be around for this. I think if you don't mind, I'll go back to Cambridge for a while. I'll leave this afternoon. You two will be fine together. Call me when it's over.' She appeared worn down.

'You only just got here, Mum,'

'I think this is madness, Monica.' There was bitter disappointment across her face. 'I can't help it, I just do. What if you kill the wrong bird? An innocent bird shot for nothing. How will you know it's the right one? This is all too much.'

Sometimes she could be overly dramatic.

'I'll know, Mum. I promise you, I will know.'

My mother sighed. Simon, who had his hand on my leg under the table so she couldn't see, squeezed my knee and said, 'You'll get through this. You're stronger than you think.'

His words filled me with resolve. Mum smiled but I could see the doubt in her eyes. It was as clear as day.

***

After Mum left, Simon and I snuggled up on the sofa. He held me and stroked my hair, occasionally kissing the top of my head. I stared blankly at the television. It had been a tough day and I felt drained. I wanted it all to be over. A part of me was willing the bird to return. It was a strange sensation. For so long I'd wished the opposite, now I welcomed the next invasion, since I knew it would be the last time the crow would get the better of me.

Lying curled up against Simon I felt safe and loved. I couldn't remember the last time I'd had that feeling with Tom. Still, it seemed strange being in his house, the home we had shared, cuddled up with Simon. Since Simon had arrived everything had felt different. It didn't feel like my home anymore. The house reminded me of the shell of my old self and it needed to become my past.

An hour later we went up to bed. We didn't make love. Wrapped together we lay in the darkness. I listened to the sound of him breathing and absorbed the scent of his skin. I felt I was home. After everything I had been through, the terrible things I had done, I began to think that perhaps my life could be good again. No more lies or pain. He was going to save me from myself and that was all I really wanted.

I understood that neither he nor my mother accepted what I told them about the crow. How could they? I couldn't be angry with them for that. Mum didn't ever really know Tom. He wore a mask around everyone but me. Only I know what happened in our marriage. I was the only one to feel his bitter disapproval. Tom had turned me into a prisoner in my own life.

Simon knows most of it. I used to confide in him when it all got too much. But he never lived through it like I did. I was so grateful to have him in my life. It was then that I had realised my marriage was over. My problem had never been coming to terms with that, it had always been how I would ever break away. Tom would never have willingly let me go.

I tossed and turned in bed. My head was suddenly flooded with images of Tom's bloodied skull flopped forward. Sickness returned with the memory. I closed my eyes in the darkness and tried to think happy thoughts. I wanted to focus on my future with Simon but the ability to do so eluded me.

Next to me Simon lay snoring lightly. I thought if I listened to the rhythm of the sound it would help. I tried to focus on the throaty purr but it was useless. My head was spinning with visions of blood, glass, twisted metal and broken bones. And then, as if on cue, the crow returned. I heard its beak scratching the glass on the bedroom window. I pulled the duvet back and jumped out of bed. Simon stirred but did not wake as I tiptoed over to the window. The thick curtains were drawn but I knew it was there on the other side of the glass. On Simon's bedside table was a retro metal alarm clock. Needing a weapon I reached for it before slowly peeling back one of the heavy curtains.

It was three o'clock in the morning. Outside, the night was indigo and a crescent moon shone high in the firmament. A scattering of stars and wispy clouds clung aimlessly to the dark blanket of sky. The bird was not there. My heart was beating in my chest as I lowered the instrument in my hand. The crow had disappeared. But looking around the garden, searching in the branches of the trees, I could feel its cold eyes still on me. Perhaps it knew I'd picked up the clock and foresaw what I planned to do. It was clever, that much was clear.

I remained motionless in front of the glass waiting for it to return. We were linked somehow. I wanted to understand why but couldn't. Standing in my underwear, trembling in the darkness, I willed myself to remember the accident. Pieces were still missing.

I remembered getting into the car and leaving the house. We were going shopping to get things for the baby. I knew that much. A memory of us arguing flitted just out of reach. The next thing I recall was waking up in the wreckage. My life changed forever.

I was so angry at the amnesia. Somehow I knew the answer to what was happening with the crow was hidden in my lost memory. I just needed to find a way of unlocking it. Shivering in the darkness, clinging to the cold chrome clock, I wondered if hypnotism would help.

Suddenly I felt something brush my lower back. I lifted the clock above my head, spun around and brought it crashing down.

'Jesus fucking Christ.' Simon rocked backwards holding his face.

'Oh my God, Simon!' My body was covered with

goose bumps. It had been impossible to see in the darkness.

'Put that fucking thing down,' he said, rubbing his temple. 'What's the matter with you?'

'Are you all right? Simon, it was an accident. I ... I'm so sorry.'

'It's the middle of the night, what are you doing?' he said as I turned on the bedside light. He squinted in the brightness. I could see a small cut and a lump appearing on his eyebrow.

'Oh Jesus, let me get you some ice.' I slipped my dressing gown on quickly and headed for the door. 'Do you need a doctor?'

He closed his eyes tightly trying to escape the throbbing pain.

'Just leave it.'

'At least let me get you some—'

'Leave it!' he interrupted.

'But it was an accident. Simon, I'm so, so sorry.'

Guilt hit me like a punch in the stomach. Slowly moving towards the door, he pointed to the bed.

'Stay here.' He was uneasy on his feet. 'I'm going to sleep on the sofa tonight.' He didn't look at me as he pushed past me and headed down the stairs.

I was alone again. What had I done? Then out of the corner of my eye I saw movement. I turned to see the large crow standing on the windowsill staring at me with dead smiling eyes. Any fight I'd had left me. All I could do was slump onto the bed, put my head in my hands and sob.

CHAPTER 17

The next morning I had a thumping headache. The wound had swollen up to the size of a golf ball and the skin around my left eye felt tight and tender. I had barely slept a wink. The sofa was too small and the pain in my face had made it almost impossible to get comfortable. I lay in my boxers under a blanket and stared up at the high ceiling feeling hopeless. Monica and I had come so far in the last few days. It was never going to be easy and I accepted that we didn't necessarily deserve to have a smooth ride. The infidelity had caught up with us. But I told myself she was worth it. I'd always loved her and always would. She didn't mean to hit me. It was an accident. She wasn't well. I felt bad for leaving her alone last night. The shock had just been too much for me at the time.

Getting up from the sofa, I wandered towards the kitchen trying to ignore the stabbing pain in my temple. I needed some relief. Fumbling about in drawers I eventually found some ibuprofen. Filling a pint glass with water from the tap, I sat down to roll myself a joint, hoping the combination of drugs would dull the pain.

The kitchen was lacking any natural light since Monica had insisted on having the blinds drawn after suffering her hallucination yesterday afternoon. I was frustrated by the insanity that clung to the walls of that house. Tom and Monica's house. I got up and opened every blind, hoping that daylight might improve my mood. But outside the world was bland. I longed for spring to return and the grey bleakness to retreat, while wishing I could take Mon and jet away to an island in the sun.

Still only in my boxer shorts, I started to feel cold standing barefoot on the stone floor. But I didn't want to go up to Monica's room. I wasn't ready to face her yet. So I retrieved my coat from the hallway. I felt ludicrous dressed like that but normality seemed out of place in that house anyway. As I returned to the kitchen, my eyes were drawn to the air rifle that stood propped up in a corner near the garden doors. A burst of rage erupted and I went over and grabbed the gun. Flinging open the doors into the garden, I stood holding the rifle on the patio in my pants and coat. The garden was still.

'Well, come on then!' I bellowed. 'Pick on me instead!'

A sparrow darted out of a bush and hurried away. I cocked the gun and pointed it in the direction of the small bird before realising it wasn't the object of my aggression. Immediately I felt foolish and lowered the gun. Turning round, I found Monica standing watching me.

I went into the house, put the gun down and pulled up a chair.

'Did you do it?'

'No, I bloody didn't. This is mad, Mon. I don't even know which damn bird you expect me to shoot.'

'You'll know when you see it.' She placed her hand on my knee. 'I really do appreciate this, you know.'

'Well, I don't. I'm going to do it because I love you but then I want us to get on with our lives. No more mention of the crow, you hear?'

I felt tired and Monica recognised the look of defeat plastered all over my face.

'This is too much for you.'

She went over to the door, looked out and hugged herself. Then a large crow landed a few feet away from the door and stared at her. It opened its beak and let out a soul-piercing screech.

'There!' She pointed with a long pale finger. 'There it is!'

Jumping out of my seat, picking up the gun, I moved towards the door.

'Don't frighten it away.' She gripped me by the arm as I slowly opened the door.

The bird stared at us both. It did not move. I lifted the gun and adjusted the sight until I could see the crow clearly.

'Are you sure this is what you want?' I said quietly, trying not to show my apprehension but never losing sight of the bird.

'Yes, I'm sure. Do it. Do it now,' Monica said.

Looking at the bird, I saw what a noble creature it was: beautiful and proud. I wanted to lower the gun and walk away but I couldn't. My finger wavered above the trigger. Then the bird hopped a step towards us. Monica retreated behind me and buried her face in my coat.

'Do it. Please, just do it,' she whimpered.

Gritting my teeth, I pulled the trigger. There was a muffled pop. I opened my eyes to see a burst of black, oily feathers.

I moved closer to the bird to make sure it was dead. The crow lay motionless on its side with wide and staring eyes. A wave of guilt and sadness hit me as I knelt down to take a closer look. Then the bird's feet begin to move. I fell back in horror and watched as the wounded, desperate creature tried to lift itself up off the ground and fly away. But it was useless. Its wing was broken. Monica watched from a distance.

'Oh Christ, do something!'

There was only one thing I could do. I stood up, lifted the butt of the gun and brought it crashing down onto the bird's skull. The noise of bone smashing made me feel ill.

'I think I'm going to be sick.' Monica darted inside with her hand over her mouth.

I turned away from what I'd done. I couldn't look at the mess of blood and feathers on the grass. My hands shook and I felt grey with sickness. Heading back into the kitchen, I poured myself a large whisky and drank it down in one go. The honey liquor burnt my throat. In the distance I heard Monica throwing up in the downstairs toilet. A feeling of resentment passed through me. She had got what she wanted, so what right did she have to feel ill?

I couldn't leave the corpse lying on the grass, so without hesitation I got a bin bag out of one of the drawers and went into the garden to clean up the mess. I felt numb as my bare hands scooped up the broken body of the crow and put it into the bag. The wet blood was on my fingers but I refused to look down. Marching back through the kitchen I took the crow to its final resting place: the rubbish bins at the front of the house. The lid came down, making a hollow sound as I discarded the corpse. It reminded me of smashing the bird's skull. I knew then that noise would be forever carved into my memory.

When Monica came out of the toilet, she looked like a ghost.

'Is it gone?' she said, wiping her mouth with the back of her hand.

'It's dead.' Monica was staring at my blood-covered hands while I poured myself another large whisky.

'I need a shower.'

'Thank you,' Monica said, but I was unable to respond. Listening to the sound of my feet padding up the stairs I wondered if I could ever forgive her for making me do that.

***

We spent the rest of the day saying little. Neither of us knew what could be said. It was over. The bird was gone. Monica told me she hoped that its death would instantly lift her but it hadn't. If anything, I could see she felt more horrible. She knew that by allowing me to participate I was also infected with the heavy feeling.

We were sitting on the sofa, not touching, watching the news when the phone rang. Monica jumped up and ran over to answer it. She was pleased to have someone to talk to. From the sofa I heard Ingrid's voice purring down the phone.

'Oh, Hi Mum.'

'Everything OK, sweetheart?'

'It's over, Mum. The bird's gone.' There was a long silence. 'Mum, are you there?' Ingrid cleared her throat.

'Well, I hope that will be the end of the matter now.' Her tone was cold.

'So do I, Mum.' I felt pangs of guilt as I remembered the bird writhing in agony. 'Would you like to come and have lunch next Sunday? Simon's still here.'

She glanced over at me. I shifted in my seat and changed the channel.

'Yes, that would be lovely.' Ingrid sounded brighter. 'What time?'

'Half twelve, one is fine.'

'OK. I look forward to it.'

'Great. And Mum, thanks.'

'See you on Sunday, sweetheart. I'll bring a bottle. Love you. Bye'

'Bye, Mum.' Monica put down the phone. 'You will still be here then, won't you?' There was anxiety in her voice as she rejoined me on the sofa.

'Where else would I be?' I managed a smile and kissed her cheek.

'Everything is going to be fine from now on. I promise.'

But I knew she was lying. As Monica rested her head on my shoulder and closed her eyes, I felt the malevolent feeling in her gut remained as prevalent as ever.

***

For Sunday lunch, Monica laid the table and made the house look good while I cooked a feast of Indian food. Both Ingrid and her daughter love Indian cuisine and happily tucked into the various dishes I prepared. It was the first time since I'd killed the crow that I started to feel normal again. I like cooking. It reminds me of my childhood, spent hanging onto the apron tails of my grandmother who had come to England from Bombay when she was in her thirties.

The wonderful smells of spices cooking filled the house bringing it to life. The three of us sat eating, chatting and laughing. It felt natural and easy. We slipped out of the routine of gloom and returned to being happy and normal. No one mentioned the crow.

The sound of Monica's laughter rippling through the house brought evident joy to her mother, who was on good form, telling tales of various adventures in her life and making Mon and I laugh. In contrast to the feeling I had had a few days earlier that Monica was still obsessed and disturbed, I felt she was at last beginning to move on from the past. I pictured future Christmases with them both and felt a bubble of excitement return. The future looked good again and it was so close I could almost reach out and touch it.

Without thinking, as she read my mind, Monica reached over and grabbed my hand. The conversation came to an abrupt halt as Ingrid raised her eyebrows and looked perceptively at us both. I looked at Monica who allowed a small smile to spread across her face.

'Well, that was simply delicious.'

Ingrid stood up and began to gather the dirty plates.

'Sit down. I'll do that, Mum,'

Monica pushed back her chair.

'Don't be silly. I'll clean up. You two go into the sitting room and get comfortable. I'll bring some coffee through. Then you can tell me what you've been up to the last few days.'

There was a twinkle in her pale blue eyes as she ran the plates under warm water, watching grains of yellow rice being sucked down into the plughole.

'You'll get no arguments from me,' chirped Monica, following me out of the room.

After coffee, followed by more wine, chocolates, cheese and three-quarters of a bottle of tawny port, the three of us were merrily drunk. I strummed on my guitar and Ingrid sang tunelessly along; she loves a singsong. The affliction seemed to have left Monica, and the burden of gloom had lifted. Perhaps, at last, the bird's curse had too.

As the volume of the singing grew, Monica lifted herself up from her spot on the sofa and tottered over to the drinks cupboard. The effect of the drink had hit her. She swayed on the spot.

'Anyone want anything?'

She poured herself a drink from the decanter of unknown contents. I declined and Ingrid was too wrapped up in the song to respond.

When my rendition of 'Like a Rolling Stone' has finished, Ingrid slumped back into her chair and gave a hearty round of applause.

'I must fish out some of my old records,' she said.

'My folks used to play Dylan all the time. I grew up listening to it,' I told her.

'How are your parents?' Ingrid leant forward.

'Very well. When Dad stopped working, they moved to the Lake District. Mum teaches yoga and Dad paints to pass the time. At the moment they are in India visiting some of Mum's side of the family.'

A thought occurred to me.

'Their house is empty at the moment.'

I looked at Monica who was sitting on the arm of the sofa sipping her drink unaware of my gaze. 'Ingrid, do you think it would be a good idea to take Monica away for a while?'

'Yes I do. Why?'

'Well, it seems to me, my parents' place would make the perfect getaway. It's wonderful countryside up there, exactly the sort of place she could have a proper break. What do you think?'

'I think it's a marvellous idea.' Ingrid clapped her hands together and turned to her daughter.

'Sure, why not?'

'You might even have fun.' I said, feeling the glint in my eye. Monica stifled a grin. 'We'll set off in the morning.'

'That soon?'

'No time like the present.' I strummed my guitar again.

'I love an adventure.' Ingrid was animated. 'I'm rather jealous.'

'We'll send you a postcard, Mum,' teased Monica.

'Don't worry about me. Just make sure you get lots of fresh air, and for goodness sake, keep having fun.'

CHAPTER 18

The next morning I woke up with quite a hangover but it had been worth it. It had been a lovely evening and the first time I'd really let my hair down since I could remember. I lay alone in the bed wishing Simon could be there with me. I'd insisted that he remained sleeping on the sofa while Mum was around. I knew she had more than a suspicion about our relationship but it seemed too soon to be open about it yet. We had all the time in the world and it was important to me that this time we did things right.

Having Simon around made such a difference to the way I felt. For the first time in ages I felt secure. He constantly reassured me how much he loved me, how he'd never leave or hurt me. I loved him in a way I'd never loved anyone before. It was the real thing – honest, brutal and raw.

I stretched, sat up in bed and looked at my alarm clock. It was eight forty. Reaching for a half-empty glass of water, I took a long sip. It was tepid and not as refreshing as I'd hoped. Then I remembered the plans we had made to go to Simon's parents' house.

A buzz of excitement rippled through me as I pulled the covers back, jumped out of bed and wrapped a dressing gown around my pale body. I went into my old bedroom and dragged a suitcase out from under the bed. It had a layer of dust on it that exploded up into the air, making me sneeze as I opened it. Inside were a pair of snorkels. They were left over from the last holiday I had taken with Tom. I picked them up and hurled them into a corner of the room. Nothing was going to spoil my good mood.

Picking up the empty case, I left the room, closing the door behind me. On the landing I found Mum waiting for me. She too looked as if she was suffering from the previous night's excesses.

'Morning, darling,' she yawned.

'Morning, Mum. Sleep OK?'

'Like a log.' She was rubbing her forehead. 'Mon, something occurred to me when I woke up this morning. I don't mean to put a dampener on this trip of yours but I was wondering if you had considered the journey there?'

'What do you mean?' I was confused.

'It's an awful long way and it will mean being in the car for a long time.' The words hung in the air and I saw my mother holding her breath, waiting for my response.

'Mum,' I said, taking hold of her hand, 'I will be just fine.'

She smiled, nodded and pottered into the bathroom to brush her teeth.

I knew I wouldn't have to drive and that was comfort enough. I still couldn't bear the idea of getting behind the wheel of a car, even though Tom had been the one driving when we'd crashed. It still felt unsettling being in any vehicle but I knew I couldn't let my phobia get the better of me. What happened with Tom had been a tragic fluke. I couldn't let the accident ruin my life any more than it already had.

Entering my bedroom, I placed the case on the bed, opened it and went over to my wardrobe. Flinging open the doors, I fingered through the rail of clothes looking for things to take. I pulled a number of warm jumpers, jeans and a dress and high heels, in case we ventured out to dinner one night. At the back of my wardrobe, I managed to find my old walking boots. Removing them from the back of the cupboard, once kept so carefully tidy to keep Tom happy but now becoming a muddle, I smiled at the sight. They reminded me of time spent travelling in the Amazon jungle with friends when I was twenty. It had been one of the most spectacular experiences of my life. I felt a surge of the old me return.

'I am Monica Whitman,' I said aloud to myself, 'and I'm not scared of anything.'

Then, without thinking about it, I removed my wedding band and put it in a box on my dressing table.

'Monica Bowness has gone. I'm sorry, Tom. It's the only way I can live again.'

At that exact moment, I felt a shiver of cold. I told myself it was coincidence and turned my attention back to packing.

When I got into the kitchen, I found Simon sitting at the table chewing on some toast. He looked handsome in his crumpled blue jumper and jeans. His hair was ruffled and his blue eyes smiled at me. He talked with his mouth full,

'All ready to go?'

'Yep. Just let me have some coffee and we'll be on our way. Shall I make some sandwiches to take with us?'

'Good idea.'

He got up, dusting crumbs off his lap.

'How long do you think we'll stay?' I asked, buttering some rolls.

'My parents get back from India on the twelfth. So we can stay until then.'

As I layered ham and lettuce onto the bread, Simon appeared behind me and slipped his arms around my waist.

'Our first proper holiday together.' He kissed my neck.

'I can't wait.' I was smiling from ear to ear. 'It feels like being a teenager again, going to stay at your parents' place while they're away.'

'We can raid their booze cabinet too, if you like.' His voice was gravelly from the years spent smoking pot. It made him sound sexy as well as a wonderful singer.

Simon let me go just in time before Mum appeared, dressed, carrying her overnight bag and ready to leave. We both kissed her goodbye and waved her on her way.

The sandwiches made and the car packed up, I went back into the house to double-check I'd locked the windows and set the timer on the lights. We had never been burgled but it was London and I knew too many people who had.

Once certain the house was secure, I pulled the front door closed and went out into the street. It was quiet and the sun was shining. I had a suede coat on and felt the warmth on my shoulders. It was only March but spring had definitely woken up. As I got into the passenger seat of Si's Ford Capri, I made sure to fix my seat belt. Although I had no real qualms about travelling in a car now, I still found it difficult to forget how dangerous it could be. Si could feel my tension and placed his hand on my knee, as he often did.

'Ready?' He glanced at me, smiled and turned on the engine.

'Ready.' I squeezed his hand as we pulled away.

'I love you, Mon.'

'Love you, too.'

It was a Monday morning and not during the school holidays, so the traffic wasn't too bad. We zipped along the North Circular until we reached the M1 exit. By midday we had passed Northampton, joined the M6 and left Birmingham behind us. Our progress was steady. It felt good being out of London. I'd never imagined I would settle there but it was the only place Tom had wanted to live. I hadn't argued, despite being a country girl at heart.

When we reached Stoke-on-Trent, we found a spot to stop and eat our sandwiches. Famous for being the home of English pottery, we passed a number of museums related to its ceramic history. It occurred to me how much Mum would enjoy visiting the various museums. Despite its rich history, the town itself was unremarkable. It had become a city of service industries and distribution centres. I'd imagined something more quaint and romantic.

Simon was desperate for a pee so we ducked into an empty tearoom where he could relieve himself and we could have a hot drink before setting off again.

It was the most unwelcoming tearoom I had ever visited. No chintz, no pretty cups and saucers and no cake. In its place, stale cheese and pickle rolls and depressingly bland-looking pork pies were on offer. It was some of the most unappealing food I'd ever laid my eyes on. The only redeeming feature was the friendly woman who served us.

Back on the road, we made good progress. We continued along the M6 passing Liverpool and Manchester. By then, the weather had sucked in and a heavy grey sky loomed above, taut with rain. We stopped at a service station outside Preston and filled up with petrol before setting off again, and the length of the journey began to take its toll.

The raindrops pelted the windscreen, making visibility difficult. I started to feel nervous about being in the car. Simon picked up on it and told me we didn't have long until we got there. Still, I felt anxious until the rain subsided. My fear was that we'd skid and end up in the abyss.

It took us about an hour from Preston before we reached Troutbeck, a small village on a hill in Cumbria. Simon's parent's house was on the north-eastern side of Windermere, with a view of the lake down below.

Si had told me Beatrix Potter once owned a farm there. I could immediately see why she had been inspired to write tales about British wildlife. We wound along the small country lane as the light started to fail, passing a cosy-looking inn boasting a menu of home-cooked meals. The houses were solid, grey stone buildings with dark slate roofs, built to withstanding the elements. On the surface it had changed little over the centuries and I couldn't get over the vibrant green of the surrounding scenery. It was as if I'd landed in a foreign land.

We drove through the village to descend along a lane passing through wooded areas and hillsides littered with sheep. Finally, at four thirty, we pulled onto a small driveway. The sign read 'Fawn's Lodge', and above was a white cottage. When the car came to a stop I looked out of my window at the view from the driveway. In between the trees I could see the hills descending to where the dusk reflected off the surface of the lake. There was not another house around. We were blissfully alone.

'Wow!' I stepped out of the car and stretched my stiff back.

'I know, right.' Simon removed our bags from the boot.

'How long have they had this place?' I stared at the white cottage with its slate roof.

'Maybe only six months. It took them a while to find it. You know how particular they are.'

It was a wonderful place. At some point a very clever architect had got their hands on it and turned it into a piece of art. I recognised the talent and felt serious envy. The original pebbledash walls housed a huge glass window that stretched from the ground to the roof. It was magnificent. Simon's parents had great taste and suddenly I found myself longing to live in and design a place like that. I would give up London in a heartbeat.

'Are you coming?' Simon stood in the open doorway, smiling.

'Of course.' I had to tear my eyes away from the view.

'Jesus, this house is cold.' Si rubbed his hands together and turned on the hallway light. The entrance hall was small and pokey, far less impressive than the exterior of the house.

'Shall I take my shoes off?'

'Don't be silly.' Old habits, taught by Tom, died hard. Simon hung up his coat. 'Let's go and put the kettle on.'

I followed Simon into the lounge. It was a large room with a very high ceiling that went right up to the roof. It included the impressive window I had seen outside, which looked just as wonderful from my new position. The floor had a thick pile dove-grey-coloured carpet. I wanted to take my walk around bare foot and feel the softness between my toes. The furniture was surprisingly contemporary. The sofa and armchairs were white leather, recognisable as Florence Knoll. A large square coffee table sat in the middle of the room, and in the centre of it was a huge green glass bowl filled with fossils, rocks and shells. The walls were painted in a soft shell pink that looked wonderful next to the grey carpet. Various colourful modern paintings adorned the walls.

'It's a great room, isn't it? Come on, I'll show you the kitchen.' He led the way and I followed like an excited puppy.

Just off the sitting room was a corridor. We passed a small office and a downstairs loo before we reached the kitchen. Simon was right, the house was freezing, and his parents had obviously turned the heating off before going to India. The room was dark and I couldn't really see anything for a moment, until a light was turned on.

The kitchen was a cook's dream. It was huge and light. The floor was laid with cream tiles, which looked unnaturally spotless. On the far wall was the biggest oven I'd ever seen. There was a vast gas range and the kitchen had an island in the middle of it which housed a double sink. The cabinet doors were beech with chrome handles, the splash-back tiles various shades of terracotta. On the other side of the room was a modernist glass table. Unusually, an indoor bench was placed near double doors which looked out over the garden.

'Coffee, my angel?' Simon asked, switching on the kettle.

'Yes please.' I pulled up one of the stools beside the island and perched on it. 'This place is incredible.'

'It cost them a small fortune.' Simon spooned coffee into mugs.

'I bloody bet it did.' I was trying to work out what the place must have cost. 'Worth it though.' I said, looking around.

'Sure. They've worked hard, they deserve it.' Simon said, opening the fridge. 'Oh shit!'

'What is it?'

'No milk, of course.' He closed the fridge door. 'It should have occurred to me to stock up. They were hardly likely to leave a fridge full of food, particularly milk, when they left. I'll nip out and get some.' He put his hand in his pocket and produced the car keys.

'Don't go now. Black coffee's fine.'

'This isn't London, Mon. Shops aren't open twenty-four seven.'

'Fine, but let's have this coffee, chill out here for a little and then go to the shop together. I'll treat us to dinner in the pub. How does that sound?'

'Sounds like a plan.' He grinned, put the car keys down on the worktop and accepted my invitation to relax.

***

We made it to the shop just before it closed at five thirty, before driving to a local pub where we had a couple of drinks, a game of pool and an early supper. The food was average but Si liked it because of the pool table and a huge fireplace that was always lit in the winter months. I had fish and chips while he tucked into a steak and ale pie. We played pool after eating and he wiped the table with me.

When we got back to the house, we unpacked the shopping bags, poured ourselves another glass of red and snuggled up on the sofa. Simon was elated by the plans he had for us. He wanted us to go to India together and to travel for a few months. It sounded wonderful and I agreed we should do it.

'It's a lovely dream, isn't' it?'

'Sure. But there's no reason why we can't make it a reality.'

'I think you are forgetting one small detail,' he

laughed. 'Money.'

'That's not a problem.'

'You haven't been at work for months, Mon. You must be pretty hard up at the moment.'

'Tom had savings,' I said, putting my glass down on the coffee table, 'and there was his life insurance.'

'Oh.' I knew Simon wanted to pry further but he held back from doing so.

'Nine hundred thousand pounds.' The words rolled off my tongue. It was the first time I'd said it aloud to anyone. Not even Mum knew how much I'd received. For some reason I felt dirty having it, and discussing it felt tacky.

'Fucking hell!' Simon raised his eyebrows.

'I know.' I started to feel that dirty guilt return. 'It feels wrong having it.'

'You were his wife, Mon.'

'Yes I know that, but I was unfaithful. I shouldn't be entitled to it but I can't tell anyone that.'

'Of course you are entitled to it. Think of it as severance pay.' Simon was grinning.

'That's not funny.'

'Oh, come on, it was a joke. Whether you like it or not that money is yours. Do something with it that makes you happy and don't feel guilty. What's done is done.'

'Going to India with you would make me happy.'

With a fingertip I touched the small area of his belly revealed by his tucked-up shirt.

'OK then. We'll arrange our adventure when we get back to London.'

'Deal.'

Si was animated as he talked about all the things we could do and the places we'd visit. We should have at least two months there, he said, and his excitement was catching. I told him I'd always wanted to get up close to an elephant and, snapping his fingers like a conjuror, he said it could be arranged. Just like that. Everything sounded so simple.

We decided to start our trip in Kerala in the south and slowly make our way north. We would stay on a houseboat before exploring some of the winding waterways. I could barely contain my anticipation and started to feel like a teenager again.

We talked on for a while then made our way up to bed. We had sex before falling asleep. It was a comfortable end to a lovely day.

CHAPTER 19

By Friday we'd fallen into a very comfortable routine. I made breakfast every morning while she had a long bath. I enjoyed looking after her. By eleven we'd leave the house and take a long walk, followed by lunch prepared by me. Our afternoons were lazy. Sometimes we snoozed on the sofa or played scrabble and discussed our trip to India. Most evenings we stayed in and cooked together.

It was the perfect escape from real life that she needed and I felt I was succeeding as a good tonic. Once or twice she did feel eyes on her, watching. She said she knew it was the bird. She believed it had survived and transformed into another being. She said it would always be there and resigned herself to never escaping it. Thankfully though, it kept its distance. Apparently it was wary of me and knew that as long as I was close to her I could protect her from harm. It sounded so crazy but I held my tongue knowing my protests would only make the matter worse.

After everything that had happened, I was glad she could share her fears with me. There had been enough lies to last us both a lifetime. She had been so sure that the threat would disappear when I killed the crow. The disappointment was a bitter pill to swallow and my lack of support would have emphasised the issue. She confessed her concern that I would force her to seek medical help when she told me about her residual fears.

But despite my apprehension about her sanity, I internalised it and convinced myself that time would tell.

That evening we made plans to go out to supper at one of the better restaurants in the area. I felt a surge of date-night excitement as I put on my best blue shirt. Being away from London meant that we were free to move about as we wished without the threat of being seen by prying eyes.

At half past seven, the taxi arrived in the driveway and hooted its presence. It was a cold evening and I wrapped myself up in a thick coat and long scarf. Mon looked great in her black dress and sexy high heels and I was proud to be her date. I helped her on with her coat and she doubled her pale blue cashmere scarf and wrapped it in a large loose knot around her neck.

We stepped out into a bitter, chilly wind and pulled the front door closed behind us. I opened the car door for her and winked as she got in. No matter what they say on female-led chat shows, chivalry isn't dead. I put my hand on her knee, as I always did. Her stockings felt silky and I looked forward to the end of the evening when we would be naked and close to one another. Chivalry may not be dead but I am still a man. The taxi pulled out of the drive and drove us to Windermere and the restaurant.

When we arrived, the town was quiet. A few people were out on the streets walking from pub to pub in the brisk spring cold. The streetlights were on and the sky was black. The taxi pulled up outside 'Hooked', a seafood restaurant where we had a reservation. I paid the fare and opened the car door for Monica, who stepped out into the cold and was hit by the current of cold air that blew down the open road.

The restaurant had a glass front behind which a number of people inside seemed to be enjoying their food. It looked good, and as we opened the door and walked in, the smell of seafood hit us and instantly whetted our appetites.

A man in a white shirt and dark grey trousers approached and took our name before showing us to the table. Despite being out of season, the place was busy. If the locals approved, I concluded the food must be good.

We took off our coats, handed them to the waiter and sat down at the dark wooden table. A tea light in the middle of it flickered in rhythm to the breeze from our movement. The room was warm with the smell of fresh hot food and body heat. I couldn't wait to get stuck in and ordered us each a vodka and tonic. We mulled over the menu as our drinks were delivered to the table. The cold bubbles fizzed in our glasses, seeming to pay attention to the momentous moment. She was mine in public. Finally.

We ordered our food and a bottle of Sauvignon Blanc and chatted like couples do. It felt good talking idly about nothing in particular. For once, our conversation could be light, and I was able to shrug off the weight I'd been carrying since discovering about my son. Monica had a sparkle in her eyes and a happy smile painted on her face. She joked and flirted and I wallowed in her beauty and her company.

After our starter and main course, we sat back in our chairs enjoying the silent haze. Saying nothing was as comfortable as speaking. I could be myself in her company. The bullshit she had been used to presenting to Tom had evaporated and the raw, real Monica shone through. The contented silence lasted a few minutes before I leant forward to ask her a question.

'Why did you stay with him if you didn't love him?'

She was taken aback and hadn't expected the evening to change its tone so suddenly. I suppose neither of us had.

'I did love him for a time.' She kept her voice down, feeling it didn't seem like the right place to be having that conversation.

'OK, but not in the end. Not when you and I got together. Then, when you found out about the baby…' I paused and shook my head. 'I'm just trying to understand it, Mon.'

'I don't know what I was thinking. My head was a mess. It's no excuse but that's the truth. I loved you, I still do, but it was complicated.'

'Because you were scared of him?' Suddenly I felt bold. Maybe it was the drink.

'Yes, I suppose so.' She shifted in her chair, looking uncomfortable. 'But what does any of it matter now? Everything's changed.'

'It matters to me.' I took a swig of my drink and banged the glass down on the table. She was as shocked by my anger as I was. It had been simmering beneath for so long.

'Can you please come out and say what it is that's eating you?' Her hackles had gone up.

'I'm not angry with you, darling. It's just when I think about him, what he did to you, it makes my blood boil. He got off lightly, dying in that accident. If I'd had my way...' My words stung with hatred. She put her hand on my arm.

'But that's all over now.'

'Is it?'

'Si, he's gone. It's just you and me now. Nothing can come between us anymore. We're free at last.'

I took her hand, looked at the scar on the back of it and rubbed it gently with my thumb.

'There are still reminders.' I couldn't hide my look of sadness. She pulled her hand away and hid it under the table.

'Let's not do this now. It's been such a lovely evening. Why spoil it?' She watched as I stiffened and sat back in my chair.

With gritted teeth, I said, 'You expect me to forget that ... that man? The man who burnt you on the hand with his cigarette? Because of an accident?'

My words seemed to bring instant pain back into her scar and she started to stroke it repeatedly like she often would.

'I'm sorry, but I find it hard to forget that you were with him for months with my baby growing inside you.' I should have predicted it. Her eyes began to fill with tears. I felt my face slowly change as she reached across the table wanting to hold my hand.

'I was scared,' she said. 'I thought he'd kill me, or you, or both of us.'

'Don't cry, Mon, please.' I wiped the tears away

from her face. 'I know it's not your fault. I'm sorry. I don't blame you. Of course I don't, but I just wish I'd known. I would have done things so differently. I would have never left you alone carrying our child.'

'You can't blame yourself, Si. What happened, happened. We both need to learn to live with it.'

It was my turn to well up. Drying my eyes and composing myself, I noticed a young waitress watching us with fascination. She looked embarrassed when I eyeballed her and signalled for the bill, red cheeked and puffy eyed.

'Let's go home. If you want to, we can talk more about it there. You can ask me anything you like. I promise to tell you the truth.'

Suddenly I was hit with a wave of tiredness.

'I know you will. I'm just not sure I'm ready to hear it.'

'But you started the conversation.' Confusion echoed in her words.

'Because I can't help thinking about it. It's there, it's always there.'

At last she understood. If we were going to move on I needed to know everything that had happened in the months leading up to the accident. I couldn't get passed it until I was able to see it all clearly. With a small nod of her head she acknowledged that and agreed to enlighten me as I paid the bill and asked the waitress, who'd been watching us earlier, to call a taxi. We were both exhausted already but the night had only just begun.

***

The next morning we both woke up feeling shattered. It felt as though we had run a marathon, except, instead of our muscles aching, it was our heads. We had talked until half past three in the morning, fuelled by some brandy I'd discovered in my parents' drinks cabinet. I couldn't be sure if I felt ropey because of all the drink or the emotional strain.

It had been arduous revisiting the past for her but it had helped me and she had said that therefore it was worth it. I felt happier once I knew it all. It was not easy but I'd asked her in detail about the final weeks spent with Tom. It was difficult for me to hear but she was honest and told me everything. Until then, she admitted that she'd done her best to forget. Remembering was painful for her but it helped us both to find closure. She felt she couldn't share the truth about her marriage with her mother. Instead it remained locked away in her head, bubbling like a poison, infecting her core. But speaking to me, like a catholic in confession, helped released a few demons. I understood her better as a result and that could only be a positive thing.

I learnt that the last few weeks spent with Tom had been very difficult. He really scared Monica. She had confessed that it was the first time in her life she had honestly felt in danger. She was unable to explain why it was but there was something about the look in his eyes that had terrified her. The man she thought she'd known, the man who she had once loved, no longer existed. Instead, she was living with a man who was constantly angry, frustrated, bitter and condemning.

Monica told me that she couldn't do anything right, from a simple task like making a cup of tea, to hoovering the carpet. Every little thing was scrutinised. She spent her days walking on eggshells. He looked at her with disgust and disappointment most of the time. She felt worthless and trapped. He had never actually hit her; his version of abuse relying mostly on mental torture and bullying.

She told me there were instances when he would lose his temper and lash out. Apparently he put his foot through doors on various occasions and would often throw breakables at the wall. Once, when she failed to remember to make his lunch to take to work, he picked up her favourite vase and smashed it on the ground. Then he blamed her for angering him and forcing him to do it. I so wished he was alive so that I could teach him a lesson. I had come across men like him before. Men who would never dare pick on anyone their own size. He was a coward, but that fact didn't help ease Monica's pain.

A few days after Tom had found the pregnancy test, he had sat her down and told her she needed to stop working. Mothers should be at home, he said. But she wasn't ready to leave the job she loved so much and had asked him to consider allowing her to go part time. His reaction had been to stub a cigarette out on the back of her neck. It was the second time he'd burnt her. The next day, Monica had handed in her notice.

When he had discovered she was pregnant his

behaviour had deteriorated further. She was forbidden from wearing make-up or going out alone. That was why she was forced to end the relationship with me. Finally, I understood why it had become impossible. Tom forced her to stay in the house practically all of the time so that he could keep an eye on her. Somehow he had managed to arrange to work from home. That had meant Monica's life was put even more under a microscope. My heart ached with pity for her.

Aside from all of that, Monica discovered he'd been checking her phone and emails too. The irony was that he had every reason to, but the more claustrophobic his behaviour became, the further away she drifted from him. In all honesty, she had known for years that he would check text messages and call history. His lack of trust had hurt her. Monica would never have dreamt of looking at his private messages. Her trust in him, as it turned out, was misplaced. People who suffer emotional abuse often idolise their tormentor. I couldn't comprehend how she could trust a man who showed her so little respect. But that was how it was.

For a long time, Monica had sought his approval and longed to make him happy. I grew to understand that every curl of his lip or sarcastic comment cut into her like a knife. He was her husband and she felt like a failure as his wife. And the weaker she became, the more his strength grew. Now I realised the severity of how nasty he was to her, it became clear that she'd married an emotional sadist. Almost worse than that, it sounded to me as though Tom was also a narcissist. His anger with Monica was always born out of concern for how her behaviour affected the way he was perceived. It broke my heart when I realised what a huge mistake she had made in marrying him. I even began to doubt how much she loved me. Was it because I represented an escape from Tom?

I must have appeared like a shining light, the opposite of Tom. But she had fallen in love with me. I knew that was true. Neither of us could fake what we felt. We were not proud of our infidelity. It was the wrong thing to do. She could have been a stronger woman had she left Tom first and started again, but life is complicated and that wasn't how it panned out.

After the accident, Monica had decided she was being punished for her mistakes. We had done a hideous thing. She had lied to Tom about the paternity of her child. I could only blame myself for the tragedy that hung over her life. Losing my son should have changed the way I felt but it hadn't. If anything, Josh's death had taught me that I had to fight for her even harder than before. I couldn't let the accident be in vain. Josh's short life needed to be validated somehow. Our son's death would not be for nothing.

Telling me all those things must have been painfully difficult. She didn't want me to see her as weak, or as a victim. It was the past and she wanted it left there but understood that I needed to comprehend what had happened. My fury with Tom grew tenfold. I am a gentle man and can't understand how anyone would treat someone they claimed to love with such contempt. Monica hadn't understood it either for a long time until realising what a strange relationship Tom's parents had had with him and seeing the way he was treated. Only then had it all fallen into place.

According to Monica, Tom's father had been a bully too. Mary, Tom's mother, had spent most of her time dancing around the men in the house, serving them and pandering to them. Fear had turned her into a prisoner in her own life. She was there only to make the men in her family happy. Sometimes, Monica said, she had seen Richard look at his wife as though she was a piece of shit on his shoe, but, contrarily, he had treated his daughter like a goddess. In response and as a reaction to this, Mary had worshipped Tom. It was a wholly dysfunctional family and went some of the way to explain why Tom had turned out so cruel. Monica accepted that as the truth and it helped her excuse Tom's behaviour. But I didn't buy it. There was no excuse as far as I was concerned.

My family life experiences were the opposite. My parents had really loved and respected one another. I grew up feeling wanted and cherished by them both. Monica had a similar upbringing and believed Tom never really stood a chance. But the strange thing was that she didn't hold Richard responsible. She laid the blame at Mary's feet. As far as Monica was concerned, Richard couldn't help being a pig. He was born that way. A leopard cannot change its spots. But Mary had no excuse. She had allowed that man to bully her and her son. She was the mother. She should have stood up to him and protected her children at any cost. Monica couldn't understand why Mary had permitted Richard to rule over the family like that. I alone saw the irony. Monica blamed Mary but had inadvertently become just like her in her subservience to Tom. Perhaps she hated Mary because she hated herself.

Monica truly believed that Richard was the reason Tom had grown up to become an insecure, controlling tyrant. Richard was the person who had kept Mary like a rabbit in the headlights. Learning this, I gently helped Monica to see her own reflection in her mother-in-law. Like Mary, she had become a pacifier, desperate to temper her husband and ease what must have been a difficult existence. Living with fear has a strong effect on people's behaviour. The crucial difference was that I knew Monica would never have allowed Tom to treat our son the way Richard had treated him. Underneath, Monica was a tigress, and by all accounts, Mary appeared to be a sheep. Responsibility had to lie somewhere. In the end, Mon believed the buck stopped with her mother-in-law. I didn't know Tom's parents so couldn't really build a solid opinion. It all sounded like a mess but as far as I was concerned, Tom had had a mind of his own and I held him responsible for his actions, not his parents.

***

Once we'd packed the car and secured my parents' house, we started the long journey back to London. There was a lump in my throat as we pulled away from Fawn's Lodge. We'd had an edifying but wonderful week, and the thought of getting back to real life was depressing. In London there were people everywhere, people Monica didn't want to see. As we wound along the country roads in silence, I tried hard to focus on the trip we planned to India. Escape from our old life was the only thing I could concentrate on. Mon was my future and I needed a way of hurrying up the inevitable.

I was sitting in the car when I realised Monica would need to leave London. It made sense for us to begin again somewhere new, away from the pain of the past. But I wouldn't push her into making a decision and so our long-term plans were left unstated. They remained between us as bars in a cage. The weight of uncertainty was somewhat harrowing but whatever happened I would wait until she was ready.

I noticed her folded hands clenched between her thighs for a while. Then she broke the deafening silence.

'Si, I don't want to go back to London.'

I flashed her a look before turning my focus back to the road.

'Where do you want to go, Mon?'

'I want to be wherever you are. Cornwall, India, wherever. My life in London has finished. It's not my home anymore. You are. I adore you, Si.'

A grin spread across my face, and reaching out my hand I squeezed her knee. She'd read my mind.

'Move to Cornwall with me.' I said.

'OK.'

The smile rang out in her words and something beat hard in my chest. Happiness rose in my body like the sun at dawn.

'We'll go to India and I'll put the house on the market while we're away. I need to rid myself of that place. I'm ready to let go now.'

I blew her a kiss before turning on the radio. The car was flooded with the sound of jazz. I whistled and tapped my foot and stared out of the window, trying to absorb the wonderful news. As though planned, the great yellow disc appeared from behind a white cloud to shine over the rolling hills.

By the time we reached Birmingham it was mid-afternoon. The motorway was busy with traffic. Out of the blue, I was compelled to confess something that had been praying on my mind.

'Mon, I want to visit the grave.' I kept my eyes fixed on the road. 'I want to visit our son's grave.'

'OK.' She rested a hand on my shoulder. 'We'll make a detour via Cambridge. Let's go there ... now.'

I wasn't prepared for it to happen so soon but after a moment of consideration, I nodded. It would be cathartic for us to go together.

'Let's stop and get some flowers.'

'Are you sure you want to do this? It's not going to upset you too much?'

'It will hurt, of course it will. But it's supposed to.'

Within seconds, the hurt I had been battling against returned and I felt the hollow discomfort of nausea.

CHAPTER 20

It was almost six o'clock when we arrived in Ickleton. The flat and unassuming countryside around there was so different from where we had come from. An early evening blanket had fallen over the quiet village. We drove past The Red Lion pub in silence. Its lights were on and it looked welcoming and warm from the outside. I suggested we went in for a drink after visiting the graveyard. I thought we might need it.

Simon's eyes were large and wide. With each yard that we got closer to the church, I watched the colour drain from his face. It was similar to the fear people have just before getting on a rollercoaster at an adventure park. Neither of us knew whether we would ever make it back from there. It was a necessary task that had been hanging over us but we weren't fully prepared for it. How could we be?

I hoped the fact that it was a spur of the moment decision would protect us both from the real horror of what we were about to face. How would Simon say goodbye to the child he had never met? It seemed an impossible question to answer.

Moments later the car pulled onto Church Street. Silently, Simon stopped the car outside the old East Anglian brick and flint church wall. He stared at it as though searching for answers. Neither of us made a move to get out of the car. We both felt unable to take the steps necessary to face what lay beyond the wooden church gates.

A streetlamp shone orange light onto the pavement nearby. It warmed the otherwise gloomy scene. Simon had never been a believer and I knew it felt surreal for him visiting his son who lay buried in a churchyard. In a moment of bravery, he pulled the handle and pushed open the car door. It was chillier than he expected and he plunged his hands deep into his pockets.

Following his lead, I stepped out of the car. Moving in front of him without speaking, I pushed open the old wooden gate. It was cold to the touch. Simon trailed after me, his head hung low, listening to the sound of the gravel as it crunched beneath his feet.

I wished it were daylight. I thought I could sense eyes on me and felt suddenly scared. The crow was watching us. I could feel it. My wide eyes searched the blackness but found nothing. We left the pathway and walked across the grass winding between new and ancient graves. The graveyard appeared spooky in the darkness. Simon regretted being there. It oozed out of him. I sensed him questioning what good this visit would do. Josh was gone. Tragically, he had never really existed.

I felt Si staring into the back of my head. He probably wondered if I felt as scared as he did. Then I stopped and pointed to a gravestone a few feet away. In the darkness it was hard to see, so Simon stepped closer to get a better view. The simple granite gravestone read:

Here lies

Thomas Matthew Bowness
23.4.1978 – 18.10.2012
And
Joshua James Bowness
18.10.2012 – 18.10.2012
Gone too soon
Rest together in peace

Simon bent down and ran his fingers over his son's name. The stone was cold and smooth. The dampness from the ground soaked into the jeans covering his knee and he closed his eyes. I stepped forward and laid down a bunch of white roses we had stopped to buy on the way. Listening to the sound of Si's shaky breathing, I thought he might collapse. We remained in silence for a few moments, scrutinising the burial site. It seemed so cold and final.

Our son does not deserve to be buried here, I thought, looking at the grave.

'I hate granite.' Simon stood up and moved away from the stone. 'It's ugly. It has no warmth.'

I was taken aback.

'I had to choose something.' My words sounded meek.

'You made a lot of choices without consulting me.'

Simon spat words that were filled hatred before suddenly turning and walking back towards the car. I didn't understand why he was lashing out at me. I told myself it was grief. I wished farewell to my son and went after Simon.

When I reached the car, Simon was already in the driver's seat. He gripped the steering wheel with his hands and revved the engine. I noticed how white his knuckles were and how his face had changed. He did not look like a man I recognised. His eyes were wild and staring. Trembling, I got in beside him. He wouldn't look at me. We remained static in the car while he continued to rev.

The car jerked forward and the wheels screeched as smoke raged from the tarmac. I gripped the seat and closed my eyes. Suddenly I was back at the scene of the accident once more, only this time it was Simon beside me.

As the car sped away, I felt my body being sucked into the seat, the safety belt cutting into my chest. I had never seen Simon so livid. The Capri hurtled through the village and back in the direction of the M11. Opening my eyes to get a look at the speedometer, I saw we were travelling at eighty miles an hour. A vision of my own death flitted across my mind. Perhaps that was Simon's intention. But why? Holding my breath as the car sped through the village of Duxford, we narrowly missed a tabby cat that sat on the side of the road.

'Jesus!'

I brought my hands up over my face and kept them there until I found the strength to address the fraught situation I was in.

After a few minutes my eyes opened. As I did so, I noticed a motorway sign signalling that the Cambridge exit was coming up. We were going the wrong way.

'Simon, what are you doing?' I asked, my voice trembling.

He sat behind the wheel, his teeth gritted and a look of thunder across his face.

'Si, please.' I waited in vain for a response. Moments later, the motorway had vanished and the car was travelling through Cambridge. By then Simon had slowed down a bit and I was able regain some composure. I reached out to place a hand on Simon's shoulder and it was batted away. I was shocked

'Don't fucking touch me.'

He still couldn't look at me. Fear returned and I was trapped in a terrified silence, feeling like a prisoner on a derailed train. I realised we were heading for my mother's house. The sight of Herbert Street evoked a feeling of sanctuary. Never in my life had Simon made me feel unsafe before.

As the car came to a sudden halt, Simon jumped out of the car, slamming the door behind him. He opened the boot and started throwing my luggage out into the street.

'What are you doing?'

I was on the brink of tears. One of the bags split open and my belongings littered the damp street. Still Simon didn't speak. He was a man possessed. I ran to Mum's front door and began pounding on the wood.

'Mum, please, are you there? Mum?' My palms ached. Moments later the hallway lights came on and the door flew open.

'Monica, what on earth is the matter?' she said, stepping forward to comfort me.

'It's Simon—' But before I could explain, Mum saw what was happening and stepped out onto the road to question him.

'Simon, whatever's going on?'

She saw his eyes were red with tears that streamed down his cheeks. Moving closer, she fixed him with her pale blue eyes. Simon stopped what he was doing and slumped forward, shaking with emotion.

'Simon' – Mum put her arm around his shoulders and led him towards the pavement – 'I think you should come inside.'

Her words were gentle and soothing. I stood in the doorway feeling helpless watching my mother comfort the man I loved.

'I don't know what I've done.' I searched my mother's face for answers.

'Simon is going to come in. Monica, go and pour him a whisky.'

CHAPTER 21

Monica rushed into the kitchen to fetch the drink while Ingrid led me into the sitting room. I was shaking as I stared at the floor, feeling as if I'd seen a ghost. Moments later Monica returned gripping a tumbler. Without looking at her, I took the drink and downed it in one. Ingrid looked extremely worried as she watched me. Neither woman spoke. They waited for me to speak but I need a moment to order my thoughts.

Eventually, I turned and looked at Ingrid. She smiled encouragingly and removed the glass from my hand, which remained shaking.

'She buried Josh with *him*.'

My voice was fragile. A wave of confusion crossed Ingrid's face as she patiently waited for a more detailed explanation. 'I just cannot believe she laid *my son* to rest with *that man*.'

Suddenly I was able to look at Monica. The truth about our relationship poured out of me. With dread plastered all over her face, Monica watched her mother absorb it all.

'I loved her. We had an affair. It was wrong but he was an animal. Tom was vile. He bullied her and made her feel worthless. I loved her and we could have been happy.'

I could see Ingrid working hard to piece the jumble together and make sense of what I was saying.

'And I know you thought he was wonderful but you need to hear the truth. But that's not it, that's not what really upset me. How could she do it?' My wet eyes searched Ingrid's face. 'How *could* she?' Overcome, I started to blub again.

Sitting stiffly in her chair, Ingrid tried to take in what she was hearing. The news clearly devastated her. I think, for the first time ever, she doubted her relationship with her daughter. They had always been so close. She had thought Monica could tell her anything and now it seemed that was a lie. She looked as though she didn't know her daughter as well as she thought she did and the realisation was hurting. I had not intended to cause her any harm and felt bad about it, but however difficult it was, she needed to know what had happened, warts and all.

'Josh ... Josh was *your* son?' I could see the words felt alien to her ears.

'I didn't know, not until after the accident when he was gone and it was too late. But at last Monica and I could be together. So we had a lovely holiday and then we went to the grave and I saw she had buried Josh with *him*. I feel sick. I'm sorry.' I stood up and moved towards the door. 'I need some air.'

Throughout this exchange, Monica had been frozen in her armchair without speaking or moving. Why hadn't it occurred to her that burying Josh with Tom would be so detrimental to me?

I reached the street and strode to my car, interested only in getting out of there as fast as possible. As I started the engine, Monica ran out of the house calling my name. Ingrid followed and stood in the road watching my Ford as it travelled away down the street.

'No! No! Wait!'

Monica ran after the car, yelling. I could hear and see her in my rear mirror, but I didn't stop. I was done. As I wound the window up to block out the sound, I heard her scream,

'Please, no!'

I glimpsed in the mirror for the last time and saw she was in a crumpled heap in the street.

CHAPTER 22

Mum stood staring at me from a distance. She wanted to comfort me but couldn't quite make herself come over. The lies were hard to forgive. The infidelity and stupidity she could set aside but the fact she had been lied to was harder to swallow. Mum could now finally understand why I had been so troubled since the accident. Slowly the pieces fell into place.

Standing on the chilly street, Mum hugged herself. The night above was low and oppressive. I remained huddled on the pavement at the end of the road. Mum could see the pain on my face but felt unable to help. She needed time to process what she had learnt. I'm sure she felt betrayed.

I whimpered in the silent street and felt more alone than ever before. This time, my life really was over. To find solace, I looked down the street for my mum but the street was empty. She had returned indoors, leaving the front door on the latch.

I looked back up the street to where the contents of one of my bags were strewn on the road outside my mother's house. The sight seemed bitterly apt. Like the scene before me, my life was a mess. From the corner of my eye, I became aware of a nosey neighbour watching the drama unfold. Finally, infidelity had caught up with me. Although it was dark, I could see that a crow had landed on a low wall nearby and was watching me sitting helpless on the ground.

With the small amount of dignity I had left, I walked back up the street, retrieved my handbag from the pavement, left the rest of my things behind and set off towards the station.

If my mother couldn't face me, then I would disappear into the night. It was the only act of kindness I had left. A shadow of the woman I'd rediscovered in the Lake District, I walked along the streets of Cambridge knowing I would have to return to London alone. For the rest of my days, I would remain in that house with the ghosts. There was no new life waiting for me. No matter how hard I attempted to escape, it was useless. My future was her punishment and so it should be.

The dark, clouded sky parted and a bitter wind began to blow, followed by a torrent of rain. Walking in the downpour, I was unaware of the elements, as zombie-like I moved along the flooded street, my shoes soaking up water as I walked slowly through deep puddles. I barely noticed the rain pummelling the flagstones and making a deathly noise. I just carried on walking, past colleges, shops and restaurants, until I reached the train station on the other side of the town.

My dark hair hung in straggles around my face and my coat was heavy with rain. People mulled about inside the station waiting for their trains and avoiding the weather. I tried not to notice the strange looks I got from people as I walked by. My trainers squelched on the stone floor as I queued for a ticket. Although I was detached from the world around me, the noise of the people moving about caused me pain and my body doubled over. I wished I were dead.

A suited man in his forties approached and asked if I was all right. Not hearing the words, but watching his mouth move, I stared blankly at him. He saw the streaks of mascara that must have lined my cheeks, and the vacant look in my eyes. He asked again, moving his face a little closer to mine. He had kind brown eyes and a soft expression.

'I'm fine.' The words were spoken in monotone. He stepped back realising that his offer of help was falling on deaf ears.

'The ticket office is free.' He indicated at an impatient looking woman glaring at me for holding up the queue. I nodded and approached the desk.

'London, please. First class, one way,' I asked, removing my wallet from my damp bag.

'Where?' demanded the rotund woman.

'London.'

'Yes, London, I know, but where? Tottenham Hale? Liverpool Street? Kings Cross?'

'Whichever is due first.'

I fixed the woman with unfeeling eyes. The lady turned her attention to her computer screen.

'Kings Cross, platform two. Due in eleven minutes. Fifteen pounds seventy.' The machine from behind the glass whirled into life and spat out a ticket. I slid my credit card into the chip and pin machine and pressed some buttons. The woman serving me pushed the tickets through, refusing to make eye contact. I picked them up and wandered off without saying thank you.

Going straight into a Marks and Spencer within the station, I had only one thing in mind. When inside I approached the alcohol counter and requested some vodka. The spotty young man serving gave me an odd look before reaching for a small bottle of Smirnoff.

I couldn't bear to be inside with all those bodies so stepped out onto the platform. It was cold and dark and raindrops dripped from the cover over the platform, splashing onto the tracks below. As I stepped closer to the edge, I thought about throwing myself under a train. The thing that stopped me was knowing that other people would be forced to witness it. I was not prepared to be that unkind.

Approaching an abandoned metal bench, I sat down. The dampness of my clothes, twinned with emotional shock, caused me to shiver. With pale fingers I unscrewed the red cap from the bottle before closing my eyes and taking a long drink. It made me gag but I did it again. Alone on the platform, I drank half the bottle. I had a strong desire to drown my sorrows.

The train arrived on time and people poured out of the station and into the carriages. I got onto the first-class carriage and found a seat. Most of the seats were empty. One or two executive-looking men took up residence but by and large the cabin was abandoned, just as I'd hoped, and I plopped down onto a carpeted seat. The rain had soaked through from my coat to my jumper and trousers. My skin looked clammy and damp but I didn't care. Continuing to sip the vodka, I watched out of the window as the train pulled out of the station.

My mind was stuck on Simon. I imagined him driving in the darkness, alone and on his way back to Cornwall. My heart was aching. I knew I would never see him again. He would never forgive me. As a last ditch attempt to explain my decision, I removed my mobile from my bag and composed a text.

I couldn't stand the idea of Josh being alone in the ground. That was all I could think about. It wasn't meant to hurt you. I will always love you. Know that I am sorry. M x

Pressing send, I hugged the phone tightly to my chest and kept it there as the train pulled out of the station, hoping I might get a response or at least an acknowledgement. But it never came. He had nothing left to say. As the train started to gain speed I felt a new kind of grief take hold.

***

May

The May sunshine was bright and offensive. My head ached with a fog, and I closed my eyes trying to escape the throb in my brain but the pounding seemed to increase. The whisky hangover was playing drums and my skull felt as if it was on the brink of explosion. My bedroom walls closed in on me, and claustrophobia hung like a shroud over everything.

When I peeled myself off the bed I realised I was still wearing yesterday's clothes. Then it occurred to me that I couldn't remember a day when I'd worn anything different. I knew my body must smell, but the alcohol that remained pumping around my system thankfully dulled my senses. Simon's blue T-shirt was wrinkled and the grey marl shorts hung loosely around my waist. During the night my hair had worked its way loose and I roughly bunched it back up into a scruffy ponytail. My fringe had grown long and I constantly had to brush it away from my eyes.

My legs felt cold as I necked the remains of a glass of room temperature water that was by my bed. It didn't quench my thirst so I tottered out of my room, my head still spinning, and went downstairs into the sitting room where I found a half-drunk can of warm beer. I took a long swig. The bubbles had vanished but the smooth bitter taste helped me lose myself again.

Still clutching the can, I wandered into the kitchen. Glasses, bottles, cans and food rubbish lay strewn across every surface. The place smelt stale and looked a mess but I didn't care. Since Simon had gone I had nothing left. My misery made itself at home in the house I'd shared with Tom. I belonged there, trapped by my own selfish mistakes. My punishment had only just begun.

A half-eaten packet of crisps was on the kitchen table. A sudden hunger came over me and I shoved a handful into my mouth. Looking up at the clock I saw it was nearly eleven. The sun shone through the double doors and the floor felt warm beneath my feet. I took another swig on the beer before deciding to go out into the sunshine.

The grass had grown long in the garden and weeds had taken over the once neatly kept borders. In among the tangle of wild plants, tulips

and peonies fought to reach the sun. I sat down on the grass and continued to drink the beer. A pigeon flew overhead and landed on the fence, followed closely by another. They sat there fat and proud, looking for food. I envied the company they shared and drained the rest of the can.
When it was finished I hurled it in the direction of the birds, who jumped into the air and flew away. I felt proud of my power to intimidate while knowing how pathetic and bitter I was, but I didn't care. I'd made a promise to myself to overcome my fear of the crow and this had left me filled with a hatred for all birds. The creature still watched me and I often felt its malevolent presence nearby.

One day in late April, the crow landed on the porch and hopped over to the kitchen door. It stood inches away, staring into my soul with its cold black eyes. I'd been drunk and felt strangely calm as it approached the house. We remained staring at one another for some time. Neither of us flinched. Time seemed to be standing still. My world was quiet and only the feeling of my heart beating in my chest reassured me I was still alive.

Without thinking, I went over to the door and opened it. The bird didn't back away. Instead it hopped into the kitchen, still looking at me. At that point I took a step back. The bird then began preening its feathers as if I didn't exist. Its long hard beak ran along each sleek feather with mechanical precision. Fascinated by the crow, I slowly sat down cross-legged on the stone floor and watched my fear melt away. Suddenly I felt a link to the bird. An invisible threat existed entwining our destinies. It was impossible to know whether our fate would lead us anywhere good, but wherever I went, I knew, in that moment, that the crow would remain with me.

Slowly I got up from the floor and edged over to the bread bin to find a crust to feed the bird. With my back to it, I began tearing small chunks of stale bread. When I turned with my offering of food, I discovered the bird perched on the back of one of the kitchen chairs. It looked larger than ever before. The fear seeped back into me like a toxin coursing through my veins. I dropped the crumbs onto the floor as I stepped back away from the crow. Slowly the bird lifted its head, pointed its sharp beak at the sky and let out a piercing scream. The glass door and the windows shattered and the flames on the hob roared into life. A bitter wind rushed through the room, blowing me backwards into a wall. My body was thrown against the bricks and an instant headache struck my skull.

Out of the corner of my eye I watched in terror as the knives in the block by the toaster began to shake by themselves. The room was alive with a raging energy and I was helpless to stop it. Seconds later, the knives came out of the block, spun around in the air and flew towards me with lightning speed, pinning my clothes to the wall and missing my flesh by millimetres. I was trapped, unable to move, and I watched as the bird slowly opened its beak again. My eyes closed in preparation for another shattering scream.

'Monica.'

A low rasping voice filled the room and

travelled through my bones. I kept my eyes tightly shut, too afraid to look.

'Monica,' it said again in an angry tenor. 'Look at me, Monica,' the voice demanded.

Without seeing what was happening, my mind was unable to process the situation. I had to understand where the words were coming from. Still pinned by the knives I had no choice but to open my fearful green eyes.

As I did, I saw the crow's beak moving and heard words echo around the room.

'You are mine.' It opened its wings in a triumphant stretch. 'Wherever you go, there I will be. I am your master now.' The voice thundered, and again flames from the gas hob leapt into the air, bursting with heat.

'Yes,' I conceded, as a large tear fell down my cheek.

With its wings fanned out, the bird lifted off the chair and came towards me with its talons extended. I'd never seen a living bird so close up and a twisted fascination prevented me from looking away.

'You cannot kill me,' the crow said when it was inches away from my face. 'I am death.' The words were carried on a listless gust of putrid air. I was reminded of rotting corpses and maggots as a surge of sickness worked its way up from my stomach, making me gag. When I'd caught my breath I looked back and the bird appeared to have doubled in size. The rest of the world was a bright, white blur. All I could see was the black crow.

The bird remained suspended in front of me

and I was frozen with terror. My eyes started to sting but I couldn't look away. I felt the tiny vessels in my eyeballs bursting and a warm trickle ran down my face past my lips. In my mouth I tasted blood mixed with bile. The two liquids swilled around, crashing together just like waves in a storm at sea. I could smell gas and feel the burning heat from the hob and wondered if the room was on fire. The scent of singed hair filled my nostrils as I remained transfixed by the bird's glare.

And then I noticed swirls of black smoke rising up from the crow, filling the air with a thick mist. As the cloud spread the crow began to disappear, each feather evaporating in front of my eyes until it was no more. With the vanishing of its beady black eyes, the knives that held me in place tumbled to the ground. The sound of steel scraping stone made me wince, and I collapsed into a trembling heap on the floor, holding my head in my hands.

When I looked around the kitchen, everything had returned to normal. The glass no longer lay in large shards all over the floor. It was back in the doors and windows as if nothing had happened. The flames vanished back into the hob and the burning smell evaporated. The set of knives that had kept me fixed to the wall appeared back in their block.

My head ached from the encounter and I wondered if I was losing my mind. Then I saw it. On the flagstones before me lay a neat pile of grey dust and one shimmering black feather.

As I sat in the garden remembering the terror

I'd experienced, I laughed aloud. I wasn't afraid anymore and I pitied the pathetic woman I'd been for so long. Under the warm spring sun I felt nothing. I was numb and that was how I would remain

***

A few days passed and showers fell over North London. I remained in the same clothes I'd been in for over a week. Every day I spent drinking, and the weeks all merged together in an inconsequential blur. My existence was futile and I had nothing to live for.

Norman Cousins once said 'Death is not the greatest loss in life. The greatest loss is what dies inside of us while we live.'

I was living proof.

Ever since the accident, my existence had been shaped by grief, in one form or another. I had lost my child, my husband, my memory, my sanity and finally the man I loved. I could see the links between all those things, like chains, but was unable to understand why any of it had happened. Somewhere in my psyche I knew that if I could remember the moments leading up to the accident I would find the answers I needed and perhaps even some peace. But it remained a fog I was lost in.

The alcohol helped though. It wrapped me in a different type of shroud, a less painful reality. My waking hours became more and more erratic. The days passed quickly and I lost all concept of time. I was unable to remember what I had for breakfast, if anything, and time melted away with the ice in my tumbler.

Mum called occasionally, I think. I seem to remember telephone conversations. Since leaving Cambridge that day I hadn't seen her though. She was struggling to come to terms with what she'd learnt. We didn't discuss it. It was left hanging in the air like a heavy veil over everything. She didn't bring it up or ask for answers. That was one of the hardest things. In a sense it would have helped if she had been angry. I felt I deserved a telling off. When we spoke, the hurt in her voice travelled down the telephone line. It was impossible to ignore and as a result I spoke to her less and less. Everything I touched seemed to fall apart and if I could spare her by keeping my distance then I would.

Sometimes, late at night when I was lonely and full of drink, I'd text or call Simon. He never answered and the silence cut through me. Yet still I tried to make contact. He would never forgive me but I needed him to know how sorry I was, if only for selfish reasons. Out of desperation, I wrote him a letter. Since I didn't have his Cornwall address I sent it to his parents' house in the hope that they would forward it to him. One week later, I got a text from Simon. I shook as I opened it. It read:

I got the letter. There is nothing left to say. Leave me alone.

I cried when I read it and finally stopped all attempts at contact. He was right, there was nothing left to say, but the hurt and disappointment took it in turns at battering me. Staring out of the window, the weather seemed fitting. The sun refused to shine and my world was grey and tired. Through my blurred vision I watched a squirrel dart about in my garden. Its grey bristly tail reacted to every movement and sound while its small hands felt about. It seemed unaware of the dull rain that trickled off its oily coat. I imagined it had young in a nest somewhere and hoped they were well looked after.

Before the accident I hadn't thought about everything in terms of life or death. I had a normal outlook, disentangled from morbidity and fear. And that is why I drank now. It was the only way I was able to return to a place in my head that felt safe and untouchable. During my drunken hours I was no longer the wife to a dead husband or the mother of a stillborn baby. I was just me: drunk, numb, angry, calm, happy, sad.

After spending some time watching the squirrel, I turned back to the fridge to refill my empty glass. As I opened the door I was hit by a strong smell of rotten food. In the salad drawer was a bag of wet green mulch that had once been lettuce. It looked like seaweed discarded on the shore and smelt worse. Holding my nose with one hand, I removed the bag with the other and marched it through the house and out to the bins in the street.

When I turned to go back into the house, I noticed my neighbour staring at me. He stood by his Mercedes and looked at me with pity. It stung and I felt impulsive anger swell. Dennis, a widower in his early seventies, quickly looked away before I had a chance to verbally explode at him, and he hastily locked his car and hurried into his house, leaving me standing there looking like a hobo.

Suddenly my knees felt weak and I needed to sit down. Tripping into the house I made it to the bottom stair just in time. The world swung between being dark and bright and my eyes stung. My surroundings appeared magnified and I could see bacteria crawling over everything, like little maggots with hairs for legs. Their psychedelic movements made my skin feel alive and I tried to shake myself free of the feeling. But it was useless. I was in the throes of another vision I was unable to escape.

For the first time since the accident a part of my mind was able to function outside the horror I was experiencing. I darted towards the kitchen in the hope of escape but when I got there the walls closed in on me and the ceiling sunk above my head. The house was alive and it wanted to swallow me. Squatting down in a corner, I put my hands up over my head and screamed for it all to stop. But the ceiling came lower and lower and the walls kept on closing inward. I noticed my breath cloud in front of me and felt a bitterly cold wind sweep around the room. My white kitchen started to bleed. It seeped out of the drawers and cupboards and came up between the cold stone tiles on the floor. I was sitting in a puddle of blood that spread across everything. A second of clarity hit me and I realised I was sitting near the drawer for the kitchen utensils. My fingers slipped in the thick oozing blood and I struggled to get a grip on the handle. The blood felt warm and pulsing on my fingertips and I could see the cells dancing in it.

Finally I managed to slip my fingers in and pried the drawer open. I couldn't see inside properly since I remained sitting on the floor with my legs tucked up, trying to escape the pool of blood that continued to grow around me. My fingers fiddled about in the drawer, feeling for something sharp to grab onto. I needed a weapon. When my palm slid over something cold and metal, I bunched my fist and pulled the implement out.

As I looked down at the potato peeler I noticed the blood had disappeared. The walls had returned to their original position and the kitchen looked normal once again. My brain did a summersault as I gazed around the room in disbelief. Why was this happening to me? The answer was out of reach and I could no longer cope with the question. Clarity dawned on me and I knew what I had to do.

With a slow and deliberate movement, I brought the peeler up to my wrist. My arm was white and bony and the veins looked like lumpy rivers pumping toxic life around my body. I didn't want to live anymore. The blade glinted beneath the electric light and promised me peace. The pools of blood I had imagined minutes ago would become real very soon.

The stainless steel hovered above the fattest blue vein, and I watched in fascination as it pulsed with every heartbeat. That was all there was to life; it was beautifully simple and my death would reflect it. Without a second's hesitation I brought the peeler down into my flesh and dragged it along my arm towards my elbow. The pain disappeared as quickly as it began. It felt like a burn doused with water.

I watched as real dark red blood trickled out of me in lines, snaking its way down my pale arm. The agony felt bizarrely pleasing. Then I cut myself again, this time harder. More blood flooded out of the wound and drops began to land on the flagstones beneath. The sound was deafening and hypnotic. Finally, I had tangible evidence of my pain. Blood dribbled out of me slowly and I knew I had not cut hard enough. For a third time, I raised the peeler and brought it onto my skin with more ferocity. The ghost of my former self floated above me watching as the skin on my arm was dragged back, revealing a layer of raw bloody flesh. I had not felt that alive for such a long time and relished the irony of the moment.

It's strange how blood smells like rust. Rust represents something dead, dying, and blood is the essence of life. But that unmistakeable scent filled my nostrils and head with a heavy thickness. I started to feel light-headed as I watched the gashes in my wrists pulse fresh waves with each beat of my heart. The flap of bloody skin hung from my arm like a slither of raw meat and a part of me had an urge to rip it off.

Then, just as I closed my eyes and sank onto the cold stone floor to embrace my death, the phone rang. Of course, I didn't answer, I couldn't.

I let it ring, the noise abrasive to my ears, interrupting my suicide. It seemed to go on forever and I screamed for the ringing to stop as my answer machine kicked in.

'Hi, Monica here. I can't get to the phone but please leave a message and I'll call you back. Thanks.' The sound of my own voice was alien to me.

'Hello, Mon, sweetheart? It's Mum. Just calling to see how you are? I was thinking I might come up to London and pay you a visit tomorrow. Let me know if you're free.' There was a long pause. 'Well, it would be nice to see you, darling, so give me a call back, OK? Love you.'

There was a click on the line as she hung up.

I sat with my back against the units, frozen in horror. That was not meant to happen. She shouldn't have called. She mustn't come to the house. I couldn't have her find my body. I looked at the blood on the floor and the river coming out of my wrist and panic hit me. I scrabbled about trying to get up and rushed over to the oven where I found a tea towel and wrapped it tightly around my arm to stop the bleeding. I pulled it taut and the cotton rubbed against my open wounds and hurt like hell.

My stomach was churning and I was dizzy as I stumbled into the hallway. Although I suspected I hadn't cut into an artery, I knew I needed to do something to stop the bleeding. With difficulty I made my way up the stairs, conscious that the tea towel was now a deep shade of red. I'd remembered that I kept a first-aid box in the bathroom and lurched over the last step, almost losing my balance. Reaching out with my bad arm, I caught the top of the banister and managed to hold myself up. The action caused a fresh surge of blood to spread throughout the temporary bandage and made me cry out in pain. After the spots in front of my eyes had evaporated, I managed to stagger into the bathroom.

I dropped the wet mess that was the tea towel onto the floor. The blood was still coming and the flow seemed relentless. With my good arm, I opened the cabinet and removed the first-aid kit. By then I was frantic and my hands were shaking. I struggled to grip the sterile wipes with my fingers and to tear open the foil wrapper with my teeth. After battling with it for a few moments I was finally able to remove the alcohol wipe and clean up my shredded wrist. My teeth were chattering and my whole body trembled uncontrollably. The blood was beginning to clot, and as I did my best to mimic a nurse, I realised how lucky I had been. The peeler could have gone much deeper. I might have heard the call from Mum but have been too late to save myself. The thought was unbearable. When I'd decided to die, my thoughts had been twisted and selfish. I had convinced myself that it was the best thing for everyone, and that I was being kind, saving Mum from having to deal with me anymore. But now I clearly saw that that was a false truth I had told myself to justify being a coward and taking my own life.

The thought of my mother coming into my house and finding me dead on the floor, in a puddle of blood, was heartbreaking. I felt sick to my stomach and found myself wanting to hurt myself all over again. I was on a torturous merry-go-round, and the harder I tried to get off, the faster it seemed to be spinning. My mother had inadvertently saved my life but I wished she hadn't. Now I had to face life knowing I had failed at suicide as well as everything else. The bitter irony was not lost on me.

Sitting on the bathroom floor, surrounded by bloody bandages, stained clothes and a raw wrist, I hit my lowest point yet. As I stared at the streaks of blood on the bathroom floor, I curled up into a ball and sobbed until I was so exhausted by the emotion I fell asleep.

***

When I woke up on the cold tiled floor, my wrist felt like it was burning. It was painfully sore. I looked down at the bandage and remembered what I'd done. Recollection made my stomach turn. I felt hollow and weak.

Out of the window I could see the light failing and a peach sky littered with lilac clouds. The sight was not enough to warm me as I picked myself up and headed into the spare bedroom. I remembered the answer machine message and wished she hadn't called. Death would have been so much easier.

I stood in the gloomy room and didn't turn the light on. The stillness felt comforting and suddenly I felt calm. I looked at the bed my mother always slept in. The room was sparse and immaculate. My eye was drawn to the painting of

London that hung on the white wall. I had always hated it. For the first time in a long while I began thinking about Tom. My head had been so blurred by drink I'd only concentrated on my baby, Simon and myself. Abruptly, now Tom existed to me again, and the calm, that had been so welcome, was rapidly pulled away from me and replaced with a desperate anger.

Suddenly I hated him. I was glad he'd died. The man I married had stopped existing a long time before his death. Everything that happened after the accident was his fault somehow. I couldn't explain how I knew he was responsible for my sadness but the feeling was as clear as my memory of his body lying in the driver's seat next to me. The only thing that remained out of focus was the memory of what happened in the moments before the crash. That still danced just out of reach and although I wasn't certain I wanted to remember, I somehow knew that it was important. It was the missing piece of the hideous puzzle my life had become.

I left the spare room shaking with rage and wanting a drink. My wrist throbbed with pain and the bandage chaffed the wound. I couldn't face removing the dressing just yet though. The sight of my cut bloody wrist could wait. I could tell that the bleeding had completely stopped and that was enough for the moment. I was worried that if I took the binding off it might start gushing again. For the moment I wanted to live, at least until my mother had paid her visit. Afterwards was a different matter.

When I got into the kitchen I looked at the pool

of blood on the floor and the discarded peeler lying close by. My stomach did a flip and my mouth filled with saliva as I steadied myself against the work surface. I knew I had to clean it up but couldn't face the task ahead without a large measure of Dutch courage. On the side, by the toaster, stood a bottle of vodka. I poured the remaining contents into a tumbler and removed some ice cubes from the freezer.

I took the drink over to the kitchen table and sat down with it. The sound of the ice cubes knocking together was reassuring to me as I took a long sip. I felt my shoulders drop. I no longer felt so angry and I noticed I'd stopped shaking. I stared out of the French windows at the creeping darkness. Sometimes I was able to forget I lived in London. It could be so quiet.

Having finished my drink, I felt stronger and able to cope with cleaning up the blood. From beneath the sink I removed a bottle of bleach, scrubbing brush and a black plastic washing-up bowl and took them over to the stain. A lot of the blood had dried but a section in the middle of the puddle remained sticky, wet and gleaming like a ruby. I tried my best to mop up the majority of it with kitchen paper before bleaching and scrubbing the remains of the mark. I scrubbed furiously but the blood was stubborn. I couldn't avoid noticing the fact that I was trying to get blood out of a stone. After tackling it with bleach, I realised the only thing I could do was lay a rug over it. I didn't have anything suitable but needed it hidden.

Eventually I worked out that I could use the

sheepskin rug from my office to hide the mark. It looked out of place in the stark, white, chrome and stone kitchen but it was better than nothing. I wanted to shield my mother from the truth of how I'd been living and needed to tidy the whole house.

After another large drink, I set about putting everything back in its place. I'd neglected to eat very much that day and the drink coursed through my veins helping me forget my sadness as I threw myself into the task of brushing all my troubles under the carpet.

I didn't hear the phone ringing over the sound of the Hoover. When I'd finished in the sitting room I returned to the kitchen to find the answer machine light flashing. I was glad I'd missed the call. The last thing I wanted was to talk to anyone. I listened to the message. It was Mum again, asking if she could come tomorrow. The thought of talking to her was too much so I reached for my mobile and sent her a text telling her to come after lunch if she wanted to. She wrote back almost immediately, saying how much she was looking forward to it. I didn't want to see her, but more than that I didn't want her to see me dead. My bid for freedom would have to wait.

I looked around my clean house and felt empty. My mother would never know what had happened or how I'd been living like an animal. All I had to do was wear a long-sleeved top and the illusion would be complete. My head felt heavy with drink, and a strong desire to sleep gripped me in a vice. Climbing the stairs, my legs felt like lead, and when I crawled into bed and pulled the covers up over my bloodstained clothes, all I hoped for was a long and dreamless sleep.

***

The next morning I spent more time making sure the house was the pinnacle of normality, much as I had done in the months before the accident. Once again, I had to force myself to appear happy. The feeling sat heavy in my gut as I attempted once more to scrub the bloodstain off the flagstones in the kitchen.

My arm was a little less sore but the throb remained. After waking, I had redressed the wound carefully, making sure not to disturb the fine layer of raw skin that had sewn itself over the cuts. I prayed I would be able to keep the wounds hidden and wore a thin powder-pink jersey with long sleeves. The deception was accomplished.

Since I was expecting my mother, I made a concerted effort not to drink too much vodka that morning. Although I did manage to exert some control, it was impossible to avoid drinking altogether. Alcohol had become a crutch and I was dependent on it. The drink helped to take the edge off my miserable reality and dulled the emptiness in my wounded heart. Unable to avoid contemplating the hundreds of regrets that swirled around my mind, instead I built them a home in my head. Physically I needed the alcohol, since without it my hands shook like leaves in a tree and left me feeling morbidly anxious.

For weeks I hadn't been eating properly. Food had lost its appeal and even my favourite things tasted bland. That day I made myself have a sandwich, if only to help soak up some of the drink that swished around in my system. The cheese sandwiched in slices of slightly stale bread was hard to swallow. I didn't have any butter in the house either, which made it drier still. It was an unpleasant experience and for some reason made me think of old people in nursing homes, eating to stay alive but not knowing why.

As a student, I'd smoked cigarettes, and in that moment I found myself longing to have one. My nerves were on tenterhooks waiting for my mum to arrive. It was vital that the visit went well. I couldn't let her see how bad things had become. Mum wouldn't ever leave me alone if she discovered the pitiful truth. But solitude was necessary. I poisoned everyone I loved and was determined to save Mum from suffering the same fate.

Looking down at the cigarette burn on the back of my hand I ran my fingertips lightly over it. Tom had stopped me smoking. But now he was gone and I could do exactly as I pleased. I got up from the table, leaving the remains of my sandwich lying there, and decided to go and buy a packet of smokes. Besides, I needed to stock up with some basics to enhance the feeling that all was well.

It had been days since I'd ventured out of the house and a strange sensation of panic began to build as I opened the front door. The world outside was bright and loud. There was a stream of traffic and the sound of sirens in the distance. I lingered on the doorstep for a moment debating whether to leave the safety of my sanctuary. The need for a cigarette won out and I pulled the door closed behind me, making sure the door was locked. Paranoia coursed through my body as though it were a disease as I walked quickly along the street, keeping my head down and avoiding making eye contact with any of the people I passed. The sun felt warm on my back and I wished I had been able to wear a summer top. I fiddled in my handbag for my Dior sunglasses, having a desperate urge to hide behind them.

Two minutes later, I reached the shop and went inside. The friendly Turkish man who was always serving offered me a warm smile.

I wandered round the shop with a basket and bought some fresh bread, butter, cheese, eggs, orange juice, coffee and a bottle of vodka and a small crate of tonics.

'Not seen you around for a while,' he said, looking past the person in front of me while handing them a receipt. 'You well?'

His accent could have been mistaken for Russian. I smiled awkwardly from behind my sunglasses.

'Fine, thanks.' I placed the basket on the counter and he rang the various items up on the till. 'And a packet of Silk Cut and one of those lighters, please.'

The Turk took the cigarettes down from a shelf behind the counter. He gestured at the lighters.

'Which colour?'

'I don't mind,' I said, and he chose a purple one.

'Nice day,' he added, still smiling and ringing the amount into the till, which I noticed was nine pounds and fifty pence and over a pound for the lighter.

Since when had cigarettes become so expensive, I wondered as I slotted my debit card into the machine and punched in my pin number. I could feel the man looking at me strangely, and suddenly heat pricked my brow. Unable to look him in the eye, I left the shop without a thank you and rushed back to the house.

When I got back to the house, my heart was pounding and my legs trembled. As I hung my handbag up on the coat hook I realised I needed another drink. The house felt dark and lifeless in stark comparison to the outside world. It seems I'd forgotten that for the rest of humanity life went on. There was a strange comfort in the realisation. No matter what I did, the world on the whole would remain unaffected and in that there was blissful unanimity.

I took the cigarettes and a drink out into the garden. The sun beat down on the patio and I could feel the warmth reflecting up from the stone slabs. The grass looked lush and green and the sky was streaked with wispy white clouds that seemed to travel across the sky with purpose. Spring was being replaced by summer.

Taking a seat on one of the painted cast iron chairs, I lit a cigarette. The smoke was warm and harsh in my mouth and lungs, and I coughed. It had been years since I'd enjoyed a cigarette. Immediately I felt light-headed and took a long gulp of icy vodka to quell the dizziness. Then I took another drag, this time with more restraint, and slowly allowed the silver smoke to slide down my throat and into my chest. It felt good and I watched the smoke evaporate as I exhaled and blew it up into the sky where an aeroplane flew high overhead, glinting like a tiny white star in the sunlight. In that instant I became a smoker again.

As I smoked I listened to the sounds coming from the park beyond the garden. Birds sang celebrating the warm weather and children shrieked and laughed, running around in the heat on the other side of the hedge. I imagined little faces smiling and small feet lying among the grass and felt my heart sinking. I used to love watching children play. Now, just hearing them made me want to cry.

Dropping the butt of my cigarette onto the stone patio, I stubbed it out with my black leather flip-flop. Just then a crow came swooping down out of nowhere and flew straight through the open French windows and into the kitchen. I was stunned and spun round to see the bird standing on the kitchen table pecking at my leftover cheese sandwich. Its beak tore through the bread and cheese with ease, making bite-sized pieces it could consume more easily. All the while the bird paid no attention to me. It seemed unaware of my presence. Its self-assured behaviour was coldly menacing.

I didn't know what to do. Getting up from my chair, I edged closer to the house. The crow remained oblivious to me until I reached the door. Then the bird stopped eating and looked up at me. It stood perfectly still, its black feathers shining in the sunlight, its dark eyes staring into my soul.

Without a second's thought or hesitation I hurled my glass in its direction. The bird leapt into the air, narrowly missing the flying glass, and flew back out into the garden. I had to duck as it skimmed over the top of my head aiming for the safety of a branch in the distance.

'Leave me alone!'

My scream echoed around the garden and park, shaking the trees. Every bird within a close radius flew up into the sky in a synchronised movement before flying south. The scream left my voice feeling hoarse. Suddenly the world around the house was quiet. The sound of my laughter disappeared with the birds into the void and I was alone again.

Just as I turned to go back into the kitchen to clean up the shards of glass, I heard a knock on the front door. My eyes were immediately drawn to the clock on the wall. It was half past one. My mother had arrived. Panic surged through me as I stood helplessly looking at the broken glass. I couldn't let her see it or she'd know something was wrong. Darting out of the kitchen, I pulled the door separating the hallway and the kitchen closed behind me. It would be fine, I told myself as I hurried along the hall trying to regain some composure. I was in such disarray I failed to notice the figures of two silhouettes standing on the other side of my Victorian stained-glass front door.

CHAPTER 23

Monica opened the door only expecting to find me standing there and looked shocked to discover I'd brought a guest with me. Mary stood behind me looking uneasy, offering a formal smile to her daughter-in-law. Reading the look on Monica's face, I bustled in, leading the way for Mary.

'Hello darling.' I kissed my daughter's cheek as I passed her but Monica didn't respond.

'Hello, Monica.' Mary's words were stiff and her round hazel eyes looked shifty and sunken in their sockets. She looked as meek and dishevelled as ever. Monica could hardly look at her, and the three of us stood awkwardly in the sitting room, surrounded by an oppressive silence.

It was the first time we had been together since the day of the argument, which had taken place beside Tom and Josh's grave.

'The house looks nice.'

My desperate attempt to fill the void of conversation only made the atmosphere tense up further. Feelings of bitterness and resentment curdled with the quiet in the room.

'How about I make us all a cup of tea?' I suggested, trying to lighten the mood.

'No,' Monica barked, 'I'll do it. You can sit down and wait in here.'

Immediately, Mary took a seat, half balancing on the edge of the large sofa, unable to make herself sit comfortably. 'How do you have your tea, Mary?' Monica's glare was cool.

'Oh, um, milk and one sugar please.' Mary wrung her hands as Monica threw me a furious look before leaving to fetch the tea.
Once Monica left the room, I leant over to Mary and whispered, 'I'm sorry about this. She'll calm down. She just needs a bit of time. She's stubborn, always has been.'

'I really don't think I should be here. She seems so angry still.' Mary didn't know what to feel.

'Oh, nonsense. I know my daughter and I bet she's regretting being so aggressive even as we speak.'

I could tell she thought that scenario unlikely given the atmosphere we'd walked into.

From the kitchen, we could hear the furious Monica stirring the teabags in the mugs, cursing Mary and I under her breath.

'How dare that woman come to my house unannounced?' she muttered. Mary and I shared a nervous look. We heard her telling herself to bite her tongue. 'Anymore outbursts will arouse suspicion. All I have to do is endure a couple of hours and then they'll go and I can stop pretending.' My daughter talking to herself like that made my stomach turn. I didn't recognise her anymore.

As Monica appeared in the living room, carrying a chrome circular tray with three mugs, Mary and I fell back into silence. Monica handed out the mugs and we sat quietly sipping the tea. After a while, Monica could no longer stand the quiet.

She eyeballed Mary. 'So,' she said, putting her mug down on the coffee table, 'are you going to tell me why you're here?' Her tone was aggressive and accusatory.

'Well' – Mary wriggled in her seat – 'I thought it was time we made friends again.' I glared at my daughter, willing her to accept the olive branch.

'Is that right?' Monica leant back into the armchair and folded her arms across her chest. A wince of pain shot across her face.

'Your mother called me a few days ago.'

Mary was a tiny woman and looked wooden, as though a string was holding up her back and head. It was an old-fashioned awkward kind of posture to adopt and I was reminded of a puppet.

'I think we need to move on. Thomas wouldn't want us arguing. He'd be so upset to think you and I had fallen out. And, well, since I've had time to think, I've realised how difficult this must be for you, and how it's affected you.'

To Monica, I think Mary appeared smug.

'Then I thought to myself I should come and pay you a visit. Today seemed fitting somehow.' Her hands were small and bony but her knuckles large and swollen.

'What's so special about today?' Monica looked irritated and perplexed.

Mary turned to face me and disbelief drained her cheeks of all colour. I felt mortified and quickly tried to salvage the conversation.

'I'm sure Monica doesn't mean to be so dismissive—' But before I could finish my sentence, Monica interrupted.

'No, Mum, don't. Please tell me what's so special about today that you felt you could come to my house uninvited?'

'Your husband's birthday!' The strength in her own voice surprised Mary. 'Tom's birthday. My son. The man you married. The father of your child, remember?'

The rage swelled in Mary as she stood up from the sofa, spilling some of her tea on the spotless cream carpet. Monica stared blankly at her mother-in-law.

So much time had passed since the accident and her days must have all melted into one another. She'd forgotten to pay attention to the date and I could see her shame under the scrutiny of Mary's hurt face. But then she evidently remembered Tom's later treatment of her and the nosedive their relationship had taken in the year leading up to the crash.

'He's dead. I hardly think it matters to him anymore, Mary.' The icy words froze the room.

'Monica!' I was horrified. Who was this person standing before me?

'What? You all want me to live in the past. I can't stand it anymore.' Her cheeks flushed red and a vein in her neck protruded as she continued to shout. 'He was absolutely not an angel and I'm sick of pretending that he was.'

Dumbfounded, Mary stood shaking on the spot. I couldn't tell whether it was with fear or rage. Stepping forward, I grabbed Monica by the arm.

'You need to calm down this instant. What is the matter with you?'

I fixed her with a glare and noticed how wild my daughter's green eyes had become. Monica shoved me away.

'I want you both to fuck off. Just fuck off and

leave me alone.'

Mary was not the kind of woman who ever swore or mixed with types that did. The shock at being spoken to like that plastered her face.

'Well, in all my life…' Mary reached for her handbag but Monica refused to allow her to finish speaking.

'It's about time you heard the truth.' Monica moved over to the doorway and stood blocking it, refusing Mary an exit. 'You son was a nasty bully. He made me a prisoner in my own home. He stopped me having friends and doing what I loved. If I didn't do exactly what he wanted, he abused me and made me feel worthless. I was scared of him, Mary.'

Monica shoved her hand out and pointed at the scar. 'He burnt me with his cigarette – Look!' Tears began to stream down Monica's face. 'Look at it!' she insisted.

Mary gazed at the small round scar with disbelief and I stepped in once more, grabbing my daughter by the shoulders.

'Go into the kitchen and calm down now. This is not helping,' I pleaded.

'But she needs to know, Mum, she has to understand. I can't keep this up anymore.' Snot dangled from her nose.

'Now, Monica. Go. Let me talk to Mary.'

I did my best to sound calm and gain control of the spiralling situation. Monica wiped her nose with her sleeve and slunk off towards the kitchen still sobbing. When I turned to look at Mary she was sitting hunched over her knees and staring at the carpet where she'd spilt her tea earlier.

'I should clean this up. So it doesn't leave a stain.'

Her sunken eyes looked vacant and her frame appeared smaller and more delicate than ever before.

'Listen, Mary,' I spoke softly as I sat down beside Mary, 'Monica isn't well. She's not coping.'

My words were not being heard. Mary remained on the sofa, her wide eyes fixed to the floor.

'I'm going to check on Monica,' I said, getting up and edging towards the door. 'Please don't leave. We can sort this out.'

I went into the kitchen to find Monica huddled in a corner of the room clinging to a bottle of vodka. Taking tentative steps towards my daughter, it took a moment to recognise the look of utter fear and madness in her eyes. I froze on the spot.

'Monica…' I bent down onto my haunches so that I was level with her. 'Sweetheart, put the bottle down and let's talk about this. Please. Poor Mary didn't deserve that. I know you've been through a lot but shouting and blaming Tom won't make you feel any better.'

Monica took a long drink, emptying a fifth of the bottle in one go. My heart hurt to see my little girl such a wreck.

'Give me the bottle, sweetheart. We can make this all better. Trust me, darling.' I realised I needed to tread softly and could see Monica was gradually beginning to respond. Smiling kindly at my daughter, I offered out my hand. Just as Monica began to lean forward, a crashing sound made us both jump. It sounded like glass exploding, and we turned around to find Mary standing in the doorway. At her feet was a photograph of Monica and Tom on their wedding day, smashed into small glistening fragments on the flagstone floor. It had broken with such force the metal frame was bent completely out of shape.

'You are a disgrace!'

Mary's voice no longer sounded quiet and meek.

'You stand here in my son's house and speak about him in that disgusting way. You ought to be ashamed of yourself.'

Her hands were on her slender hips and she appeared taller than usual. 'I told him you were a waste of space. I told him a hundred times that you weren't good enough. Foolish boy never could do anything right. Pathetic, just like his father.'

Monica and I looked at Mary as if she were a stranger. We had never seen any side to her but meek and never imagined she was capable of such power.

'I told him he could do better. I begged him to get a divorce, to come home and live with me. I was the only one who ever knew what was best for him. I knew how he liked his coffee, the way his bedsheets should be folded properly, what clothes suited him. I was the only one who ever understood how to make him really happy.'

She spoke with venom and seemed to tower over the two us, while we remained crouched on the floor listening in disbelief.

'You are a disgrace to the Bowness name' – Mary's pupils expanded – 'and your son would have been too.'

It only took a second for Monica to lurch towards a large shard of broken glass and pick it up. She stood face-to-face with Mary, holding the fragment like a knife, which shone in the light, reflecting like a mirror.

'You have no right to talk about my son. Get out of my house before I kill you.' Monica was trembling with adrenaline.

'This is my son's house, you little bitch.'

Mary was too angry to see how serious Monica was but I could. I jumped up and put myself between the women.

'Monica, put the glass down.' I'd never felt so frightened in my life and felt my bottom lip quiver. I thought I might pass out.

'Monica, please, you don't want to do this. Put it down.'

From behind me, Mary chuckled a patronising laugh. For a moment she sounded like Tom.

'She's too pathetic to see anything through.'

Monica lunged forward with the glass in her hand cutting through the clothing covering Mary's arm.

'Get out, get out!' she screamed, trying to cause further injury as Mary fell back onto the floor and landed in the fragments of glass from the broken picture. She shrieked as she looked down at the palms of her hands, which were splintered with glass and beginning to bleed. Monica pushed me out of the way and hovered over Mary, who'd returned to looking helpless.

'He wasn't Tom's.' Monica was breathless. 'Josh wasn't Tom's. Your son failed as a husband and was never going to be a father.'

'Then I'm glad your bastard died!' spat Mary. I watched in disbelief as my daughter attempted to stab Mary. The scene played out in slow motion. Without thinking, I reached for a plate that lay on the work surface, stood up and brought it crashing in to the side of Monica's head. Monica dropped the shard of glass she'd been holding and fell to the ground unconscious.

The room was deadly quiet and for a moment no one moved. Realising what I'd done, I rushed over to Monica's body and hurriedly felt for a pulse.

'Call an ambulance, now!' I barked at Mary, never taking my eyes off of my daughter, who lay motionless on the cold kitchen floor.

CHAPTER 24

I don't remember the trip in the ambulance to the hospital. Sirens didn't sound. The nurses weren't there. Doctors didn't treat me and the police didn't guard my bedside. As far as my memory is concerned it didn't happen. There is a large gap, a space void of vital information that would help explain why I am here today. But parts of it visit me like visions from a bad dream and I almost remember. Almost.

Now I sit in my pyjamas staring out of the window as the summer passes me by. There are a few benches on a patch of green outside. Beyond the walls are rooftops, and in the distance I can see skyscrapers, towers of industry. It remains surreal. My world is a bubble caught between one world and another. I watch myself float from space to space aimlessly. My legs don't feel like my own and my thoughts belong to another. I barely exist.

Then I see a nurse patrolling the ward and I am brought back to earth. I remember where I am but not why. Others hover around consumed by their misery and madness and I watch them. Poor souls, I think to myself. Pity helps me distance myself from my reality. As long as I can build a wall between myself and the other patients I will remain an outsider. I am not one of them.

It's unusually hot for this time of year. Damp cotton clings to my back making it itch. I want a bath but they won't let me without supervision. I feel like a child and like a child I'm at a loss to understand what is happening. The air in the room feels uncomfortably close and I need to escape. There are too many people, clouding my space and my judgement, so I head to my private room to escape the scrutinising looks from everyone around. They are watching me, waiting for something.

When I reach my room at the end of the long corridor I go in and sit on the bed. I cannot close the door and be alone. It's not allowed. As I look around I am reminded of being in a cell. There is nothing there that belongs to me. No pictures on the wall; nothing that states I even exist. Perhaps I don't.

The single bed on which I sit is made with military precision. The clean crisp sheets are folded exactly and pulled tightly across the mattress. My pillow is plump and beautifully ironed. Were it not for the bareness of the room it might be mistaken for a hotel. I smile at the thought, if only, and run my hand over a fold in the sheet. It feels cool and smooth. I wonder who made my bed?

Ten minutes pass and a nurse appears in the doorway. She is holding a clipboard and marks me down as present. As she leaves she smiles sympathetically and I want to throw my pillow at her head. Every fifteen minutes one of them appears to check on me. I'm being closely watched. The attention is as stifling as the heat.

I get up and go over to the window. Outside, the oppressive sky is low over London. The pale brown clouds gather slowly, insulating the hot air.

A bead of sweat is running down my neck and the hairs on my arms stand up. Suddenly I feel alive and then I look down and see the bandages around my wrist and think of death. Then I remember the peeler and shudder. The medicinal sickness I am suffering increases tenfold and my legs turn to jelly. I support my weight by leaning against the window and the surface feels cool on my forehead, but not for long. My warm breath is reflected off the glass and bounces back into my face. I can't remember the last time I brushed my teeth. I look over to the small sink in my room and see a lonely toothbrush in a mug – my only possession.

From the corridor I hear a radio turned on. A husky voice cuts through the stale air announcing it is the hottest summer in forty years. But I don't care. I stroke the fabric of the curtains. They are ageing chenille – that smell of smoke and sickness. For some reason it makes me think of an old man's pub. The short pile feels warm and slimy and I take my hand away and close my eyes. The dizziness is unbearable and I feel I'm going to faint.

Then a familiar sound distracts me from my thoughts. I know that voice. I stay glued to the spot and listen for a while, craning my neck in order to hear.

'Doctor, please tell me you have some good news?'

'Well to be honest with you, progress has been very slow. She still refuses to communicate.' The male doctor sounds grave.

'No improvement at all?' The voice sounds

fragile.

'I wouldn't say that. We have her heavily sedated, and as a result she is calmer. The violent tendencies she was displaying when we admitted her are now under control. This is progress.' The doctor clears his throat. 'It is going to be a long, slow road. She is very ill.' I am deafened by the silence.

'But she will get better?'

'I am sure with time and work we can get her back on her feet. It often takes a while to find the right combination of medication and treatment. It's still early days.'

I go back over to my bed and sit down. My days are spent living outside of myself, and listening to people discuss me only exacerbates the feeling.

'So what is the next step?' the shaky female voice asks.

'I have spent a long time looking through her notes. It's clear that she is suffering from post-traumatic stress disorder but I feel it has been compounded by dissociative amnesia. This occurs when a person blocks out certain information, usually associated with a stressful or traumatic event. People with this condition often suffer with depression and anxiety and it is not uncommon to see an extreme fluctuation in mood. The way in which she lost her husband and child was particularly disturbing, and it is no surprise that she is now suffering mentally as a result. Having spent time with Monica I feel our best bet is to concentrate on a mixture of psychotherapy and cognitive therapy backed up by a course of anti-psychotic drugs. She is plagued by nightmares and hallucinations. Her sense of self was lost when her family died. We need to go back to the grass roots of the problem if we are going to help her.'

His words mean nothing to me but he sounds so sure of himself. What I am hearing is laughable.

'So you think you can help her?' Hope pours from the quiet voice.

'I believe so. But you need to be aware this may take some time. The outlook for her is positive. She has a good network of support. Most people with this condition eventually remember the event and are then able to recover. Often this takes time, but I must warn you that in some cases the buried memory can remain locked out of reach.'

'So what does that mean?'

'We have no reason to think this will be the case with Monica.' The doctor bats the question away. 'Now if you will excuse me, I have another patient to attend to.'

'Oh, thank you so much for your time. If there is anything I can do…?' the words trail off and I hear footsteps disappearing on the carpet.

I look down at my battered slippers and realise my feet feel clammy. Then a quiet knock on my open door brings me back to reality.

'Hello, Monica, sweetheart. Can I come in?' My mother stands looking sheepish in the doorway. I look out of the window as she comes into the room. She stands over me for some time, waiting for me to speak. My silence speaks for itself.

'I brought you some magazines,' she says,

putting a carrier bag down on the bed, 'and some grapes.' I find her close proximity suffocating and get up and move over to the window again. I can feel her hurt and disappointment as she perches on the edge of my bed. There is a long empty silence and the room feels more claustrophobic than ever. I want to run out screaming. Instead, I scratch at my bandages.

'Mary won't be pressing charges.' Her voice is calm and serious. Still I don't respond. I have nothing left to say. What is the point? In this place I am deemed insane and no one will listen to me anyway.

'The doctor tells me you're doing well.' The lie spins like a web and I am trapped in the centre of it. I close my eyes tightly, willing her to disappear and the nightmare to end.

'OK, that's fine. You still don't want to talk. But I'm not going anywhere. I'm going to read my book for a while and if you want say something you can.'

She gets a thick paperback out of her handbag and opens it to a bookmarked page, just as she has done so many times over the last few weeks.

She stays for a long time. We don't speak. She reads while I lose myself in the changing sky out of the window. I have never understood how grey days can be humid. I associated heat with the sun, but the sun remains hidden, refusing to shine over the city. I refuse to move or look at my mother the whole time she is there. Eventually, once she feels she's done her duty she gets up and moves over to the door.

'I'll be back at the same time tomorrow.' She

waits for a response that will never come. 'I love you, Monica, and I won't give up on you.'

My eyes fill with tears as I hear her footsteps fade into the distance. The emotion surprises me. I am not used to feeling anything and long for the return of the drug-induced numbness. The tears feel warm running down my cheeks, hanging momentarily from my chin before tumbling soundlessly to the floor. I return to looking out over Mile End. It is an area in the east of London which received some funding for improvement during the year we hosted the Olympics, but it remains an abyss. I've been sent here to reside for an unknown period of time in the Psychiatric Intensive Care Unit in an ageing hospital. It's a female only ward and I'm glad. I don't like seeing men. Every one reminds me of what I've lost: Simon and Josh. I see their faces everywhere.

Looking out over the concrete jungle, I think about what I heard the doctor say. I am a diagnosis to him, something to be studied, something to be fixed. It seems impossible to imagine a time when I felt normal. It's been so long. But he said there is hope and I suppose that is what I should concentrate on. I've always known that it all goes back to the accident. It's nice to have that confirmed. Perhaps I'm not so crazy after all.

Just as the unfamiliar feeling of optimism creeps beneath my skin, I see it. On a slate roof a stone's throw from my window, it sits. Preening its feathers, it looks larger than ever. I step away from the window, hoping it hasn't noticed me. My heartbeat quickens and nervous energy rushes around my body. It feels like vertigo. I stop when I reach a safe distance and continue to watch it with horrified fascination.

Its body glistens like crude oil and I am transfixed. It stops what it's doing and slowly moves its Jurassic head to look at me. Those black eyes are as cold as hell and I am struck by a violent headache which leaves me dropping to a paralysed ball on the floor. I can hear its dark thoughts penetrating my mind.

From out of nowhere, I feel something touch my shoulder and I fly out of control, waving my arms and hitting out at the unknown entity. Then I hear a wail and open my eyes to find a nurse cowering. I run screaming out of my room, and behind me I hear her shouting for assistance. I don't know where I am going but I continue to run until I find myself at the end of a corridor of locked doors. The three nurses approach me cautiously and I feel like a trapped animal. One of them is brandishing a syringe and I start to plead and beg.

'No, don't, please. You don't understand, it's come back, it's there outside.' But the look in their eyes tells me they've heard it all before and suddenly I see myself the way they see me. I stop trying to escape. I sit down on the floor and sob as they surround me. Two male staff nurses gently handle me and hold me face down to the floor while another administers the drug. The world starts to fade and blackness takes over.

CHAPTER 25

18 October 2012

When I find her phone, I'm fuming. I'd been suspecting for some time that the bitch was lying to me. I'm not stupid. It was obvious. Her sneaking around in the night, pretending it was just the baby kicking, keeping her awake.

It's in a hidden compartment in her desk. I hardly ever go in there but for some reason I'm drawn to it. I had to know what she was up to. I hacked her account and checked her emails. I've been doing it for months but come up with nothing. Letters she received, I'd monitored too but she was cunning, like a feral city fox.

She's ironing in the kitchen, pressing creases into my shirts as usual; hopeless fucking excuse for a housewife. I stand watching her and realise how fat and ugly she's become. After the baby, she'll need to go on a diet. I'll have to watch what she eats and make sure she doesn't balloon more. I'm not going to have a whale as a wife. I stare at her. She stops ironing and looks up.

'Don't you fucking burn my shirt,' I growl at her, 'it cost me a fortune.'

'Oh, sorry, Tom. I'm sorry.' She sounds pathetic, and I see she subconsciously rubs the cigarette burn on the back of her hand. I can't help but smile to myself.

'I'm going out. I'll be back soon,' I tell her, picking up my house keys from a bowl on top of the fridge. 'Make sure the ironing is finished when I get back. Oh, and Hoover the sitting room will you? It looks like a pigsty.'

'Yes, of course,' she says. That mousey voice isn't fooling me.

'I want pie for supper so make a start on that too,' I call out as I march along the hallway.

'What sort of pie would you like?' I hear her say.

'Be a good girl and try and think for yourself for once.' I open the front door. 'Just as long as it doesn't taste like shit, like the last one.' I step out into our small front garden and pull the door closed behind me.

I turned out of our street into Priory Road and walk along until I reach the entrance to the park. There's an autumn breeze blowing some of the leaves off the trees. Above me the sky is pale blue and low white clouds gather above my part of North London. As I walk along the path past silver birch trees that sway in the wind, I come across a few clucky mothers with their brats playing with a ball. I sit down on a bench nearby and remove the mobile phone from my pocket. I examine it properly for the first time. It's a cheap one and I'm revolted by her lack of taste.

As I turn it on the screen bursts into life and welcomes me with a cacophony of musical notes. After a moment the menu appears in front of a picture of colourful flowers. She really doesn't have any style, I think as I begin a search through her text messages. To my disappointment I find none. They have all been carefully deleted. I will find no evidence there, so I open the photo folder on the phone. Again it's empty. I can't understand the point of keeping a phone hidden if it has nothing significant on it. I'm wrong; she's more stupid than I've given her credit for.

I'm chuckling to myself just as a soft football comes flying through the air, narrowly missing my head. It instantly angers me. I scowl at the little sod responsible, who has a disgusting snotty nose, and turn my attention to his mother, who is flapping like a hen around an obese baby dressed head to toe in a hideous shade of pink. She looks like a bloody cupcake.

The phone is still in my hand when I have one final thought. I open up the call history to see whom the lying snake has been talking to. Then I see it. Simon. His name over and over again, hundreds of calls, and I know it makes sense. So, Monica has been fucking him all this time. It's the worst kind of betrayal I can imagine. *Him over me*? That dirty snivelling wimp who can't rub two pennies together?

A violent rage comes out of nowhere and I scream up at the sky. The other people in the park stare at me as if I'm deranged.

'What the fuck are you looking at?' I holler, stomping off out of the park. Those stupid cunts have no right to look at me like that.

Reaching Priory Road, I realise I need to calm down. This needs to be dealt with efficiently, and as I walk along the pavement back to my house, I hatch a plan. She won't get away with this. I know exactly what I need to do.

When I get back into the house I rush up the stairs and return her secret fuck phone into the compartment in her desk. When I come downstairs I find her in the sitting room hurriedly winding up the cord on the Hoover.

'Tom, I'm sorry, I didn't know you'd be gone for such a short time. I've just finished.'

She sounds out of breath and I wonder if she's been fucking him in my bed while I was in the park.

I inspect the carpet and see she has missed a patch, but bite my tongue.

'I'll put the Hoover away, my love,' I say, bending down to pick it up. She flinches as my arm brushes against her leg and I relish the power I have over her. 'You sit down and put your feet up.' She looks at me, confusion crossing her face.

'But I haven't started the pie?' She is nervously edging towards the door.

'Don't worry about that now.'

I strangle the Hoover hose with my hands and try to smile as she sits down tentatively.

I put the Hoover away in the cupboard under the staircase and return to the sitting room where I sit down on the sofa beside her. She hasn't plumped the cushions properly and the usual wave of disappointment comes over me.

'I was thinking we should go out to lunch,' I say rubbing her lower back with the palm of my hand while she remains sitting upright, as stiff as a board. 'You deserve a treat.'

I speak the words through clenched teeth and try to hide my bubbling fury. She doesn't say anything and I want to slap her for the lack of gratitude.

'Would you like that?' I try to keep the tone light.

'Well ... well ... yes, that would be lovely. Thank you.' I can see the caution creeping into her eyes. 'Anywhere you choose I'm sure will be perfect.'

She trips over her words, trying to placate me. But it is a waste of time, since now I know everything.

'Go upstairs and brush your hair,' I say standing up. 'We'll leave here at twelve.' She jumps to her feet and rushes up the stairs. It sounds like a herd of elephants charging through the house and I want to shout at her but manage to control myself.

While she is attempting to make herself look less of a mess, I go into the kitchen where I discover she has folded my ironed shirts over the back of one of the kitchen chairs. I ball my hands into fists and curse her under my breath. What is the point in doing the fucking ironing if you are going to instantly crease the clothes again? And then I remember how very stupid she is and realise I am wasting my time worrying about it.

I think back to when I first met her and how impressive she seemed. The woman I live with is a long way from the girl I met. She's let herself go in so many ways and as a result let me down. I'm embarrassed by her most of the time now. She showed so much promise back in the day but turned out to be a waste of space. The woman isn't even capable of ironing a shirt properly. She can barely call herself a woman at all. And I think to myself if she's failed so miserably at being a wife, what sort of mother will she make? I deserve better.

I go over to my pile of shirts and carefully pick them up on their hangers. I brush the silky cotton with the back of my hand and move them over to the hooks in the hallway where I can hear her, upstairs, moving around, no doubt making a mess in the bedroom. From the bottom of the stairs I get a sudden waft of her perfume and realise it's coming from her coat that hangs just a few feet away. Does she put it on for him, I wonder? And then I have a vision of the two of them, together naked, and I want to punch the wall.

A second later she appears at the top of the stairs. I can see her pale ankles beneath her long green skirt. She stands there smiling at me and I smile back. She has no idea what's coming.

'Come on then,' I say jangling the car keys. 'Ready?'

'I am.' She waddles down the stairs, her large belly looking more like a balloon about to burst than ever before. As she reaches the bottom step I offer her my hand and she takes it gingerly. The feel of her fingers intertwined with mine makes me sick to my stomach but I push the nausea away. 'You look nice,' I say helping her with her coat.

'Thanks.'

Then we step outside and walk towards the car. The air feels closer than it did before, as if an electric mist surrounds us. My car is parked a few yards down and as I hold up the key to unlock the doors I am struck by its beauty. The silver paintwork gleams in the sunshine and warmth is reflected off its sleek body. I run my hand over the roof admiring my clean metal machine.

I bought the BMW just two years ago. It was the result of my hard work and sweat. Monica was not allowed to drive it. God forbid a stupid woman should be trusted behind the wheel.

We get into the car and I start the engine. It roars into life and I'm excited by the powerful sound.

'Where are we going?' she asks in a quiet voice.

'It's a surprise,' I say enjoying the supremacy I have over the situation.

I pull the car out of our road and turn the radio on. I know how much she enjoys music and I want her to feel relaxed. Some pop drivel floats out of the speakers and I can see in my peripheral vision that she is gently nodding her head in time to the beat. I clench the wheel with my hands until my knuckles turn white. I want to stop the car and strangle her right there.

I drive us towards Turnpike Lane and the traffic is slow. This part I haven't planned, and I wonder how best to put my scheme into action.

'Are we going to that Turkish restaurant on Green Lane?' she says hopefully. It helps to focus my mind.

'No,' I say taking a left at the traffic lights and driving through Wood Green, passed the shopping mall.

'Oh,' she sounds disappointed and I'm pleased. We carry on through the busy shopping district and drive on by Wood Green underground. I'm not sure where it is I am going to take us but I will keep driving until I make a decision. Then suddenly I have an idea and know what I want to do. I find a quiet street and pull in. She looks around, wondering what we are doing there, but isn't brave enough to ask. We sit in silence for a while and I can feel her wriggling anxiously in her seat. With each slow passing second I feel more empowered. She stares out of the windscreen, dead ahead, too scared to look at me and I smile inside. I turn to look at her profile and suddenly see that she is still beautiful.

'Have you spoken to Simon recently?' The question hangs in the air like a noose. I see her whole body tense and her eyes widen like a deer in headlights. Patiently, I wait for a response but she is quiet.

'Have you?' I ask again. She looks down at her hands in her lap and I see a large tear roll down her pallid cheek. She is unable to speak. I slap her face hard and her bottom lip splits, revealing fresh red blood.

'I asked you a fucking question,' I bellow in her face. She turns to look at me.

'So you know.' The fear I am grown accustomed to has disappeared. She is hollow and drained of any fight.

'Yes, you fucking despicable bitch. I know. I found your phone.' My hands are shaking with rage as I turn the keys in the ignition and start the car again. She says nothing. 'Aren't you going to explain at least? Apologise and beg for my mercy?' My foot is pressed hard on the accelerator.

'No,' she says at last. 'No, Tom, I'm not.' I ball my hand into a fist and hit her on the side of the head. She gasps and holds her face.

'My mother was right about you,' I spit. 'She told me you weren't good enough. I should have listened, you lying cheating worthless whore.' I am so angry I'm losing control. I'm hardly able to concentrate on the road. I swerve to miss a pedestrian crossing the road with her shopping and give her the finger. Everywhere I go, I'm surrounded by stupid bitches.

'Tom, please, you need to slow down. Stop the car. We have to talk about it.' But I speed up, enjoying the rush it gives me. One hand is gripping the handle of the door, her other is holding her belly.

'Tom, please,' she cries. 'It's over. It has been for weeks.'

'You think I care about that now? After you've lied to me, humiliated me.' The car is travelling really fast now and I'm overtaking a lot of traffic.

'You think you can cheat on me and get away with it? I picked you up out of the gutter! You are nothing without me.' We pass Alexandra Palace station on the left and continue along South Terrace, passing Alexandra Palace standing proudly at the top of the hill. 'You are going to pay for what you've done, you fucking little cunt.' On the horizon I can see over the whole city of London.

'I'm sorry, I'm sorry, it was a mistake, a horrible mistake,' she whines like an animal in a trap.

'Not yet, you aren't. Not yet. But you soon will be,' I tell her. We begin to wind down the road leaving the palace behind us. There is little traffic and the road is lined with trees on either side. We are gaining speed and I see the speedometer reads nearly seventy miles per hour.

'I'm going to fucking kill you for what you've done to me,' I shout as I pull the wheel hard and aim the car right at a large tree. 'Fucking die!' I scream just before we collide.

CHAPTER 26

The drug-induced haze lifts slowly. I open my eyes and look around the small room, squinting at the shining light. My mouth feels like a desert and my limbs are heavy. I fan my fingers in front of my face, trying to block out the bright white light and notice how my head is thumping. Is this limbo? Have I died?

It takes a moment for my eyesight to adjust. I am lying on a mattress on the floor in my pyjamas. The room I am in has no windows, only a mirror put into the wall. Sitting up slowly I notice how stiff my neck is. I try to shake the heavy feeling from my skull. Opposite me I see a clock up high on the wall. The red second hand ticks by slowly and the sound seems unbearably loud. I rub my temples with my fingertips and close my eyes. My heart is beating hard in my chest and I think I am going to faint. My stomach knots and sickness hits me like a bus. Where am I?

I remain sitting on the floor in the white room and inspect my surroundings again. Next to the huge mirrored panel I notice a door without a handle. I crawl on my knees, too weak to stand, and try to push it open but it won't budge. Exhausted, I collapse in a heap and try to think clearly.

And then I remember the crash. And Tom. He tried to kill me. Suddenly I find the energy to sit upright and the last year of my life flashes before my eyes. I come crashing into the present like a comet and I realise I'm in hospital; in seclusion. Looking at the mirror, it occurs to me that people are on the other side, watching. My bones ache and I move back over to the bare mattress where I lie down again. I know who I am and how I got here. It floods me with clarity. Suddenly a voice appears from nowhere. It sounds magnified. 'Monica, it's Doctor Rush.' I recognise his voice. 'To the left of the mirror is an intercom. If you press the button and speak into it I will be able to hear you.' I'd never noticed his voice was kind until that moment.

Gingerly, I get to my feet and take slow deliberate steps over to the speaker and press the button, which is labelled 'Talk'.

'Hello, Doctor.' I lean against the wall for support.

'Do you know where you are?'

'Yes. Mile End Hospital.' I try not to feel patronised.

'Good,' he says, 'and do you know why we put you in seclusion?'

'Yes, because I hit that nurse.' I shudder at the memory.

'That's right, Monica.' His words echo around the room free from judgement.

'I'm sorry,' I say, sounding pathetic. 'I didn't mean it, I'm sorry. Is she OK?'

'Yes, she is fine.' He is so calm. 'We've informed your mother that we've had to separate you from the rest of the patients.' As I listen I hang my head, feeling ashamed.

'I'm sorry,' I mumble into the intercom. 'Please,

when can I get out of here?'

'That is entirely down to you,' the doctor says. 'This is a last resort. We will not tolerate violence towards our staff.' Disdain creeps into his voice.

'I was scared,' the words tumble out of me. 'I saw the crow again. She surprised me and I panicked. I'm sorry. It was an accident.'

'That may well be, but until I am certain you are no longer a danger to yourself or anyone else, we will keep you in here for observation.'

I want to cry and scream but I know it won't do any good. I walk over to the two-way mirror and look at my reflection. I nod my head, hoping he is watching.

'Someone will be outside the door at all times,' he reassures me. 'If you need the toilet or want to have a cigarette, press the button on the intercom and someone will come and accompany you. Your meals will be delivered, and if you require anything extra to eat or drink, you just have to ask.'

This is like being in prison, I think to myself. There is a long silence.

'Is there anything else, Monica?' I shake my head but then remember and rush over to the speaker.

'Yes, yes. I remember. I remember the crash. I remember it all!' I can't hide my excitement and hold my breath waiting for him to answer.

'Well, that's very good, Monica.' He speaks softly. 'That's good.'

'Can I come out now?' I feel like a child put on the naughty step.

'Not just yet, Monica.' With his gentle words,

he pacifies me. 'We will talk about it very soon.'

'OK.' I'm relieved. 'I'm going to get out of here. I'm not mad, you know. It's all just a big mistake,' I tell him. 'Everything is going to be fine. You'll see.'

'Of course it will.'

From my side of the glass I feel him leave. I return to the mattress, which sits in the middle of the room like my private island. The clock on the wall is my friend. I make myself comfortable and watch as her hands track the circle of time. Everything is going to get better. I am not mad, I tell myself, and when I look at my reflection in the mirror, I notice I am smiling.

THE END

OTHER WORKS BY BETSY REAVLEY

Poems: The Worm in the Bottle
Beneath the Watery Moon

Betsy Reavley is currently working on her third novel.

You can follow Betsy on Twitter **@BetsyReavley**

For more great novels visit

www.bloodhoundbooks.com

16093414R00190

Printed in Great Britain
by Amazon